THE HIGHWAY DINER

MARK PAUL SMITH

North Carolina

Published in the United States by BQB Publishing
(an imprint of Boutique of Quality Books Publishing, Inc.)
www.bqbpublishing.com

ISBN: 979-8-88633-031-1 (p)
ISBN: 979-8-88633-032-8 (e)

Library of Congress Control Number: 2024938700

Book design by Robin Krauss, www.bookformatters.com
Cover design by Rebecca Lown, www.rebeccalowndesign.com
First editor: Caleb Guard
Second editor: Allison Itterly

This book is dedicated to my beloved wife of forty-six years,
Jo Ellen Hemphill Smith,
January 10,1945 - October 23, 2023.

Special thanks to alpha reader/editor,
Brenda Fishbaugh, who has provided insight
and encouragement for each of my five novels.

CHAPTER ONE

Murray daydreamed while looking through the restaurant window, wondering how she could paint the clouds to light up on the canvas just like they brightened in the morning sun. It would take a light blue underlayment before she added gray tones to shape the cumulus. No silver linings. The color contrast could do all the work.

"I think I'll have me an omelet." The voice brought her back to earth, where she stood in her apron over the truck driver who was trying to order. "What do you think? The Denver or the Meat Lover?"

She raised her eyebrows slightly. "That depends on how much of a meat lover you are, or if you're headed to Denver."

The driver grumbled and looked back at the menu. "I can see you'll be no help at all."

"No, no. I'm sorry," she said. "I'm just being a smart ass. The Meat Lover is my favorite. It's got lots of bacon and sausage and big chunks of ham."

He smiled as his eyes ran up and down her twenty-year-old body. She hated the way he looked at her, even though she was quite used to it. She wanted to tell him she wasn't on the menu. He was old enough to be her grandfather. He was fat and gross, hadn't shaved in days, and his teeth were crooked and yellow. She tried to smile but only crinkled her nose.

After much too long a lecherous pause, he returned his gaze to the menu, holding her hostage with his indecision. Other diners were trying to attract her attention, looking for coffee refills. "Do you need a little more time?"

"No," he finally responded. "I'll have the Meat Lover omelet with an English muffin, side of your house potatoes, and coffee black. Oh, and an ice water and a large tomato juice."

She pretended to write down his order and hurried to the kitchen to yell over the wide metal counter, "Meat Lover, potatoes." That was all the cooks needed to know. She'd get the muffin, coffee, water, and tomato juice at the server station.

She heard her mother's gentle, but firm voice of authority over her shoulder. "Write it down, Muriel. Make the ticket now. How many times do I have to tell you? And make sure you get all the drinks, so I know what to ring up."

Murray hated the name *Muriel*. By the age of fourteen, she went by Murray. Her mother said Murray sounded too much like a boy's name. "That's why I like it," Murray always responded.

She shook her head in exasperation as she filled out the ticket, clipped it on the wire over the counter for the cooks, and hustled to the tables with a fresh pot of coffee in one hand and a pitcher of ice water in the other. She smiled and bobbed a playful curtsy as she passed her mother. "Happy now?"

Isabel chuckled. "Why, yes, I am. Thank you very much, Muriel."

Murray's mother, Isabel Paterson, owned The Highway Diner and the truck plaza on the northwest edge of Fort Wayne, Indiana. She had been running the struggling business like a broken-hearted ship captain since her husband died two years ago in 2020.

Murray knew it was going to be a long day. It was only 9:00 a.m., and she had to work straight through to closing at 10:00 p.m. She didn't mind the extra hours and tips. She was saving up for art school. For once, the breakfast crowd was so busy that all Murray could do was dash from table to table, carrying heavy trays of buttermilk pancakes and smoked sausage, while dodging clumsy flirtations from a few of the men who had forgotten about their wives back home. She had no time to think about art.

A heavy-set man wearing denim overalls motioned her over to his table. "I wanted to thank you for being so friendly," he said as he handed her a ten-dollar tip. "Just wanted to make sure you got this. I see they got you hopping."

"Thank you, kind sir," Murray said, recognizing the kindness in his eyes and the sincerity in his smile. "Can I give you a warm-up on your coffee?"

"No thank you. I'm on my way out. Gotta make it to Madison, Wisconsin, today. You keep up the good work."

"I'll do my best," Murray said as he got up to leave. "Be safe out there."

Once the man paid his bill and left, Murray walked up to the cash register and showed her mother the tip. "Ten-dollar tip on a nine-dollar bill from that older guy who just left. Said he liked me being friendly, sweet as can be."

"That's nice," Isabel said. "Most of our guys are good people. I know the ones who heckle you. Their bark is worse than their bite. They're trying to be friendly, and they don't know what else to say." Murray rolled her eyes as Isabel added, "But you already know that."

"Because you tell me all the time," Murray laughed. She handed her the ten-dollar bill. "Can you change this for two fives? I'm gonna split it with the guys in the kitchen."

"That's my girl, Muriel."

"We've got to keep the crew happy if we want the ship to sail."

"That's what your father always said." Isabel smiled.

The room was filled with good-natured conversations among drivers who were happy to be taking a break from the road. The half-moon counter was centered in front of the kitchen and spanned the twenty-two four-top tables of the main dining area. The room had a ten-foot ceiling, but it never felt crowded, even when it was. The walls were painted a cheerful honey amber and decorated with sepia-toned photographs of historic trucks and trains.

Murray smiled as she approached the table of a casually elegant middle-aged couple. "May I start you off with coffee and water?" she asked, handing each of them a six-page, plastic-coated menu.

"Yes, coffee please." The woman raised her head from her slumping shoulders. "Jack's been driving since we left Chicago and the road construction's been brutal. I'm afraid I've been a bit of a backseat driver."

"From the front seat," Jack said. "Black for both of us," he said before Murray had a chance to ask.

Murray began pouring. "So, where you headed?"

"We're headed to an art show in Cincinnati," the woman said. "It's an Oil Painters of America show that looks fantastic."

"That sounds so exciting," Murray said. "I'm an artist myself. Or trying to be, anyway."

The couple looked at her like they wanted to ask what she was doing working as a waitress at a truck stop. Murray answered the unspoken question to break the awkward pause. "I'm saving up for college to major in art."

The woman smiled. "Good for you. There's a fantastic art school in Chicago, you know."

Murray nodded and went off to get their waters, adding a

lemon slice just in case. The woman was impressed. "Thank you so much. How did you know we love lemon?"

"I can tell you have good taste."

"Oh, Julia," Jack said. "Listen to this one." Turning to Murray, he said, "You're gonna go far in this world, kid."

"Don't call her a kid, Jack. She's obviously a talented young woman."

Murray laughed. "Actually, I still feel like kind of a kid a lot of the time."

She took their orders, then served them French toast with bacon and fruit cups. Murray thought about how wonderful it would be to travel around the country buying art. She let the couple enjoy their breakfast in peace without quizzing them about their art world.

Her mother always warned her about being too chatty with customers, but Murray usually managed to have a little fun with them. It never ceased to amaze her how many different types of people came into the diner. From truckers to traveling salesmen to visiting royalty, The Highway Diner served them all. The only thing they had in common was being hungry and ready to eat.

Isabel motioned Murray to join her at the register. Murray was sure she was about to get a lecture about daydreaming on the job, but her mother surprised her as she took her in her arms and hugged her tightly. "I just wanted to tell you how much I love watching you work these tables. You get it all done, and you're never in too much of a hurry to be friendly and kind."

Murray hugged her mother back. "Thanks, Mom. I love you too."

With that, Isabel seemed slightly embarrassed at her

outburst of maternal emotion and steered her daughter back into the dining room. "All right, that's enough of a mother-daughter moment. Go get 'em, Muriel."

Murray went back to her tables with more bounce to her step and a tear playing at the corner of her eye.

Just before noon, a young truck driver caught her attention as he eased his lanky frame into a small table near the server station. He wore black biker boots, faded black jeans with no designer tears, and a black-and-red flannel shirt. His eyes were blue and intelligent. His chin and forehead had a strong Viking look. His hair was blond and shoulder length. He looked to be in his mid-twenties. She noticed his hands and fingernails were clean, no wedding ring.

"Coffee?" Murray asked as she handed him a menu and wondered what this gorgeous man was doing driving a truck. Or maybe he was on a motorcycle or driving a car? She instantly wanted to know everything about him.

His eyes widened as he gazed up at the captivating young woman handing him the menu. Murray was five eleven, with long legs and the athletic build of the volleyball spiker she had been in high school. Her eyes were hazel and sparkling beneath softly angled brown eyebrows that were perfect for her oval-shaped face.

Murray hated to feel herself blushing as she laughed in embarrassment at his stunned reaction. "Should I repeat the question?"

"No, no need." He tried to recover with a shake of his head. "Yes, please. Coffee, black."

Murray took a couple steps to the server station and brought him back a coffee and an ice water. "Nice to see you've got everything close at hand," he said as he toasted her with the water.

Murray breathed a silent sigh of relief. He wasn't coming on to her; he was being friendly. "I'll give you some time to look at the menu." She detoured into the women's room to check herself out in the mirror. "Oh, please," she scolded as she splashed water on her face and retied her long brown ponytail. "Why would you bother?"

It was easy getting to know the young man as she took his order and served him the Big Breakfast. He was ready to talk after hours of being alone on the road. "Name's Benjamin Fitzgerald," he said. "I'm driving a Peterbilt semi from Oakland, California, to Detroit, Michigan."

"I'm Murray. How long you been driving a truck, Benjamin?"

"Actually, it's just Ben," he said. "I don't know why I said 'Benjamin.' My mother's the only one who calls me that." Murray smiled and waited for him to continue. "I been driving truck less than a year," he said. "Dropped out of college after my junior year, got into advertising for a few years. Long story. I won't bore you."

As Murray wondered how and why he got into trucking, Ben looked around her and asked, "Is that your sister working the register?"

Murray laughed. "No. I get that a lot. She's my mother. We own this place. Or, I should say, she owns it. I'll tell her what you said. She always gets a kick out of it."

"She reminds me of my mother," Ben said. "They both still look so young."

"Well, she still treats me like her baby girl. She just gave me a hug and told me what a good job I was doing. But usually I can't get through ten minutes around here without her telling me how to do something better."

Ben laughed in delight. "That's the thing about mothers.

They're always going to be our mothers. They're going to worry and try to protect us, no matter what we do. I used to think I could get my mother to stop being so motherly. Now, I hope she never does. Like, I used to hate it when she ran her fingers through my hair to spruce me up. Now, I don't mind it at all. In fact, I miss it when she doesn't do it."

Murray knew she needed to be moving on to the next table, but she was curiously attracted to Ben by the way he talked about his mother. He looked so rugged on the outside. She was surprised and flattered by how quickly he showed her his gentle side. Murray noticed him becoming self-conscious as he stroked his chin with his hand. "You probably think I'm some momma's boy now."

Murray realized she had been staring at him. She straightened up and pulled on her ponytail. "Not at all. Not in the slightest. It's just downright refreshing to hear a man talk about his mother like you do. I want to hear more, but I got tables to cover. Don't go away. I'll be back."

As she floated from table to table, Murray tried hard not to look at Ben to see if he was watching her. Every time she caught him out of the corner of her eye, he was following her every move. She was slightly out of breath when she got back to him. "So how am I doing?" she asked. "More coffee?"

"Yes, please," he said, shifting awkwardly in his chair. "And I know I shouldn't be this forward, but it feels like it would be good for us to—I don't know—take some time and get to know each other."

"Are you asking me out?" Murray spoke more bluntly than she had intended.

"Not like on a date or anything. I mean, I'm not trying to pick you up. Oh man, I'm messing this up."

"A date sounds like fun," Murray reassured him. "You are not messing anything up."

Suddenly, a young woman in a short skirt with black fishnet stockings and a pink shirt torn half off her back came screaming into the restaurant.

"Isabel, Murray . . . call the cops. Red's trying to kill me. He's after me. He's got a gun."

At the mention of the word *gun*, several diners drew handguns. Isabel grabbed her cell phone and dialed 911. Murray produced a Glock 9 mm pistol from a waistband holster in a bread drawer by the coffee pot. As she was pointing her weapon toward the door, she noticed Ben pointing his own Glock in the same direction.

The screaming woman ran into the ladies' room. It was Anita, Murray's good friend from school and a former employee of the diner. Whoever was chasing her would be a dead man before he made it through the door.

"Hold your fire until you see a weapon," one of the armed diners commanded.

Just then, a man in flip-flops, jeans, and a T-shirt came strolling innocently into the restaurant, fresh from the showers at the convenience center and store adjoining the restaurant. He did a triple take and dropped his towel and gym bag as he saw what looked like a firing squad pointing their weapons at his chest. He looked around nervously, but quickly dropped to his knees and put his hands over his head. "Don't shoot. Don't shoot. I didn't do anything."

"Hold your fire," the diner who assumed command shouted. He was stocky and bald, with a dark shadow of a beard, wearing black jeans and a blue sport coat. "This is not our guy." He pointed to the man. "Get under that table and keep your head down. Might be trouble headed our way."

Diners sitting near the only window on the front wall screamed warnings and hit the floor when they saw a man in the parking lot with a handgun taking aim at the diner.

Gunshots ripped into the outside wall of the restaurant. A bullet shattered the window and whizzed through the diner, smashing an old International Harvester truck photo on the back wall. Diners covered their heads with their hands and arms as the crashing cymbals of breaking glass shattered the peace.

"Stay low," roared the diner who had taken charge. "Get on the floor."

The shooter methodically emptied an eight-shot clip into the building. Most of the bullets hit the wall. He took his time. There were long pauses between shots. He was screaming, "Anita. I know you're in there." *Blam!* "Get your sorry ass on out here. I'm not done with you." *Blam!* "You stole from me, girl." *Blam!*

Each shot shook the restaurant with its thunder and shuddering impact. A few terrorized diners shrieked and wailed. Others were stunned into silence by the threat of sudden death. A bullet entered the roof and ricocheted down through the ceiling, exploding a full coffee pot and the machine that was keeping it warm. People at the half-moon counter had slid off the chrome stools with red Naugahyde seats and hit the floor when the first shot rang out. Diners who were on the floor crawled under tables. There was no safe place to hide. Murray was on her hands and knees, crawling toward her mother across the ceramic-vinyl tile floor. *There is no way some crazy fool is going to take my mother out. No way. Not today.*

The shooting and screaming stopped after the eighth shot. Murray froze and held her breath to listen, assuming that the shooter must be reloading. The silence seemed more deafening than the shooting. Her ears were ringing. The spinning world was slowing down like a merry-go-round running out of energy. Just when she thought the shooter had left, a much louder shot rang out that sounded like a hunting rifle. She worried the shooter had switched to a more powerful weapon, but no additional bullets struck the restaurant.

An eerie quiet descended outside. Nobody said a word until the silence was broken by a man calling out, "All clear. We got him. All clear. Show's over."

"Don't anybody move," the take-charge man said. "It could be a trick."

Traumatized diners huddled in fear on the floor until they heard sirens as police and paramedics arrived. Isabel had the dispatchers on the line. "It is over," she said loud enough for everyone in the diner to hear. "The shooter is down. A trucker shot him in the back with a rifle. They're advising us not to leave the restaurant for now."

A wary trucker in a jean jacket with motorcycle club insignia on the back looked out the shattered window and said, "I see the shooter is down in the parking lot. Some people are . . . no wait, it's the medics. They're all around him. Looks like he's not getting up any time soon."

Murray got off the floor as Ben rushed to her side. They collapsed into each other in a brief embrace of relief, each still holding a handgun. Ben was bigger and stronger than he looked sitting down. He was six-three, two hundred pounds. Murray felt herself catch her breath as she realized how wonderful he smelled. She couldn't place it. It wasn't cologne or deodorant. Maybe a body wash. *Oh my God*, she thought, *I smell like bacon and onions.*

Her mother's voice brought her out of the embrace that had

lasted a little too long. "Come on, you two. At least holster your guns before you start making out in my restaurant."

Murray and Ben separated quickly, embarrassed at falling into the arms of a near total stranger. Ben tried to recover. "Man, that was intense. I thought I was going to have to shoot somebody. I mean, I thought we were going to shoot somebody."

Isabel put her hands on her hips, threw back her head, and laughed.

"What's so funny?" Murray demanded as she tucked the handgun behind her back. She wondered how her mother could laugh when she was still shaking in her shoes.

Isabel had to bend over at the waist to catch her breath from what had turned into a hoot and howl. Her nervous laughter was exaggerated by the adrenaline of a near-death experience. When she raised up, Ben was holstering his pistol beneath his shirt. Others who had drawn handguns were doing the same. Murray glared at her mother, failing to find humor in the traumatic situation.

"I'm sorry," Isabel said, catching her breath. "It's just, I never saw love at first sight while locked and loaded."

Murray looked at Ben. They smiled at each other but were still in too much shock to understand the emotions of the moment. Ben turned to help an older couple out from under a table. The gray-haired man tried to make a joke as he grabbed his wife's arm. "Getting down was a lot easier than getting up," he said as they stood up and began sobbing in each other's arms.

Murray and Isabel checked on their customers as they emerged from underneath booths and tables. Everyone was dazed. The gunshots had been so loud as to be disorienting. People were quivering and weeping tears of relief at having survived. A husband-and-wife truck driving team held each other's shaking hands, trying to regain their emotional equilibrium. Isabel sat them down at the counter and brought them water and fresh coffee. The cooks came out of the kitchen to help calm everyone and try to settle their own racing hearts. Everyone was shell-shocked by the gunfire. The electrifying experience had been terrifying.

Gregor, the head cook, was trembling so badly he could barely hold a cup of coffee. "I thought we were all going to die," he moaned as Isabel helped him take a seat at a table and rubbed his shoulders. "It was so loud I thought it would never end." He buried his face in his hands, embarrassed by his loss of control.

The take-charge guy turned out to be a retired detective. He let out a puffy-cheek breath that became a low whistle. "That was some serious action. All that combat drama makes me want to say the first round's on me. I hope somebody in this place has some whiskey."

"I've got a bottle of Jack Black," Isabel said. "We're only licensed for beer and wine, but what the heck! Drastic times call for plastic measures." She lined up plastic cups for shot glasses on the counter and poured a round. At least ten people stepped up for a shot. Most hands were unsteady as they raised the whiskey cups. Isabel proposed a toast. "Here's to surviving the insanity," she said solemnly.

Her toast was saluted by a subdued chorus of here-here's and amen's. Once the drinks were downed, Isabel followed with a more somber thought, "And may God help the troubled soul who lost his mind today."

No one responded to her second gesture. Several diners held out their cups for a refill.

As the retired detective left to check outside, Murray heard pounding on the ladies' room door and realized her frightened friend was afraid to come out. "Hold on, Anita. I'm coming."

She tried to open the door, but it was locked. "Anita, unlock the door. It's okay. It's all over now."

"Did they kill him?" Anita was sobbing as she opened the door. "Oh, please God, tell me they didn't kill him." Mascara was running down her face. She took one look at Murray and collapsed in a heap of sadness under the sink opposite the toilet. "It was Red. Red Mavis. You met him. He's a sweet, sweet guy. I might even love him. Always pays in advance. Tips great. Then he got so crazy it wasn't him anymore. He got into the meth way too heavy. Please tell me they didn't kill him."

Murray helped Anita to her feet. "What did he do to you? Are you hurt?"

Anita looked at herself in the mirror. She was five inches shorter than Murray, but every bit as pretty: full, smirky lips, slightly turned-up nose, and wide-set hazel eyes. "Oh my God. I'm a mess," she said, beginning to wash her face gingerly. "I was smoking crack and meth with him. I'm shaking so bad. I don't know what I'm doing. Please tell me he's all right."

"We don't know how he is," said Murray. "We can't leave the restaurant right now." She gritted her teeth. "Oh, God, Anita. You've got a nasty cut on your right cheek. It's bleeding bad. It's bruising up already. Did he hit you? Don't tell me he hit you with his gun. You're lucky he didn't kill you. We're lucky he didn't kill us all."

Anita swooned and fell to her knees. She would have collapsed to the floor if Murray hadn't scooped her up. "Look at you, Anita. You're skin and bones. How could we let this happen to you? I told you a hundred times to quit tricking, but you laughed in my face. Now look at you. You look like a ghost—a beat-up ghost."

Anita sobbed. "Don't, Murray. Don't say it. Don't say 'I told you so.' I know I should have kept working with you. You were always the strong one. And I was weak. I'm still weak. Look at me. I went for the easy money. I was going to get out. But look at me now. I'm a mess. I didn't quit. And now it's too late."

Murray wrapped her arms around her friend and hugged her gently. "I'm not going to say I told you so. I should have seen this coming. We all should have gotten you into rehab a long time ago. It's not too late, Anita. You just got a wake-up call, that's all. You're going to be fine. Go ahead and cry. It's good to cry. Everything's gonna be all right."

Isabel knocked on the bathroom door. "Muriel, are you in there? Everything okay?"

"Come on in, Mom. It's open."

Isabel walked in carrying two shots of whiskey and set them on the counter. Murray released Anita from the hug. "Oh, my sweet Jesus," Isabel said. "Anita, look what he's done to you. Your eye's red with blood. Your whole face is battered. Good Lord, we'd better get you to a doctor."

"No, no, no," Anita's voice was desperately hoarse. "I've got drugs in my purse, and they'll find my fingerprints all inside his truck. I can't get arrested. I'm still on probation."

Isabel handed a shot to Murray, who swallowed it whole. She handed the second shot to Anita. "You look like you could use this, but are you sure you want it?"

Anita blasted back the whiskey like a gunslinger in a saloon.

"Okay, now. You're okay?" Murray asked Anita. "You're not going to puke?"

"I can cope," Anita croaked.

Murray picked up Anita's purse off the floor and emptied it on the sink counter. Several bottles of pills, a small bag of weed, and two baggies of crack and meth spilled out. Isabel gasped in horror as Murray emptied out the contraband, poured it into the toilet, and flushed the evidence.

"There," Murray said. "So much for violating probation."

Anita collapsed on the floor before Murray or Isabel could catch her. The sight of her drugs going away in a swirl was too much for her. "It doesn't matter," she swooned. "They're gonna drug test me anyway."

A knock on the door startled the three women.

Ben cracked open the door. "Sorry to intrude, but the cops are wanting to talk to the owner and all the witnesses."

Murray looked at her mother. "You go, Mom. I'll take care of Anita."

Isabel pointed her finger at Murray. "Don't even think about sneaking her out of here. She's hurt. She needs a doctor. She's in shock. Stay down, Anita. I'll get paramedics to come in here and carry you out on a stretcher. You're the victim here, nothing else. And, by God, you'll look like a victim getting hauled out of here. God damn it, Anita, I don't know why you wouldn't listen to me. I told you this kind of trouble would happen. You could have gotten us all killed."

Anita put her hands over her face and sobbed. She sounded pathetic and hopeless. Isabel softened and kneeled beside her. "Come on now, girl. I'm sorry. I don't mean to be hard on you. Guess my nerves are still pretty shot. You know I love you."

Anita pulled her hands off her face and sniffled somewhat hopefully. "I love you too, Isabel."

Ben backed out of the door as Isabel rose and offered one last bit of advice. "Just remember, Anita, don't confess anything to the police. You weren't tricking, you weren't doing drugs, you were on your way to lunch when you got attacked. You got that?"

Anita raised her right hand in appreciation as Isabel left the restroom.

CHAPTER TWO

The ambulance arrived with flashing lights and a screaming siren. Paramedics turned off the siren but kept the lights flashing as they jumped out and rushed into the diner with Murray showing them the way. The medics took one look at Anita and loaded her onto a stretcher. Anita lifted her head up as much as she could with the brace around her neck and safety straps across her body.

"Did they kill him?"

Murray was by her side as they lifted Anita into the ambulance. "Don't you worry about that right now. Relax as much as you can." She whispered in Anita's ear, "Don't say anything. The cops don't need to know you care about Red. The less they know, the better."

Anita closed her eyes, understanding. Murray stepped away from the ambulance and waved as it pulled away. The front window of the diner was shattered, as well as the long, narrow sign on top of the building that said, "The Highway Diner." She had hand-painted the black letters on a white background six months ago. *How could anyone violate such a wholesome, homemade place as this?* Her fear and shock were simmering into an angry stew.

Ben walked toward her with open arms. She leaned into him for a careful hug. Only then did she cry. The gunfire had been whipping her emotions into a fine frenzy for the last hour. She settled into a terrible sadness.

She'd never felt this way before: humiliated, abused even. One crazy man with a gun had scarred so many lives. The coffee pot shattering could have been a person. She pulled away from Ben.

Isabel's face was drawn and distraught. The adrenaline had worn off. She'd been crying too. Murray grabbed her mother like they hadn't seen each other in years. "Oh, Mom. I was crawling across the floor with my gun to get to you."

They cried in each other's arms. "Your daddy would've been so proud of you, Muriel," she said. They stared at each other in the silent relief of shocked survivors. Ben turned to walk away, but Isabel grabbed his arm and brought him into the hug. "Get over here, young man. You're in this too."

The detective in charge of the investigation walked over to ask a few questions. Isabel wiped her eyes with a tissue and beat him to the punch. "How's the man who shot up my restaurant?"

The detective looked at the ground as if deciding whether to respond. He loosened his tie, kicked at a piece of gravel, and blurted, "He's dead. One bullet in the back, straight through the heart, massive exit wound. They took him out in an ambulance, but he's going to the morgue. The guy who shot him is a deer hunter. It's his first human, though. He's pretty shook up."

"We all are," Isabel said. "More than shaken up. We're devastated. You never think something like this could happen here. Then it does, and you wonder why you didn't see it coming. Guess this means the restaurant shuts down. How long do you think? One week? Two?"

"We'll be done by late tonight," the detective said. "After that, it's up to you."

"Okay," Isabel said. She turned to Murray and said, "Looks

like we'd better get back in there to clean her up and close her down. We're out of business for now."

"Couple questions first, if you don't mind," the detective said. He took a note pad and pen out of his wrinkled sport coat. "What can you tell me about the woman he beat up? What was her relationship to Red Mavis?"

Isabel straightened as if someone had poured cold water down her back. "You're talking about Anita. Anita Montgomery. She's beat up bad. She's only nineteen years old. She'll be twenty soon. I know her well. She used to work here as a waitress."

"What about her relationship to Mr. Mavis?"

Isabel frowned. "If you're talking about the asshole who beat up my girl and shot up my restaurant, I don't know anything about that."

The detective looked at Murray, and she responded, "She stopped working here about a year ago, but she still comes in to eat pretty regularly."

"She's a friend of yours?"

"I'd say so, yes."

The detective tilted his head and leaned in ever so slightly. "Then you know she's on probation for a prostitution charge?"

Murray didn't flinch. "I do know that, but I also know she was cleaning up her act to make it through probation."

The detective looked at Ben, who shook his head. "I'm just driving through, Oakland to Detroit. First time here."

The detective wrote down his information. "Any idea why Red was so mad at her?"

Murray answered, "Probably looking for a trick and she wouldn't cooperate."

"Okay, then," the detective said with an exaggerated exhale

as he put away his pen and notebook. "This isn't really about Anita, anyway. And the only one who committed a crime is deceased. So, I guess that's all the questions I have for now."

Murray and Isabel thanked the detective. "I'll be done in a couple hours," Murray said to Ben.

Ben smiled. "See you then."

———

The diner was quiet by the time Ben walked back in at 4:30 p.m. Chairs were stacked on the tables, and the floor was still shining wet from mopping. Murray pretended to be surprised to see him. "Ben. You came back. I was hoping you would. We're closed now, for how long we don't know. Maybe we can go somewhere and talk."

Isabel came out of the kitchen and opened her arms for Ben. "I need a hug," she said. "My restaurant has yellow police tape all around it. Looks like I'll be closed for who knows how long. Give the public a little time to forget somebody got killed in my parking lot."

"Oh, Mom, I shouldn't leave you here tonight."

"No, no. You two go. Talk it out. Try to make some sense out of this crazy day. I've got Lois and Jean coming over for a little red wine support group."

"Are you sure?" Murray gave her mother a kiss on the cheek.

"Yes, I'm sure." Turning to Ben, she said, "Make sure you have her home sometime tonight."

Ben gave her a grateful smile. "I'll have her home by midnight."

———

Murray drove her trusty, rusty Toyota pickup truck. They swung by her house so Murray could change out of her work clothes. Ben waited in the pickup, but he didn't have to wait long. Murray raced into the house looking like a truck stop waitress and emerged a few moments later in black skinny jeans and a red tunic sweater, two inches taller in black suede ankle boots.

"Whoa, Wonder Woman," Ben said as he jumped out of the pickup to fully appraise her new look. "You're making me feel underdressed."

Murray got back behind the wheel and looked at Ben. "You look fine. You don't smoke do you?"

He laughed. "What is this? A job interview?"

"No, I just don't let anyone smoke in my truck."

"Neither do I," Ben said. "Not even marijuana."

"So, you do get high?"

"Nah. The company drug tests its drivers. How about you?"

"I stay away from that. I see what it does to people. Mom and I stick to booze."

"But didn't you tell me you're not twenty-one?" He poked her playfully on the shoulder.

"Please," Murray laughed. "It won't be long. And by the way, I know this is a little weird, but I've got to stop at the hospital to see Anita before we go anywhere else. You could come in with me or you could wait in the car."

"I'll do whatever you want."

"Good answer," Murray said. "So, okay. Come in with me. We won't be long."

Ben pretended to open the automatic front door for her as they walked into the hospital. Murray bobbed a playful curtsey before sobering her mood at the information desk. She was pleased when he got serious and offered his hand as they walked down the hall to Anita's room. Murray accepted his emotional support. The shooting had shaken her to the core.

Anita was resting fitfully on a morphine drip for a broken cheekbone, multiple facial contusions, and two broken ribs. Her right eye was bruised purple and swollen shut. Murray bent down closely to whisper the good news about the police investigation not focusing on her. Anita nodded weakly and said, "I hope nobody checks the blood they've been taking from me."

"Don't worry," Murray said. "Remember, this is nothing but a wake-up call. By the way, this is Ben. He was in the diner when the shooting started."

Anita nodded to Ben. "I hear they killed Red," she whispered.

"Afraid so. I'm sorry, Nita. I know you cared about him."

"Did he suffer?"

"No, he probably didn't even feel it."

Anita closed her eyes. A tear worked its way down her bruised cheek.

"How are you doing?" Murray asked.

Before she could answer, a nurse came in and suggested Anita needed to rest. Murray kissed Anita on the forehead and said goodbye.

Neither Ben nor Murray said a word until they were out of the hospital and back in the pickup. "What a day," Murray said. "I'm completely drained. I feel so sorry for Anita. Somebody she really cared about got shot to death, and here I am saying he probably didn't feel a thing. Was that insensitive?"

"Not at all," Ben responded quickly.

Murray drove them to the Old Crown Coffee Roasters Bistro. "It's a nice, quiet place. We can have coffee and talk, or we can have cocktails. The food's good here too."

"I could use a beer myself," Ben said. "Maybe two or three beers. I've never been shot at before. You can see it in the movies your whole life and never have any idea what a game changer it is."

"It paralyzed me at first," Murray said. "Then I thought about Mom, and I got so mad I wanted to kill the bastard. And then he was dead, and we all felt bad about it. It's been a real roller coaster of a day. I've been sick to my stomach since the shooting, but now I'm famished."

"A burger would hit the spot," Ben said. "I'm hungry too. It's not every day you get involved in a shootout and meet a woman who takes your breath away." He paused to check her reaction.

Murray glanced at Ben and smiled as she undid her seat belt. "And now I'm ready for a shot of whiskey and a beer. I need to blow off a little steam. They won't card me here. I know the bartenders. And, yeah, a burger does sound good."

Ben paused, then said, "There's something you need to know, Murray."

Oh no. He's going to tell me he has a girlfriend.

"I'm not the kind of guy who gets serious with a woman on the first date. It's just that everything feels so right with you. And what a bizarre coincidence! What are the chances of us getting together in the middle of a shootout?"

"I know," Murray said, breathing a sigh of relief. "It's almost spooky."

Before they got out of the car, Ben switched conversational gears and said, "Hey, you mentioned you're an artist. What kind of art are you into?"

"I mainly draw now, but I want to be a painter someday."

"I'd like to see your artwork sometime."

"You can see it right now," Murray said as she reached over

and retrieved a nine-by-twelve-inch sketch pad from behind the passenger seat.

Ben opened the book and studied the first few drawings, nodding appreciatively. He paused when he came to a figure study of a young woman staring up at a light and holding her hand over her head. "This is good. It looks like she's reaching for enlightenment."

Murray nudged him with her shoulder. "Thanks. That's from when I was in high school. Keep going, they get better."

"I can see that," Ben said, turning pages until he came to a landscape drawing of an oak tree on a hill with a man on horseback in the distance. "Murray, you are really talented. Look at the perspective. The rider, the tree. It's perfect. I love the shadow shading."

"I see you know something about art."

"My mother was a painter when I was growing up. She always joked about how people say they don't know much about art but they know what they like. Then later, she came around to saying that's all that matters, what you like. It's all about whether a painting speaks to you. And, let me say, your work speaks to me loud and clear."

"You said your mother was an artist. Does that mean she's not with us anymore?"

Ben thought about the question so long that Murray wished she hadn't asked it. Then he closed the sketchbook with a heavy sigh. "She's still with us, but she doesn't paint anymore. She stopped when my father ran off with one of his nurses." He paused as if to let the sadness sink in, then said, "That was a few years ago. Mom and Dad are divorced now. She's planning on getting back into her art, but she hasn't been able to do it yet."

"I'm sorry to hear all that, Ben," Murray said. "I hope she gets back to painting. It's what I want to do more than anything. It makes me feel so . . . I don't know . . . so alive, I guess."

Ben's eyes widened. "That's exactly what she always says. Amazing. It must be something artists say."

"Not just artists," Murray said. "People say that about what they love to do. I'll bet there's some happy plumbers out there who say the same thing."

Ben laughed with her. "No doubt. So, how does waiting tables at a truck stop fit into your plan?"

Murray considered his tone. It was straight forward. He wasn't asking the question like working at a truck stop was a bad thing or beneath her. He seemed genuinely interested in what she wanted to do with her life. "Mom really needs the help right now. It's been hard on her since my father died. But what I'm really doing is saving up for art school."

"Sounds like a good plan." He leaned in and kissed her gently.

CHAPTER THREE

"Heard you come in around midnight last night," Isabel said as she poured herself a steaming hot coffee and sat down at the kitchen table in her purple pajamas and blue kimono robe. "You two were on the front porch so long I was afraid you were going to invite him in for a sleepover. Then you left and came back. What happened?"

Murray was puzzled until she remembered. "Oh, that's right. I forgot about that. Ben walked me to the front door and we got so carried away talking that we forgot he was riding in my truck so I had to take him back to his truck."

Isabel nodded and smiled.

Murray smelled bacon in the oven as she headed for the coffee in her oversized Notre Dame sweatshirt. "You slept in. It's almost nine thirty. Smells like you've been busy. What time did you get up?"

"I was up at the usual five o'clock until I remembered we don't have a restaurant today. Damn fool shot us up and right out of business for who knows how long." She took a pouty sip of coffee.

Murray pulled her mother into a hug. "It's going to be all right. We'll be back in business in no time."

"I don't even want to turn on the morning news," Isabel said. "Everybody thinks we're trucker trash anyway." She put her elbows on the table and held her head in her hands. "My head is pounding. Me and the girls had a good cry and too much to drink over the whole thing. I got up at five, had three glasses of water and a couple of aspirin, and went back to bed. Slept til eight thirty. I haven't slept in like that in I don't know how long. Maybe never. Not since you were born, anyway."

Murray grabbed her coffee and sat down at the table. "Aren't you going to ask me about Ben?"

"I don't have to ask," Isabel said. "I can see it all over your face. You're in love. To tell the truth, I'm amazed you didn't spend the night in his sleeper and run off with him in the morning."

Murray spit the too-hot coffee back into the cup. "Is that the kind of girl you think I am? You know I wouldn't run off and leave you alone after all this."

"Oh, honey, I was only teasing," Isabel said. "I wish your father were still around. We need him now. I miss him so much. I keep waiting for him to walk in the door and help us figure out what to do."

"What are you cooking?" Murray asked. "It smells delicious. I'm starving."

"It's the sausage and egg casserole we have at the restaurant. I haven't made it at home in a long time. It smells even better here, don't you think?"

Murray jumped up. "I'll set the table and make the toast. You dish that stuff up and let's talk about Ben and Daddy and how to make a comeback at the restaurant."

Breakfast was served in a flash, as only two pros could organize. Mother and daughter savored the food and the moment. They weren't ready to talk about yesterday's trauma, but they were alive and together and eating the perfect breakfast. Isabel served up seconds on the casserole before she asked the big question.

"So, how was Ben?"

Murray had a big bite of casserole and toast on the way to her mouth. "He was good," she said with a full mouth, then swallowed and took a sip of orange juice.

"Don't talk with your mouth full, dear." Isabel couldn't help herself from treating her daughter like a child who needed to learn her manners.

Murray took a big gulp of juice and wiped her mouth with an exaggerated flourish of the napkin before continuing. "He was perfect."

"You said that."

"He was a perfect gentleman. He rode in my little truck and didn't make any jokes about it. We went to see Anita. She got admitted with some broken facial bones and two broken ribs."

"That bastard," Isabel said, referring to the shooter. "He got what he deserved."

"Then we went out for a couple drinks and a long talk at the Old Crown. He loved my sketches. He said we should turn the restaurant into an art gallery, and I could sell my art if I did paintings of guys' trucks. His mother was an artist, and he kind of lost her like we lost Daddy, and we talked about you and Daddy."

"Hold on," Isabela said. "That's all well and good. I can see how excited you are. But did he kiss you?"

"We kissed in my pickup, if you must know. He was very respectful."

"Good. I knew I liked that boy," Isabel beamed. "He didn't invite you into his truck, did he?"

"No, he did not," Murray said. "And if he had, I would not have gone. I'm not like Anita, bless her heart."

"That's my good girl." Isabel took Murray's hands across the table. "I know it hasn't been easy for you with the boys."

Murray had her heart broken by her first boyfriend in the ninth grade who took a liking to one of her best friends. Then, the young man who took her to the junior dance lied to his friends about having sex with her. Worst of all, her volleyball coach tried to put the moves on her several times until she finally notified school authorities.

"We both know what pigs men can be," Isabel continued. "It sounds like you might have found a good one. Does he have any tattoos?"

"Don't try to trick me." Murray shook her hair back over her shoulders. "But yes, he's got some ink. He's got a sleeve from his right shoulder to his elbow. It's a tiger in a tree. And no, I didn't see it. He told me about it."

Isabel shook her head. "I'll never get this tattoo thing. You know how much I hated it when you got that dragonfly in the middle of your back. I'll never understand why people want to wear the same shirt for the rest of their lives."

Murray sidestepped the never-ending tattoo debate with her mother. "But here's the best part about Ben. He's got great ideas for more art in the restaurant and even a line of clothing in the store."

"Hmm," Isabel mused. "Jeans and flannel shirts, maybe even some leather jackets. We could do better than the baseball caps and socks we've got now. That's for sure."

"Ben thought we could reopen and make it an event. Have a stage and let our drivers get up and talk about how much the truck plaza means to people from all around the country, and have a preacher say a prayer for the man who died, and use microphones, and have musicians, and do a press release, and invite the media, and turn the tragedy into an advertising event. Ben knows about this stuff. He worked in advertising for a couple years after he dropped out of Stanford."

"Stanford?" Isabel said. "That's a big-time school. You've got to be a genius to get in. Why'd he drop out?"

"He was pre-med, and he didn't want to turn out like his asshole father."

"Pre-med? What's he doing driving a semi?"

"He thought he'd go see the world, but now he realizes you don't see much driving the interstate highways. He's about to give it up for something new."

Isabel looked dumbfounded as Murray paused to take a breath. "Do you think we could pull off an event for re-opening?"

"Oh yeah," Murray said. "We could invite the mayor and the chief of police and talk about how the trucking community is coming together to make the world safe for democracy, or whatever it needs to be safe for. Tell the people what really goes on here at the crossroads of Middle America. We're not trailer trash or trucker trash. We're only trash if we think we are. And we are most definitely not trash. Ben called us the backbone of the supply chain. Said the world couldn't survive without what we do to keep product rolling down the road."

Isabel buttered another piece of toast. "You know what? I think he's right on. That's what your father always said. We're the most important cog in the wheel. Anyway, where is Ben now?"

"He's halfway to Detroit by now. He's a hardworking guy. And, man, is he organized. You should see the inside of his truck." Murray stopped, realizing she'd said too much.

Isabel put down the toast. "I thought you said he didn't invite you into his truck."

Murray squirmed in her chair like a fifth grader caught passing notes in class. "No, he didn't invite me in. I just looked in when he went to get his jacket."

"Murray," Isabel used her stern voice to keep from smiling.

"Okay, I got in for a little while, but only to show him I knew how to drive a rig. He made me show him my commercial driver's license first. Then, I backed him into the best spot on the lot, between the restaurant and the truck wash. He was impressed. I was smooth as silk, even in reverse. I had to show him I could do it after I bragged about Daddy teaching me."

Isabel smiled at the mention of her late husband. Then she asked, "What's this about Ben losing his mother? Did she die?"

"No, his dad is a surgeon who ran off with one of his nurses, and divorced his wife. She stopped painting when he left her with the two kids, Ben and his older sister."

"Surgeon, huh? Kid comes from money. Good job, Muriel."

"Mom, don't be crass."

"So, what's he doing driving a truck? Why isn't he in med school?"

"He doesn't want to be anything like his father. I told you that already. He's off to see the world."

"In a semi?" Isabel raised her voice.

"What's wrong with that? Daddy drove an eighteen-wheeler."

"For fifteen years," Isabel said. "He made good money, but then he started to hate it. Too much alone time. You remember, he said it all the time. That's why we got into the restaurant business. Then we bought the land and opened the store and the truck wash."

"Oh, Mom, I miss him so much. He always knew what to do."

"Well, he didn't always know, but he never let that stop him. He was turning this truck stop into a gold mine when he died." Isabel paused in a moment of silent sorrow. "He would have hated what happened yesterday. It would have broken his heart like it did ours."

Murray finished her orange juice and set the glass on the table. "What would he do now?"

Isabel looked Murray in the eye. "He'd tell us to get up and running as soon as possible."

"What about Ben's idea of a press conference?"

"No, I don't think so," Isabel said. "But we'll open when the cops give us the okay and we get the window fixed. I need time to think about this. I might call the media in for a visit to see how we're doing. I'm not going to sit around and mope. We do have our truckers' numbers from the overnight parking registration. We could call them and get a rally going."

Murray jumped up to start clearing the table. "That's the spirit. I'll call the staff and see if they'll come back when we need them."

"We might have some trouble there," Isabel said. "Some of our people might be afraid to come back."

"Then we'll get new people," Murray said. "This whole thing will blow over before you know it."

"Don't be too sure of that, Muriel. It's going to take us all quite a while to get over what happened yesterday."

CHAPTER FOUR

The Highway Diner reopened three days later with enough food and staff to handle what Murray predicted would be a massive truck rodeo. She had no idea how right she would be. Tractor-trailers rolled in from Detroit, Indianapolis, Chicago, and as far away as Louisiana. Traffic was snarled for miles. Parking was impossible. The rally turned into a regional media event.

Big Ed from Shreveport, Louisiana, told the ABC reporter from South Bend, "I detoured from my Maryland route to make it for this. Not sorry I did. Look around. Everybody's here. It's truck-stop Woodstock. We all come for peace. We're the backbone of this nation—hell, of the world. One crazy shooter, who happened to be a truck driver, doesn't make all of us dangerous. We're family men. And we all love The Highway Diner. Isabel takes care of us real good. Food's tasty, gas is cheap, and the showers are clean."

Isabel gave Big Ed a hug. She had tears in her eyes as she looked directly into the camera. "Hey, y'all. This here's Big Ed. Old friend of mine and my husband's. All the way from Louisiana. Come to support The Highway Diner. It's drivers like Big Ed that make this country great. So, tell 'em, Ed, how far away did you have to park?"

Big Ed looked at the sky and let out a hoot. "Man, I'm two miles down the road at the Holiday Inn. Me and three other drivers shared an Uber to get here."

The reporter tried to regain control of the interview. "So,

you're Isabel, owner of The Highway Diner?" Isabel beamed as the reporter continued. "How are you going to feed this crowd? There must be more than a thousand people here."

"We're gonna switch over to takeout," Isabel shouted. She was dressed for the occasion in a red cowgirl pantsuit with white fringe and silver stallion embroidery. She looked and sounded like a country star. "We got a great country band—The Long Road Band—about to kick it off on a stage in the parking lot. They got here from Nashville, Tennessee, last night. They're big-time good, and they're playing for free to support the cause. Thank God the weather's good. It's almost seventy degrees out. Feel that sunshine? That's God shinin' down on the little old Highway Diner."

With that, Isabel was completely engulfed by a cheering throng. Five other television outlets were filming the wild scene. The reporter from South Bend wasn't about to lose her story. She jumped into the fray, holding her own camera, and got next to Isabel.

"You said people are here to support the cause. What is the cause?"

"The cause is Trucker Nation," Isabel shouted. "Peace and freedom and Trucker Nation."

Murray had not thought about the term "Trucker Nation" until it came rolling off her mother's tongue in the heat of the moment. Murray knew right away it had the staying power of a memorable slogan. Murray saw her mother disappear into the crowd and fought her way through the crush of people to reach her. The crowd was chanting "Trucker Nation" as Murray wrapped her arms around her mother from behind. "Mom! Come on. We need you in the restaurant. This isn't even safe out here anymore. You can do interviews inside."

Isabel nodded, and the two women tried to make their way

back inside. It was no use. They were trapped between a crush of enthusiastic people. Murray felt claustrophobic and panicky until she saw a large man parting the waters, one person at a time. She didn't know who it was, but she got the distinct feeling he was coming to her rescue. Then she recognized the voice when he yelled, "Make way, make way, coming through. Mission from God. Coming through. Official business. Make way. Murray! Isabel!"

It was Ben. She wondered what he was doing in Fort Wayne. He wasn't due in until tomorrow. She wanted to kiss him, but too many people were pushing in on them. She grabbed his arm with her right hand and her mother's arm with her left. With Ben leading the way, they were able to get back inside the restaurant.

Isabel took command of the food operation. "Ricky, tell the cooks we're shifting to takeout only. Limited menu. Cheeseburger and fries or fish and chips, five dollars. That's it. Do it now. We'll move all drinks out to the parking lot. Junior, set up wine and beer by the band, five dollars a drink. No coffee. Martha, get three big tubs of bottled water and soft drinks out there. Two bucks a bottle. Cash only. Go."

The cooks started grilling burgers and deep-frying fish and fries, faster than fast food. Ben set up a do-it-yourself condiment array on the wall next to the registers. Murray was amazed at how efficiently he moved.

"You look like you been doing this your whole life."

He flashed her a sly smile. "I worked in the cafeteria when I was in high school. It got me out of class early, and I got as much free food as I could eat."

Murray wanted to hug him, but they were too busy passing out lunch bags at the serving tables. "By the way," she managed to ask him, "What are you doing here today?"

"Are you kidding me?" He laughed. "This is the biggest thing to happen in a long time. It's all anybody's talking about on the CB. I dropped everything and came as fast as I could. I'll probably get fired because I didn't get enough sleep time on the electronic logbook."

Murray chuckled and returned to the task at hand. The crowd was mostly truckers, men and women who understood how to keep things moving. They paid quickly, grabbed their order, and moved on to the condiment table to keep the line moving. A tall driver with long hair and a full beard opened his bag of fries and took a deep, satisfying sniff. He held out the bag to Ben. "Here, buddy, have a couple of fries off the top. They smell better than McDonald's."

With a sweeping flourish of his arm, Ben took a fry and made a big scene by dangling it over his open mouth and taking it in like a fish on a worm. The line applauded as it kept moving. "Oh man, that is tasty beyond belief," Ben howled. "Come on, people, step right up. We got the finest fish, fries, and burgers in the land." Then he grabbed Murray by the arm and lowered his voice. "Seriously, we need some of those fries for ourselves."

Murray reached into a bag and grabbed an order of fries to set between them. "How about that for service?"

Isabel joined them at the table as the band outside kicked off their set in the parking lot. "Eating on the job, I see." She shoved three fries into her mouth. Her eyes widened. "Oh my. I had no idea. They taste even better than they smell. That's the new vendor out of Idaho. And you know what I always say about potatoes." She paused and raised her voice to make sure everybody within listening distance was paying attention. "What I always say is if you want good potatoes, buy 'em from the people who grow 'em."

The crowd cheered. Murray got into the act as she danced and yelled like a carnival barker. "Step right up and get your red-hot Idaho fries, straight from the farm. All the way from Idaho. Don't be shy, have a fry."

Murray and Isabel continued entertaining as the spirit moved them. Ben fit right into the family shtick. Servers kept bringing them tall beers. Spirits soared. Murray and Ben eventually took a break from their serving frenzy to go outside and listen to the band.

"Good Lord," Ben said, "I've never seen anything like this. Look at the crowd." He jumped up. "I can't even see the end of it."

Murray hugged him. "My mother loves you. Did you see the way she looks at you?"

"I love your mother," Ben said. "She looks like Loretta Lynn in that cowgirl outfit. How long can she keep all this up?"

Murray shrugged her shoulders and held out her hands. "Indefinitely. The woman works harder than any three people I know, except for maybe you and me."

The band sounded big-time good. Murray and Ben had to shout at each other to talk until The Long Road Band brought a hard-rock country song to a drum-thumping, guitar-crunching finale. The crowd erupted into a screaming, foot-stomping ovation. Blake Dawson, the lead singer, bowed until the applause died down. He wore a tattered straw cowboy hat with an American flag headband that dangled down to his golden boot spurs. He was tall and handsome in a Clint Eastwood way. "Let's hear it, Fort Wayne, for the greatest truck stop in the country: The Highway Diner!"

The audience went wild, and Dawson waved his arms and asked them to settle down. "Easy now, y'all. We got a very special guest who wants to say a few words to reflect on the importance of this occasion. We got none other than the Big Kahuna of this fine city, Mayor Harry Balls."

The crowd roared in delight at the semi-obscene introduction. The mayor raised his hands over his head in triumph, undaunted by the laughter, as he took the microphone. "That's Baals for you out-of-towners. Baals, like in bales of hay." The crowd drowned him out with good-natured jeers.

The mayor beamed at the crowd, unafraid to laugh at himself. "Don't worry, people. This isn't the first time I've heard jokes about my last name. The good thing is people don't forget it."

Now the applause was genuine and respectful. The mayor had passed his stage test under fire. "But I didn't come here to talk about myself. First of all, I want to thank Isabel and her daughter, Murray, and all the good people at The Highway Diner." The audience cheered for a good thirty seconds. "What we're doing here is showing the world the fortitude and resilience of the people of Fort Wayne and the trucking community nationwide." More cheering.

"Three days ago, a terrible act of violence disrupted our peaceful community. An act of violence that could have torn us apart. An act that could have shut down this vital hub of commerce. But did we let that stand in our way?"

As the crowd thundered a collective cheer of defiance, a thin man wearing eyeglasses and clerical garb with a white collar eased his way between the mayor and the microphone.

"My name is Cal Mavis. My brother, Red Mavis, was shot to death right here. For no good reason. It was murder, plain and simple."

A plainclothes police officer from the mayor's detail grabbed the clergyman from behind, but the mayor held him off, saying, "Let the man say his peace."

A hushed silence came over the crowd.

The clergyman looked surprised to be allowed to continue. "My brother . . ." He choked up, then regained his voice as boos and jeering began popping up in the crowd. He raised his voice. "My brother wouldn't hurt anybody. I know he was shooting a gun. But not at anybody. He was shooting at a wall when they gunned him down. He had a terrible drug problem. They never should have killed him. It was murder!"

The mayor nodded for his police detail to remove the clergyman, who was quickly hustled away from the stage.

The mayor didn't miss a beat as he regained the microphone. "The priest, or whatever he is, does have a point. It is important to remember that a life was lost. And we, as a God-fearing community, must take notice of that life. I call on everyone here to observe a moment of silence for the life of Red Mavis."

The silence didn't last five seconds before someone shouted, "Fuck Red Mavis. You shoot up our truck stop, you die."

A storm of obscenities interrupted the mayor's attempted eulogy. Blake Dawson mercifully took control of the microphone and said, "Thank you, Mr. Mayor. I think we can all agree with the mayor that it takes more than one bad apple to spoil the Trucker Nation barrel. But let me add this on behalf of the band: we came up here from Nashville to support The Highway Diner, not the damn fool who shot her up. And that's all I got to say. So, hit it, boys."

The band kicked in hard and fast, soon drowning out the delirious and triumphant roar of approval from the crowd. Ben grabbed Murray and twirled her smoothly. The boy knew how to dance. It had been a long time since Murray had fun dancing with a guy. All her athletic moves came together as Ben spun her around and caught her in his arms, again and again. It felt so natural and easy and free. They would have cut a much wider rug if the crowd hadn't been so tight.

By the time the band took a break, Murray and Ben were exhausted and ready for a cold beer. They got two frothy cups and took big gulps. Murray gave Ben a beer-foam kiss that lasted long enough for envious onlookers to begin applauding.

CHAPTER FIVE

The Highway Diner rally didn't break up until 11:00 p.m., long after the band had packed up, but shortly after Isabel stopped serving beer and wine. The giant party moved to the strip clubs and hotels surrounding the truck stop and to high- and low-class bars all the way downtown. The revelry spread like wildfire.

By midnight, Ben, Murray, and Isabel were the only people left inside the restaurant. They stared at each other in exhausted silence until Murray wondered aloud, "You know, what do you think about that preacher guy saying they shouldn't have killed his brother, Red Mavis?"

Isabel took a long sip of beer. "He probably wasn't a preacher or a priest."

"And he probably wasn't his brother," Ben added.

The three of them laughed tiredly. Isabel filled their glasses from a pitcher of beer.

"My, my," Murray said. "Aren't we the skeptics?"

Ben looked up at the ceiling, puffed his cheeks to blow out a deep breath, and said, "Whether he was a brother or a preacher or whatever probably doesn't matter. The question is, should the guy with the hunting rifle kill the crazy man with the drug problem?"

"He could have at least shot him in the leg," Murray said.

"He was shooting up a restaurant full of people," Isabel

protested. "He didn't know where those bullets were going. We're lucky he didn't kill somebody. Besides, if they shot him in the leg, he'd probably just return fire."

Murray and Ben looked at each other and nodded. *Mom's right again*, Murray thought. *When she's right, she's right.* And no doubt about it, the crowd agreed about using deadly force against an active shooter. So did the police and the news media.

Ben echoed her thoughts. "Did you hear the crowd when the band said they were here to support The Highway Diner, not the damn fool who shot her up? I've never heard such a roar."

"The whole day made me realize what we've got here," Isabel said. "Ever since my husband, Brodie, died, the diner's been a heavy weight on my heart. It's like I've been running this place to keep him alive. I felt like a slave to his ghost, sailing a ship without a rudder."

Murray and Ben were stunned into silence by her revealing confession, waiting for her to continue.

"Well, let me tell you," Isabel said. "Today changed all that. Oh my, how Brodie would have loved today. I heard his big laugh in my head all day. He was cheering us on, reminding me how important all this is, what a wonderful service we provide. We built this place up out of nothing, you know. Brodie and me. Nobody else. When we bought the place, it was nothing but a few diesel and gas pumps and a shabby, little convenience store with a leaky roof. It took a couple years, but we eventually laid the block ourselves to add this restaurant. Muriel helped. Remember that, hon? You were only thirteen years old."

"Like yesterday," Murray said. "The blocks were too heavy for me, but Daddy taught me how to string a level line and slop mortar."

"Slop mortar?" Ben asked. "That doesn't sound good."

"That's just what Brodie called it," Isabel said. "Muriel actually got to be quite the little mason on that job."

"Your late husband sounds like a good man," Ben said. "How did you two meet?"

Isabel chuckled, took a long swig of beer, and set her glass down hard on the table. "Funny you should ask. I was just thinking about that. I met Brodie the same way you and Muriel met. I was waiting tables in a truck stop south of Chicago when Brodie came rolling in like a hurricane. He was just out of the Marines, tall and lean and rugged, and driving the most beautiful purple rig I ever saw. I fell so hard for him I never got over it. I'm still not over him."

She began to tear up and lowered her head. "He used to call me Izzy, but after he died, I made everyone call me Isabel. It was my grandma's name on my mother's side." Murray took her mother's hand across the table. Isabel looked up and wiped her eyes with a napkin. "But you know what? Today was a major step for me. I'd been thinking I was keeping this place going for Brodie. But as we all pitched in to handle that huge crowd, I began to see it's all the truckers we're doing this for. Not just Brodie."

Now Murray was crying. She grabbed Ben's hand with her other hand so the three of them formed a loop.

Isabel went from crying to laughing as she recalled, "We saw each other for a couple years, then one day he told me about a business opportunity in Fort Wayne, Indiana. That turned out to be this place. Then he got down on one knee and asked me to marry him and be his partner and run the restaurant. He didn't even have a ring."

"So you said yes right away?" Murray asked even though she had heard this story many, many times before.

"Said yes? Hell, no. I got down on my knees and kissed him so hard we both fell on the floor and rolled."

The three of them laughed until they were too tired to laugh anymore.

"You know how much we sold today?" Isabel asked. Murray and Ben waited for her to answer her own question. "We sold 753 burgers and about 250 fish sandwiches. How's that for a record? That doesn't count the ones we gave away or ate ourselves."

"How about drinks?" Murray asked.

Isabel's shoulders sagged slightly. "I'm not sure about that. Things got so crazy out there we lost count. We've got a big bag of money, though. It's in the safe. I'll count it tomorrow and try to figure it out. I know we went out and bought twenty-six kegs of beer and it's all gone. We stopped serving when the beer ran out."

Isabel stood up slowly and stretched her arms and back. "Well, I don't know about you two, but I'm going home to bed. I'm too tired to think about all that. I've got to get out of this scratchy old cowgirl suit and into my silk pajamas."

"I'll lock up," Murray said as Isabel headed for the door. "I'll be home in a little while."

Isabel laughed as she walked out the door and hollered back over her shoulder, "Don't do anything I wouldn't do."

As soon as her mother left, Murray and Ben leaned into each other for a kiss that had been all day waiting. Ben held the embrace for what seemed to Murray like a perfectly long time. Then he stood up and took Murray's hands. "Let's go somewhere," he said.

"Wherever could we go, my dear sir? All the hotels are booked."

"My truck will do just fine."

Ben's truck cab shined cherry red under the lights of the truck wash. The grill up front was massive and steely with a winged hood ornament on top that looked like a flying goddess.

He guided Murray up two steps and into a cab that felt like a space capsule with computer screens, a keyboard, and a dashboard full of gauges and GPS equipment. The sleeper had a freshly made bed. Everything was spotless. Ben lit a small lavender candle in a center cupholder. Murray recognized the scent that initially attracted her to Ben.

"Looks like the maid's been here," Murray said as she rolled into a bed barely big enough for two.

Ben crawled in gently and straddled her on his hands and knees. "I am the maid. I got it ready just in case." They pulled each other's shirts off before they had time to wonder how things would go. Murray gasped as their naked chests touched for the first time. Her heart was beating wildly. His body melted into hers.

Ben was gentle, and Murray was surprisingly eager. She didn't feel clumsy or anxious. There was no doubt in her mind. Instincts and hormones and pheromones took over. She never dreamed she could be so ravenously hungry for a man. *This is crazy*, she thought. *I'm not sure what's happening with this beautiful man. It's like he's setting me free. Like we were meant to be together. I can't believe this. It scares me, letting go, giving in too deep, maybe, but it feels so right, so perfect.*

They took their time with each other. Murray surrendered more fully than she ever thought possible. The universe wrapped her in its loving, infinite arms and made her forget everything that had gone so terribly wrong. Ben was right there with her until they were both floating. In the delicious aftermath, their bodies melded together like they were made for each other. They fell asleep in each other's arms.

CHAPTER SIX

"Eat up you two lovebirds," Isabel said as she stood over Murray and Ben's table at the diner. "I'll bet you're hungry."

Ben nodded and Murray said, "Like you can't believe."

"I've got two Meat Lover's omelets coming right up with sides of French toast and fruit. Why look, here it is now. Eat up. It's gonna be a big day. Here's your coffee black with two giant orange juices."

Ben and Murray dug into the food while Isabel continued. "I already got a call from Blake Dawson with The Long Road Band. He's going to introduce us to an agent. Says we're gonna need one. We've already gone national on the news. We're viral on social media, whatever that means. Blake says it's the best thing that ever happened to him and his band."

"We gotta be careful what we say today," Ben said. "It could end up defining the brand. You've got a big platform now."

Murray looked at her mother. "Do you know what he's talking about?"

"Not in so many words," Isabel said. "But I think you're talking about what our message is gonna be. Right, Ben?"

"Oh man," Murray said. "It just hit me. This is bigger than all of us. It's our chance to make a statement. It's all about Trucker Nation. One nation, under God, indivisible and all that other stuff. But it's about bringing the country together. No more politics and religion splitting us apart and making us hate everybody who's not in complete agreement." She slammed her hand on the breakfast table for emphasis so hard it rattled the silverware.

"Now you're talking," Ben said. "You know there's three and a half million truckers in the United States, and we're all part of the same supply chain. Most of it starts in China or Europe. It connects sellers to buyers. It doesn't get any more important than that."

"We see all kinds at The Highway Diner," Isabel said as she refilled Murray and Ben's coffees. "We serve all kinds. We got blacks and whites, gays and straights, country rednecks and city slickers, young and old, Hispanics and Asians, men and women, hookers and johns, Democrats and Republicans. We are the goddamned melting pot."

"That's it then," Ben said. "The Highway Diner, Trucker Nation, *e pluribus unum,* baby."

"What does that actually mean?" Murray asked. "I forget."

"It means 'out of many come one,'" Ben said. "It's the motto of the good old USA. It's on the back of every coin you've ever spent. Lots of people have forgotten it lately. Looks like it's up to us to remind them. Which reminds me, we need to raise a giant American flag around here. Please tell me you've got a flagpole."

"We've got a tall one right in the center of the parking lot," Isabel said. "There hasn't been anything on it for years. And I know we don't have a flag around here, let alone a big one."

"Where can we find one?" Ben asked. "We're already swamped with media today. In fact, where can we hire security guards? Somebody needs to keep traffic moving."

Isabel walked outside while Ben and Murray finished breakfast. A few moments later, she came back in a hurry, looking aghast and nearly panting. "There are news trucks all over the place. I thought you were crazy about security, but now I see your point. I don't think anyone can get through to the diner. I'll start making calls. I know the people we need to contact, and I'll bet they'll be ready to help."

Murray got up from the table. "Let's get showered and cleaned up. Then what do you say the three of us hold a little press conference? We'll announce there's gonna be a flag raising at noon. They'll eat it up. Great pictures and footage. How long since a good old-fashioned flag raising made the news?"

"How do I look?" Isabel asked. She was wearing black pants, red cowboy boots, and an embroidered velvet jacket.

"Like you dressed for the part," Murray said.

"I haven't worn this outfit since your father and I used to line dance at the country bars. It's a little tight, but how do I look?" She twirled around.

"Like a million bucks," Ben said, holding his hands over his head as if to signal a touchdown.

Murray laughed and applauded. "You still got the moves, Mom."

Isabel rested her hands on her hips. "Cut it out, you two. You don't want me getting a big head, do you?"

"Way too late for that," Murray teased.

Isabel eased out of showbiz mode and got on the phone. It wasn't long before she had security guards and an honor guard detail on the way with a massive flag. "They want to be part of the flag raising. The Highway Diner is big news now. I can't believe it. They even have a bugler lined up."

Two extra cooks and five new servers were on the way. No staffing shortages at The Highway Diner. No one seemed afraid of another shooting.

The Highway Diner was packed and had a three-block waiting line by 8:00 a.m. Isabel worked the front door as hostess and found herself signing autographs. She kept the media at bay by announcing there would be a press conference at 10:00 a.m. Guests walked into the diner and craned their necks in awe as if they were visiting a holy shrine. *Amazing what a few days of news coverage can do. Turn a truck stop into the Indy 500,* Murray thought.

Promptly at 10:00 a.m., a phalanx of cameras and microphones were set up in the parking lot near the entrance. Isabel took the lead. "Good morning. I'm Isabel Paterson, owner of The Highway Diner. This is my daughter, Muriel, and our friend and advisor, Ben Fitzgerald. We're here on behalf of Trucker Nation. That's Trucker with a capital 'T' and Nation with a capital 'N.' One nation, under God, indivisible, with liberty and justice for all. And we're here to tell the country that it's time to come together. It's time to stop the hate. A terrible thing happened here a few days ago. Something that could have shut us down. But Trucker Nation rallied to the rescue. There are 3.5 million truckers in this big, beautiful country of ours and millions more supporting them. We're Republicans and Democrats, black and white, young and old, gay and straight, Asian, Hispanic, male and female. We're all part of the same thing. We're all in this together. And we all work as one to keep the entire economy moving on down the road. We don't let politics, race, or religion tear us apart."

Then Murray stepped up to the microphones. "It's time to stop the hate, people. Yesterday, Trucker Nation showed up in force to rally for The Highway Diner and to show the country what we're all about. And I'll tell you what it's all about. It's *e pluribus unum*, baby. *E pluribus unum*. And if you don't know what that means, look it up. It's the motto for the United States of America, and it's high time we all started remembering what it means."

Ben stepped up and said, "There will be a flag-raising ceremony at high noon. Don't miss it. The Highway Diner is sending out a wakeup call to the nation. The bugler will be playing 'Reveille,' not 'Taps.'"

With that, Isabel, Murray, and Ben walked back into the diner, ignoring the questions from the reporters. Once inside, they hugged each other in triumphant relief. "I'd say that went as well as it could," Isabel said.

"Was I too much?" Murray asked.

Ben laughed. "My favorite was the *e pluribus unum* like it was your favorite saying."

"I liked Mom reciting, what was that, the Pledge of Allegiance?"

Isabel smiled. "I don't know where all that came from. I was just speaking from the heart."

"That went extremely well," Ben said. "You two are fantastic. Just remember, the media is going to try to pin you down on issues so they can attack."

"Like what?" Murray asked.

"Like everything from abortion to teaching critical race theory in schools. Vaccinations, cruise ships, reforming the police. You name it, they'll try to get an opinion out of you. Don't fall for it. Stay on message. We don't get involved in politics or religion. It's like what you don't talk about at a dinner party when you don't know the other guests."

———

The flag raising was breaking news on national television. The story was irresistible. The determined women of an embattled truck stop, rallying Trucker Nation, and sending out a beacon of hope to a hate-weary world.

The bugler arrived as part of a full color guard from a local post of the Veterans of Foreign Wars. The color guard also had four riflemen and a giant flag carried by two uniformed men who knew how to properly unfold and raise it up the pole. "No gun salute, please," Isabel said. "We're still trying to get over a shooting here."

The color guard wore deep blue dress uniforms with white service dress caps. They looked sharp, as if they just stepped out of Arlington Cemetery. The uniforms fit quite nicely on each member of the unit, except for the bugler. His uniform was the same design as the others, but it was two sizes too big. He was skinny and slouchy, and his hair was a little too long. He looked like he couldn't blow a bugle to save his life.

Murray nudged Ben. "Where did you get that sloppy little bugle boy? Looks like he's gonna ruin the whole thing."

When the flag started going up, the bugler raised the instrument to his lips with what almost looked like a flourish. Murray held her breath. *Please, God, don't let him sour note the entire ceremony.*

What came out of the bedraggled bugler, loud and clear, was the most beautiful and perfectly played version of "Reveille" ever heard by man or beast. The crowd of more than two hundred people did a collective double take at how such a poorly postured character could perform so flawlessly. The CNN reporter howled with breaking news overstatement that the boogie-woogie bugle boy of company B had performed a musical miracle.

The entire crowd was at attention, either saluting or holding their hands over their hearts. Everyone cheered when the flag reached the top. It was almost as big as the giant flag at the Chrysler dealership. It flapped and snapped like a bullwhip when the wind caught it just right. All it needed was the rockets' red glare and bombs bursting in air. There wasn't a dry eye in the parking lot. Patriotism was puddling up on the pavement.

The bugler finished his song. Everyone was still eyeing him in wonder when, suddenly, the bugle began playing "Taps" on its own, loudly and perfectly. Cameras zoomed in to catch the bugler frantically fumbling to turn the damn thing off. The crowd laughed and pointed with glee as they realized how the sad sack bugler had played so beautifully. The bugle was equipped with an electronic insert that played recordings by jazz great Wynton Marsalis.

The bugler fled the scene, fake bugle in hand. Nobody tried to track him down. "That was some baggy bugler we found," Isabel said with a huge grin. "Could you believe that bugle going off on its own? What a turnout! What a great show! We did good. The flag raising was a perfect touch, a little corny until the bugler provided comic relief. You don't think he ruined the whole thing, do you?"

Murray was still laughing as she managed to say, "It was funny. It's still funny. Thank goodness that bugle didn't go off until after the flag had its big moment at the top."

Isabel, Murray, and Ben shook every hand they could reach until they were surrounded by nothing but cameras and microphones and reporters with too many questions. Isabel finally had to say, "That's all, folks, we're not taking any questions. We're gonna let the flag speak for itself."

The gathering dispersed quickly after that because no stage or public address system offered a forum for any of the gathered politicians and community leaders. The CNN reporter, who had been fooled by the fake bugler, caught up to Isabel. He was out of breath from running after her.

"Since you're obviously another victim of gun violence, how do you feel about gun control?"

She was walking away when she said, "Gun control? What are you talking about? Everybody's got a gun."

The CNN reporter stopped dead in his tracks as Isabel kept walking. He turned to the camera. "So, there you have it," he gloated. "Trucker Nation is heavily armed and proud of it."

CHAPTER SEVEN

Murray felt ripped apart when Ben had to leave for Oakland the day after the flag raising. She was embarrassed to be clinging to him as tears streamed down her face. She hadn't felt so forlorn since she was nine years old when her father had to leave in his truck.

"It's not right," she cried. "We just got together and now you're going away."

"Oh, Murray," Ben said, wiping tears from his own eyes. "I'll be back before you know it. I'll call every day. And next time you see me, I won't be driving a truck. I'm coming back for you in a big camper, and we're taking off for the Wild Wild West."

Murray was so shocked by his one-sided plans for her that she let him go without another word. Did he really think he could decide what they would be doing without talking it over with her? They'd only known each other for a few days. She waved goodbye as his semi wheeled out of the parking lot. He let out a long air horn blast that sounded like a ship heading out to sea in a deep fog. She wondered how long he would be gone, and she worried about how she would ever leave her mother, or if he was even serious about the Wild West.

The diner was crowded, at least forty people waiting outside in line. Murray had no time to deal with her conflicting emotions. Her mother was sitting at the round table in the corner with Blake Dawson of The Long Road Band and a man and a woman who were dressed in the Nashville showbiz look: fancy boots, slim-fit tan suits, and matching blond hair. They looked like middle-aged Barbie and Ken dolls.

Murray grabbed coffee and water and sidled over to eavesdrop and offer refills. Isabel was relieved to see her. "Hey, everybody, this is my daughter and right-hand woman, Muriel. Come sit with us. We're talking about how to handle the gun-control mess from yesterday."

Blake reintroduced himself to Murray, then introduced Leona Ryder and Chase Marshall as two of the top talent agents in the country. "They represent several of Country Music's biggest stars, for heaven's sake. It doesn't get any bigger than that."

Leona held out her hand. "And now we might be representing you and your mama, not to mention The Long Road Band." Her Southern drawl did not endear her to Murray.

Isabel brought the conversation back to her main concern. "I wanna set the record straight on this gun thing, and these folks are trying to keep my mouth shut. Can you please tell them, Muriel, how hard it is to do that? All I did was restate the obvious: everybody's got a gun."

The table laughed politely and settled into an uncomfortable silence until Chase spoke. "I know you want to say it's not just Trucker Nation that has guns. Everyone in the country has guns, from women with designer pistols in their purses to old men with canes packing .44 Magnums. I totally get that. But everybody already knows that. What you don't want to do is feed the news loop that reinforces the stereotype that truckers are gun-toting rednecks."

"What we need to do," Leona said, "is let the whole thing blow over. You could come out and say this country was born by the gun and it's gonna die by the gun, and all they'd want to know is what are you going to do to stop school shootings. What we need to do is keep you out of politics and focused on Trucker Nation."

"Let's not talk about the negatives," Chase said. "What you did yesterday was a masterstroke of public relations. I saw that flag go up with the perfect bugle call. It gave me goosebumps, I tell you. I wondered who put that show together. Even after they showed the bugle playing on its own. Anyway, it made me realize what you've got here."

"What do we have here?" Murray asked.

"Besides a damn good truck stop and a national following?" Leona said. "You've got merchandise sales, radio and television talk shows, and extremely lucrative endorsement deals."

"Endorsement deals?" Isabel asked.

"Okay," Chase said. "What's the most popular tire for big rigs?"

"Probably Road Warriors," Murray said.

"Good," Chase said, leaning into the table in a confidential tone. "How much do you think Road Warrior would pay to have Isabel from The Highway Diner say truck drivers who care about safety trust Road Warrior tires?"

Isabel closed her eyes and grimaced like someone had shined a bright light in her face. "Oh no. That would make me look like a money grubber."

"We wouldn't do that right away," Leona said. "The first thing we need to do is get a trademark on Trucker Nation and start selling hats and T-shirts. Come to think of it, better get ownership on The Highway Diner. I love that name. It says it all. It's on the highway and it's a diner."

Murray tried hard to keep from rolling her eyes.

"We could sell out right here at the store," Isabel said.

Leona and Chase looked at each other with knowing grins.

Then Chase said, "We're talking nationwide, Isabel. We've got lawyers to get the rights, set up the corporations, and obtain the financing for manufacture and distribution."

"Oh my God," Isabel said as she looked helplessly at Murray.

"This whole Trucker Nation is good for the truck-driving image," Leona said. "It's taken quite a hit since those truckers in Canada did their blockade of the bridges to the US last winter. All the truckers I know thought it was a bullshit move. Why protest Covid vaccines when all you have to do is get the goldarned shot for heaven's sake."

"They shut down Ford Motor for a good while," Isabel said.

Feeling pressured, Murray stood up abruptly and grabbed her coffee and water. "Anybody need a refill? I gotta get back to work."

Leona put her hand gently on Murray's elbow. "I hate to say this, because I know a good woman doesn't need to get by on her looks, but you and your mother would make a mean modeling team. You look like twins."

Murray smiled tightly as Isabel said, "Thank you, Leona. That's so nice of you to say."

Murray couldn't get away from that table fast enough. Several diners were trying to get her attention for coffee. As she poured out the pot from one customer to another, she felt sick to her stomach. The Nashville people were like vultures. The problem was, they were right. Birds of prey know where the food was, but she hated seeing her mother surrounded like fresh roadkill.

Please, God, she thought, *don't let her sign anything today. But why worry? Mom knows what she's doing. Look at this place. It's packed. Everybody wants to say they saw us on TV.*

The line outside is getting longer by the minute. What am I going to do about all these people?

Suddenly, the gunshots from a week ago blasted away again in her head. She jumped when her phone rang. It was Ben. With a shaky hand, she answered. "Ben, thank the Lord. We need to talk. Mom is surrounded by agents who want to sell T-shirts and do tire commercials and, oh God, I don't know what to do."

"Hold on, Murray. Settle down. Take some deep breaths. It sounds like you're in the middle of a panic attack."

"No, no, I'm okay. It's just that every time I get flustered, I hear those gunshots again. It's going to take some time to get over that whole mess. That's all. I'll be fine. And I'm so glad you called. I was thinking about calling you, but I didn't want to sound needy."

"I had to call. I miss you already. And I know what you're saying about the gunshots. I hear them too. Ben took a deep breath. "Remember what you said about how painting makes you feel alive? Well, I just now figured it out. You know what makes me feel alive?"

Murray waited breathlessly.

"You," he said. "You make me feel alive. And I've got to say, it's so good to hear your voice. It feels like we've been apart for days when it's only been a few minutes."

"Oh, Ben. Come back here right now."

Ben laughed. "You know I want to, but I can't. So, what's going on at the diner?"

Murray outlined the agents' plans in detail.

Ben said, "I think it's a good idea to move on the trademarks and the merchandise right away. We don't want to lose our momentum. On the other hand, there's no need to rush. You'll need to talk to a couple of people before you make any decisions. Let me call my old ad agency, and I'll get back to you."

"No, no, no," Murray begged. "Don't get back to me. Stay with me. I need to talk to you about us. And about Mom. You said that you wanted me to go with you to the Wild West. But I can't leave my mom."

"Nobody's talking about you leaving your mother," Ben said. "We'd just be taking a road trip together, that's all. And we won't go anywhere until you decide. Don't mind me. I get a little impulsive sometimes. In fact, I want you to meet my mother. She needs to meet you. She needs to know her son is really in love and not going to run out on her like my dad did."

Murray talked to Ben until she saw diners raising their coffee cups for refills. She said a quick "gotta go," tucked her phone away, and hustled back to work. Isabel was getting up from the table, and the Nashville people were leaving their cards and promotional materials. Murray pretended to be too busy to say goodbye. She tried to get away with a wave, but they all came over to tell her how wonderful everything was going to be.

Once they were gone, Isabel took her daughter by the arm and whispered, "Don't worry about those agents. I didn't let them talk me into anything. I had a hard time working around their matching blond hair. But what about that Blake? Don't you think he's a hunk?"

Murray looked away in disapproval as her mother continued. "One thing I'll say about all three of them: they're on it. You know those agents flew up in their own private jet. They are the real deal, Murray. Blake's along for the ride at this point. But you watch. He'll be flying the plane before long."

CHAPTER EIGHT

Over the next two weeks, Isabel and Murray were convinced they didn't want any more national attention. All aspects of the truck plaza were completely overrun. Drivers were fighting to get parking spaces and fuel. The six shower spaces were in constant use, and the hot water started running out by noon. The line to get into The Highway Diner was so long, even the McDonald's across the street couldn't handle the overflow. Regular customers were starting to complain and claimed they weren't going to come back because the plaza was too crowded.

"What can we do, Murray?" Isabel asked after a driver stormed out.

"I don't know, Mom. We can't keep going like this. The cooks and servers are totally burned out. It's like the world is spinning out of control. I'm getting cranky. I snapped at a guy this morning for taking too long to order."

Isabel grabbed Murray by the shoulders. "We need to hire more people and take some time off before we lose our minds."

"Let's take it one step at a time for now," Murray said. "This crush of people can't last forever. We can ride it out and see where it goes."

"Yes, of course, you're right," Isabel said. "But I am going to start looking for a manager. Somebody who's handled bigger places than this. I'm in way over my head. And, by the way, that somebody's gonna be a woman. I don't need a man running around here telling me what to do. Your father was good at treating me like an equal, but most men aren't."

———

Two days later, Isabel called Murray over to the cash register. Murray knew something was up. Her mother looked like a teenager with a secret she was just dying to tell. "Muriel, there's something we need to discuss."

"Mom, I'm super busy here."

"Just listen. This won't take long. You'll be in charge of the diner this Friday, Saturday, and Sunday."

"What? You know how slow I am on the register. You can't do it?"

"No, it's just that Blake called." Isabel waited for Murray's reaction.

"Blake from The Long Road Band? Oh no, Ma. Don't tell me you're hitting the road with a country band."

Isabel laughed nervously. "No, his band is doing a television special at The Grand Ole Opry in Nashville. A lot of big names are going to be there. It's a benefit for the homeless."

"Since when do Blake Dawson and The Long Road Band play at the Grand Ole Opry?"

"Since he signed with Leona and Chase."

Murray threw her hands in the air. "The evil blond twins? You can't be serious. Those people give phony a new look. I thought we were done with them."

Isabel flashed Murray a look of disapproval. "I never let you sass me before, and you're not going to start now. So hold it right there, Ms. High and Mighty. They're sending a private jet for me, and there'll be a limo waiting for me at the Nashville airport, and guess where I'll be staying?"

Murray's shoulders sagged. She could see her mother was

excited. God knew she could use a break, and why not be happy for her? She tried to brighten up. "I'll bite, where?"

"The Joseph. It's the best in town, according to Blake. They've got a huge indoor pool. I'll have to buy a new swimsuit."

Murray shook her head slowly, deciding not to sarcastically suggest a thong.

"Oh, and guess what the really exciting part is?"

Murray raised her eyebrows as her mother did a little dance and song. "I'm part of the show. I'm the guest of honor, in fact. Carrie wants me to join her on the stage."

"Please tell me you're not going to sing."

"No, they want me to say, 'Greetings from The Highway Diner,' and wait for the applause to die down and then yell out, 'Long live Trucker Nation.' Then Carrie will ask me how things are going at the diner, and I'll invite everybody to come visit. And that's it. I'm done."

Murray had to smile, seeing her mother so gleefully happy. She hadn't seen that since before her father died. "That's wonderful, Mom. You're gonna knock em' dead. And don't worry about the diner. I got you covered. And, by the way, you'll need to go a couple sizes smaller on the bathing suit because you're doing so well on your diet."

Isabel hugged her. Murray wasn't being sarcastic about the diet. Her mother was losing weight, and not just from the stress of recent events. Blake was the first man to spark her interest since her husband passed.

Murray got back to her tables. *Gotta hand it to those Nashville agents*, she thought as she refilled cups. *They do know how to bribe a girl. Mom's got stars in her eyes already.* She wondered how much the agents were paying her.

A table of drivers brought her back to the tasks at hand.

"Hey, you're Murray," one driver said. The man across the table chimed in. "Yes, indeed. Woo-wee! You look even better in person." A third driver had a mouthful of biscuits and gravy when he tried to say, "What's a big celebrity like you doing waiting tables?"

You know, he has a good point, Murray thought as she moved on to the next table. *If Mom can start steppin' out and steppin' up, so can I. Problem is, I don't want to be somebody's showbiz monkey.*

Murray felt herself getting angry, which surprised her. She wasn't one to be jealous. *What is it?* she wondered. *This feeling is new. I can't explain it. It's more than being mad about the shooting. I want to run out into the parking lot and scream. That's not like me. I'm an artist, not a fighter. It's that Blake Dawson. She doesn't even know who he is. He doesn't even live here.*

Murray marched over to her mother and said with mock sternness, "I'm sorry, Mom, but I've thought it over and I'm afraid I have to tell you something."

"What is it?"

"No dating. Especially musicians. You know they're trouble."

Isabel threw back her head and let out her big, fun-loving laugh as Murray went back to her tables.

CHAPTER NINE

Isabel was already in Nashville on Friday afternoon when Anita asked Murray to come back in the kitchen for a talk. Murray could see from the frown on Anita's face that something was wrong. So, even though she was super busy as temporary manager, Murray followed her back to the walk-in cooler.

"Step inside with me," Anita said. "This has to be totally private."

Murray could see her own breath as she followed her friend into the small, refrigerated room. "Make this fast, Anita, I'm freezing my ass off."

Anita grabbed Murray by the shoulders. Murray could see for the first time that she'd been crying. Her face was healing nicely, but she was frowning, and her eyes were puffy from crying. "I got a terrible phone call last night," Anita said. "It was from Cal Mavis, that guy who said he was Red Mavis's brother. You know, the one who interrupted the mayor at the rally? Turns out he is Red's brother, but he did tell me the priest outfit was just a disguise."

"How did he get your number?"

"He's Red's only heir. At least that's what he says. He's getting the truck and the bank accounts and the whole bit. He not only found my number all over Red's notes and address books, but he found . . ."

"Go on, Anita. What else?"

"He found naked pictures of me and the two of us together. Videos too."

"You let Red film you? Are you out of your mind?"

Anita lowered her head and stared at the floor. "Well, yes, in fact. I was out of my mind. We were smoking crack and meth for days at a time. But that's not what I'm talking about. He's not after me. There's nothing to get. I've got nothing to lose, except my clean time."

Murray began to sense something was wrong. Anita took a step closer and said, "He's after you and your mother. Says you've done nothing but profit off his brother's murder. He saw an ad for this Nashville thing your mother's doing."

"What? She's part of the advertising?"

"Here it is on my phone."

Murray was stunned. Her mother's photo was on the promo poster, big as anybody's, with a headline that read, "Trucker Nation's Isabel Paterson, owner of The Highway Diner."

Murray tried to ignore the sharp pang of jealousy she felt. *They're laying it on thick*, she thought. *Figure they'll nab her as a client once they get her onstage. She does look good. Those Nashville people know what they're doing. Hope she doesn't sign up with them before she talks to me.*

"Did you get his phone number?" Murray asked, forcing herself to return her thoughts to Anita. "Did he make any specific threats or demands?"

"I called the number back, but it was some gas station in Michigan. All he said was, 'If she keeps this up, she and her daughter are going to pay the ultimate price, same as my brother.'"

Murray felt an angry heat rising inside, hot enough to make her forget she was standing in a cooler. "Did he say anything else?"

Anita lowered her head. "He said he loved the photos and wanted to hook up. Said he'd pay twice as much as his brother."

Murray put her hands on Anita's shoulders. "Well, that's not going to happen now, is it?"

"No way. I love my new life. Working thirty hours a week, and it feels good to have a clear head and make some honest money."

"Do you think he'll follow her down to Nashville?"

"I don't know, but he did say she might not make it out of Nashville alive. And then he said he's already been in contact with some people who can get the job done."

"What kind of people?"

Anita scrunched up her face and closed her eyes. "Yes, yes, he did talk about some militia group in Michigan that hates unions, especially the teamsters. And now they hate The Highway Diner. Turns out my dead friend, Red Mavis, was a lifelong buddy of the guy who runs the militia."

"Good Lord," Murray said. "That's all we need. A fight with the far-right militia. We're all still trying to get over the shooting. And now we're getting death threats. I'm telling you, this bull crap's enough to push me right over the edge."

"I know," Anita said. "I didn't want to ruin your day. But I knew I had to tell you."

"Thank you for telling me," Murray said. "I'm not mad at you. I'm mad at hateful people. And if they're coming after my mother, I swear to God, I'll kill them first."

Anita grabbed Murray by both arms. "Hey, slow down. I've never seen you like this. We don't want to be just like them."

Murray hugged Anita hard. It felt good to feel her warmth. "Okay, you're right. I've got to cool down. But right now, I'm more than cool. I'm freezing. Let's get out of this refrigerator and get back to work. And thank you for telling me all this."

Murray felt a cold fear tightening her back even as she began to warm up from getting out of the cooler. She hated to call her mother and spoil the fun, but it had to be done. She called her as soon as she got a chance. No one answered, not at 1:00 p.m., 1:15, or 1:25. Every time the phone went to voicemail Murray got more nervous. In desperation, she looked in her mother's little office at the diner.

The desk was piled high with mail and accounting papers. Murray dug through the disorganized mess for a good five minutes, realizing her mother really did need some management help. Finally, in the desk drawer, she found Chase Marshall's card. She called as fast as her fingers could punch in the numbers.

He wasn't at the office, but Murray talked his assistant into finding him as fast as possible. "We've got some guy making death threats against me and my mother," she said.

Chase called Murray within ten minutes. "Who is this guy? Is he a real threat?"

"He's the brother of Red Mavis, the man who got killed shooting up The Highway Diner," Murray said. "Cal was crazy enough to get up at the rally and say his brother was murdered."

"I heard about that guy. I don't like the sounds of any of this. I'll get security on your mother right away. I'll have her call you. She's checking into the hotel right now. What about you? Should I send some people to Fort Wayne?"

"That won't be necessary," Murray said. He sounded totally military-like, crisp and in charge. She softened her tone. "Thank you so much for taking care of my mother and for everything you're doing. Don't worry about me. I can take care of myself."

"Okay," Chase said. "I've got to get on this right away. Don't worry. Guys who talk on the phone are almost never dangerous. We deal with this kind of thing all the time. I'll have your mother call you ASAP."

Murray was impressed by Chase's professionalism. *Let's see how fast he can track down Mom*, she thought as she hung up the phone.

Isabel called within ten minutes. "What's going on? All of a sudden, I've got a cop guarding my door. Chase called me to say that Mavis man is threatening to kill us both."

"Mom, I gotta say, this Chase guy is starting to impress me. I couldn't get you on the phone. He had you on the phone pronto. Why weren't you answering?"

"I don't know," Isabel said. "Let's see. Oh my, the ringer's off. Now I see you called. I'm sorry, honey. I wasn't expecting all this trouble. So how did you find out about the death threats?"

"The guy called Anita. He found a bunch of naked pictures and videos of her in Red's truck. And he wants revenge on us for killing his brother and making money on it."

"That's ridiculous."

"Right," Murray said. "Ridiculous as Charles Manson. He said he's talking to people who can kill us, some militia group from Michigan."

"Militia group? What are you talking about?"

"Mom, they're all over the place. They run shooting ranges and bars and play war games and stockpile ammunition for civil war."

"They wouldn't bother with us."

"Mom, they tried to kidnap the governor of Michigan so they could execute her."

"Oh my. Do you think I should call this whole thing off and come home?"

"No. No way are we caving into threats from a crazy man.

There's a million more like him out there, and we can't run away from all of them."

"I like your spirit, Muriel. You know I love you so much and, if anything ever happened to you, I would never forgive myself. But you're right. We're not the running kind. Chase says not to worry—he's putting two security guys on me for the show. Security's tight at the Opry. Meanwhile, how are you doing? How's the diner?"

"It's all good here, Mom. I don't want to worry you. Ben's coming in tonight. We'll be fine. The diner is busier than ever and running smoothly. The hard part is counting the money and getting it to the bank."

———

Ben rolled into The Highway Diner parking lot just before closing that night. He was driving an Accolade XL Recreational Vehicle with enough room for a family of six. He called Murray to come out and look.

Murray ran into his arms. He lifted her up over his head and lowered her down slowly to kiss her. His lavender aroma enveloped her as she kissed him. Then she wriggled free to look at the forty-foot vehicle. "My God, Ben, it looks like a semi that's all connected. It's gorgeous. The blue-and-white swoops look like it's flying even when it's standing still."

"You ain't seen nothing yet. Step inside, my queen, and behold your new castle on wheels. All the conveniences of a showplace home. And it's got a 360-horse Cummins Diesel engine for all the power we'll ever need, even in the mountains."

Murray stepped up into the luxurious RV, wondering when she would ever have time to go see the mountains. She gasped at the sight of sleekly styled tables and sofas and cabinets. A lavender candle was flickering gently in the cupholder between two deluxe front scats. That made her smile as she walked to the back, past the full kitchen and lavatory, and flopped into the king-sized bed in the very back. "This is big enough for a rock band."

Ben jumped on her and kissed her lips and ear and neck. "You smell good enough to eat."

Murray jumped up, remembering she hadn't showered since this morning. "I'm sure I smell like bacon and onions. Like the first time we met. Come back to the diner with me. I can't be gone long. It's closing time. But answer me one question. And I hope it's not too personal."

Ben stood up so straight he had to duck a little as his head brushed the ceiling. "Ask away."

"How did you ever afford this thing?"

He laughed and wrapped his arms around her from behind as she tried to walk out of the motor home. "It's my mom's. It's a 2020 model, but she's never driven it. It's been in a garage gathering dust. She was hoping to use it for painting trips."

"That's so great," Murray said. "I know how much you want her to paint again. Has she started?"

"A little. She started on a big one just before I left. She's excited to meet you, by the way. I've told her so much about you."

"You didn't tell her everything?"

"None of the really good stuff," Ben said, and then looked embarrassed. "So, anyway, I quit truck driving. They offered me more money to stay, but there was no way. Driving a big rig is nowhere near as exciting as I thought it would be. In fact, it's mostly boring. So, I've saved money since I started working, and I was going to buy a car to get back here. Mom said I should take her RV. She said I could use it if I promise to bring you home to meet her."

"I can't wait to meet this woman," Murray said as she wiggled out of his grasp.

Ben followed her out of the RV. "I may have prejudiced her in your favor since you're all I talk about. And she's seen you all over television and on social media. Did you know there's video of you playing volleyball in high school that's gone viral?"

Murray turned around with wide eyes and an open mouth. "No, I haven't seen any of that. Not even when I was playing volleyball." Her eyes narrowed in suspicion.

Ben held out his arms in surrender. "You look great in those short-short shorts. I'm just saying."

Murray pushed him playfully with both hands on his chest. "Is that all you men can think about?"

Ben chuckled. "I don't see why they have to be so short and tight. I'm not complaining. Just wondering."

They walked to the diner together in silence. The staff greeted Ben happily. His team spirit had always been popular. Without missing a beat, he pitched in and helped stack chairs and mop floors to close the diner until the only people left in the restaurant were himself, Anita, and Murray.

They sat down at the circular table in the corner. Ben and Murray poured themselves tall beers. Anita stuck to water with lemon. "Don't mind me. I'm trying to get my thirty-day-clean chip. And you know what we say in Narcotics Anonymous: Alcohol is a drug."

Ben toasted her new life. "Here's to you staying clean and serene." After they drank to Anita's sobriety, Ben asked, "So, what's this I hear about Cal Mavis threatening Isabel and Murray?"

Anita told him the whole story, including the drug-crazed, naked videos. "He wants to get with me. He's gonna call me back. What should I do?"

"First of all," Murray said. "You need to start recording his calls."

"How do I do that?"

"Good question," Murray said. "Let's ask Siri. She knows everything."

Sure enough, in a matter of moments, Anita got the Ring Central app on her iPhone, along with detailed instructions on how to use it without letting the caller know he was being recorded.

Anita got quiet and Murray knew what was wrong. "All right, Anita," Murray said. "I totally get why you don't want any part of going after Cal Mavis. Really, I don't either. The more I think about it, the more it feels like a terrible idea for us to play FBI on this whole thing. We were already freaked out by the shooting and now the death threats only make it that much worse. How about we all worry about our mental health and let the police do their job?"

"Sounds like a plan, Murray," Ben said.

"Thank you for understanding, Murray," Anita said.

After a good, long talk about everything, from Cal and Red Mavis to future plans for the diner, Ben and Murray said goodnight to Anita and drove the RV to Murray and Isabel's house. Ben parked on the grass in the backyard between the garage and the screen porch. "They call this boondocking in the RV world," Ben said.

"What does that mean?"

"It's camping in your RV without water, sewer, or electrical hookups. We obviously can't do it forever, but it'll do for now."

Murray unlocked the back door of her house and led him inside. "We won't be boondocking, or whatever they call it. Mom's in Nashville, and I live here too. We won't be camping at all."

She led Ben upstairs to the walk-in shower off Isabel's master bedroom. They were naked and in each other's soapy arms in a steamy, foggy flash. Afterward, Murray wrapped her legs around Ben as he carried her to the bed. She relaxed completely in the moment, releasing a day full of tension as he kissed her all over.

"It's so good to have you back," she moaned. "I've been missing you too much."

"Murray, you have no idea how much I need you. Just like this. I'm telling you, the drive here was surreal. All I could think about was you. I started seeing your face in the clouds and even in the mountains. I've never felt this way about anybody. Not even close."

Murray rolled him over onto his back and got on top. They moaned in unison as she eased him slowly and deeply inside her. "Oh God, Ben. You feel so good. So perfect. You can never go away again, ever, I mean it."

The rhythm of their union intensified into a wild roller-coaster ride. They climbed up the steep track to the highest peak, then plunged down and through the turns, holding onto each other for dear life. They were only able to catch their breath as the coaster slowed and glided into the sweet bliss of sexual exhaustion.

CHAPTER TEN

Isabel returned from Nashville a changed woman. She was smiling like the Cheshire Cat with a mischievous twinkle in her eyes. Murray took one look at her on Sunday night and realized her mother had found a man.

"So, how was Blake?" she teased.

Her mother looked at the ceiling and bit her lip gently. "He was magnificent in every way."

"Looks like somebody had a good time," Ben said.

"A good time would be putting it mildly," Isabel said. "I'd never flown in a private jet. Blake and Leona had champagne on ice and a charcuterie board with the best blue cheese I ever had. The flight was over so fast, I didn't want it to end. And then the limousine at the airport. The hotel and my own security guards. But the best part was being in front of four thousand people and hearing them scream when I said, 'Greetings from The Highway Diner.' They all know who we are. And then I said, 'Long live Trucker Nation,' and they started chanting, 'Trucker Nation, Trucker Nation, Trucker Nation.' I had no idea we were this big."

"Oh my God," Murray said. "It's all going to your head."

"Don't worry, Muriel. I was just having fun. I know it's not all about me. The Highway Diner and Trucker Nation are what it's all about. And you're just as big a part of all this as I am. And guess what?"

"What?" Murray asked, afraid of what her mother might say next.

"No, honey." Isabel laughed. "I'm not running off with Blake. He is a lot of fun, but that's not happening anytime soon. So, here's what's exciting." Her eyes grew wide with excitement. "Chase and Leona found us a manager for the diner—subject to your approval, of course. She's the assistant manager at The Joseph hotel. She runs the entire dining operation. She's got a degree in hospitality management from the CIA."

"The CIA?" Ben asked.

"That's the Culinary Institute of America."

"Of course," Ben and Murray howled in unison.

"Why would she want to manage a truck stop?" Murray asked.

"She's as excited about us as everybody else," Isabel said. "You should have seen her going over maps with Chase and Leona. They want to buy the old hotels around this place and all the land between here and the Interstate. They're even talking about building a casino once they tear down the hotels."

"What about the good old diner in the meantime?" Murray asked.

"Plans for the diner are huge," Isabel said. "We'll expand the restaurant and the service center. The plaza will have more pumps and mechanics and truck washes. It'll be great."

Murray looked at Ben with a frown. "What if we like it the way it is?"

"Wait a minute," Isabel said. "I'm supposed to be the one against change. You're supposed to be the youngblood pushing for expansion. But don't worry. I see your point. We don't want to lose what we've got here. So, you and I will make sure the best things remain the same. I, for one, am glad to have some help coming in. You'll get a chance to meet our possible new manager in about ten days. It'll be totally up to you if we hire her. She wants to start off as a waitress and run the register so she can get a feel for the place."

"I like this woman already," Ben said. Murray frowned at him for being too agreeable. Any new manager would have to pass her test of trial by fire.

"Will you show her the ropes, Muriel? That's the best way for you two to get acquainted to see if you get along."

"It doesn't sound like you'll be needing me anymore," Murray said. "You could show her yourself."

"No, no. Don't be like that," Isabel scolded. "Of course, I need you. We've been partners since your father died. And we need to stay close with all these death threats flying around. I've been looking over my shoulder a lot lately. And when I do, I need to see you by my side."

Murray was pouting inside. Her mother had a new man and a new manager. She didn't need a daughter anymore. Murray stomped her little feet mentally until she stopped and tried to get a hold of herself. *I shouldn't feel this way. I've got a man of my own. Why am I feeling left out and thrown to the curb? This could all work out just fine for everybody.*

She straightened up with a smile. "You're right, Mom. I'm just getting a little swept away in all the excitement. I don't see how we're gonna feed all the people lining up outside every day, let alone worry about building an empire. And by the way, we're running low on those Idaho potatoes. The last delivery got delayed."

———

Isabel got a dozen red roses from Blake Dawson on Monday.

She cried when they arrived. "Oh, Muriel. Your father used to buy me roses every year for our anniversary. Look at these beautiful flowers. They make me so happy."

"Then why are you crying?" Murray asked.

"These are tears of joy, Muriel. I thought I could never feel this way again." She set the bouquet next to the cash register and beamed radiantly as she rang up the next customer.

Murray was amazed. Her mother was a smitten kitten. As a good daughter, she wanted to be happy for her mother. But she wasn't. It was happening too fast with a man nobody knew—a musician, no less. Murray was suspicious.

Later that week, she caught Isabel sitting in her cluttered office. "Mom, what is it about this Blake guy that's got you so head over heels?"

Isabel leaned back in her chair and sighed deeply as she pondered the question. "Well, let's see. First, he's a romantic. I need that. I didn't realize how much I missed being wined and dined. Blake's a kind and gentle soul underneath all that tough-guy, country-singer image. He's a talented songwriter. Knows half of Nashville." Her smile broadened as she looked at Murray. "He's writing a song about me."

"Oh, come on, Mom. That's the oldest trick in the book."

"It's not a trick, Muriel. He's got songs coming out on a couple of big records. Of course, he is thirty-eight, which makes him five years younger than me, but that's a plus as far as I'm concerned. And you know what's great about him?"

"What? Like that's not enough already?"

"He taught junior high English for ten years before he went full-time into songwriting. Oh, and he's got twelve-year-old twins, a boy and a girl, and he gets along just fine with their mother."

Murray was stunned. The more her mother talked, the more she realized there might be more to Blake Dawson than met the eye when he was singing with The Long Road Band. He did look good on stage: strong, cleft chin, compelling blue eyes, and a bit of a hawk nose. He was six-foot-three, same as Ben. She and her mother were tall and never got along that well with short men. Isabel always said they had Napoleon complexes. "A man gets angry and intimidated by a woman who's taller than he is," Isabel said. "Not all men, of course. I don't want to overgeneralize. But it takes a confident man to date a taller woman."

Murray couldn't help thinking about her father when she heard her mother talking about a new man. She would never forget the unreal ordeal of her father's death. One day he was her invincible hero, healthy and strong and happy. The next day, it seemed, he was in bed dying from cancer. It only took three months. Murray was alone with him when he passed. She was just sixteen. Isabel had gone home to get some rest. His dying words were, "Take care of your mother."

Daddy could not have known what a huge job that was going to be, she thought to herself. *And now, I can't protect her from a hound-dog musician, let alone a lunatic threatening to kill us both.*

"Muriel." Her mother called her back to the conversation. "Are you still with me? Come here and give your mother a hug. You're still my favorite person in the whole world. After we lost your baby sister, you've been my only girl. And that's not going to change. Don't you worry."

Murray took comfort in her mother's arms. The squeeze was always just right, not too loose, not too tight. She loved the smell of her mother's hair. It was fresh and reassuring.

It took her back to being a little girl. Ben walked in to see mother and daughter embracing. "Hey, is everything all right? Should I give you two a moment?"

Isabel stood up and pulled Ben into a three-way hug. "I'm just telling Murray about Blake, and we're thinking about her daddy and how much we still miss him. I don't think Murray likes the idea of me dating again."

"No, Mom, I'm happy for you," Murray said. "I really am. If Blake treats you right—and it sounds like he is—I'll take him in just like you took Ben in."

"Thank you, Isabel, for everything," Ben said. "But especially for raising this wonderful woman."

"That's a good way to put it, Mr. Benjamin Fitzgerald," Isabel said, putting her hands on her hips. "You know, I think I like Benjamin better than Ben. Maybe I'll start calling you Benjamin. Would that be all right?"

"Sure," Ben said. "That's what my mother calls me. And I hate to break up this love fest, but Naomi Robinson is here. You know, the Nashville restaurant manager."

"Oh my heavens," Isabel said. "Isn't she a couple days early? Come on, let's go welcome her to The Highway Diner."

Naomi was African American. Her hair was short and curly black. Her eyes flashed with intelligence and minimal makeup. She looked about thirty years old. She was five-four, with a dancer's build and a beautiful smile. She greeted Isabel and Murray and Ben warmly.

"Thank you for having me. I had a little trouble getting in the door. So many people waiting to get in. What can I do to help?"

Murray liked Naomi right away, even though she was prepared to hate her. Naomi was a team player, not someone who thought she could come in and start running the show.

Murray gave her a quick tour of the kitchen and restaurant, then turned her loose to wait tables.

It was obvious right away that Naomi had skills that couldn't be taught. She moved quickly and efficiently without seeming to be in a hurry. Her food orders were detailed and legible, and she dealt with the customers in a friendly but no-nonsense way. She did not hesitate to bus her own tables, and she never seemed to get tired.

The entire staff at the diner was amazed by how well Naomi fit into the diner's fast-paced environment. She looked like the best new server they'd ever seen, not the new manager. The best thing was her easy and gentle laugh. She even laughed at herself when she asked Murray about the restroom situation. "I mean, I can see where the ladies' room is," she chuckled, "but I wonder if there is an 'employees only' space."

"That, my dear, is an excellent idea," Murray said. "Definitely one to include in our expansion plans."

Later in the day, Naomi caught Murray staring at her from across the diner. She came over to Murray and said with a big grin, "What are you looking at?"

Murray held up her right hand for a high five. "I'm watching you work. I like what I see."

The two women laughed together. "So do I," Naomi said.

Once the restaurant was closing for the night, Murray said to Naomi, "It's so nice to have you with us. You fit right in. What's your first impression of The Highway Diner?"

"It feels like home," Naomi said, wiping down a table. "You've got a national treasure here. It's a relief to be with down-to-earth folks after all those stuffy people at The Joseph restaurant in Nashville. You know, I got my start in a place a lot like this, the Redwood Inn in Lansing, Michigan. My parents owned the place. They had me doing dishes at ten years old."

Isabel joined them. "Naomi, I'd put you up against any two of my best servers, besides Murray. Did I hear your parents owned a restaurant?"

"They still do," Naomi said.

Isabel sat down and motioned Murray and Naomi to join her. "Come on, girls. Let's take just a minute. What I want to know right off the bat is why aren't you working with your parents?"

Naomi's smile came out more like a grimace. "That's a tough one for me," she said. "My father is, shall we say, a very stubborn man, and he is not open to new suggestions, especially not from his daughter, or any woman, for that matter."

"How does your mother handle him?" Isabel asked.

Naomi grinned. "Oh, Momma knows how to handle him. She's so good he thinks what he's doing is his own idea."

Isabel and Murray had a good long laugh at that.

"Don't get me wrong," Naomi said. "I love my daddy. He's a good, hard-working man. He's just old-fashioned. Fact is, he never wanted me to go into the restaurant business. He came up out of the South. He always wanted me to be a doctor."

Murray and Isabel nodded sympathetically and let the truth of Naomi's situation settle in. Isabel broke the silence. "Well, you won't have that problem here. I mean, we're not old-fashioned. We're ready for new ideas. Whatcha got?"

Naomi laughed. "Oh no. It's my first day. I still don't know what I'm doing. I'm nowhere near making suggestions, but I can make an observation."

Isabel nodded for her to continue.

"This place has the best vibe ever. You and Murray make customers feel comfortable and welcome. I mean, you're celebrities and you still do the hard work. And I love the oldies rock music. It feels like a party going on. People are excited to be here. That is so rare. And thank you, Murray, for treating me with such kindness. It's been a super fun day."

Murray was relieved by Naomi's attitude. This wasn't going to be a competition. It felt like the team had acquired a talented new player.

CHAPTER ELEVEN

Murray was humming a song she'd just heard on the radio as she arrived to open The Highway Diner at 5:30 a.m. She couldn't believe how fast things had progressed in the four months since Naomi Robinson came on board. Most noticeably, the office was neatly organized and nearly paper-free. Records and receipts were now computerized.

Plans were underway for a major expansion of the restaurant and bar. The restaurant would take over the entire storefront. The expanded store and showers would be modernized in a new adjoining building. Truck fueling, washing, and maintenance would be upgraded and tripled in capacity.

Legal reorganizing was also well underway. The Highway Diner Corporation would be owned by Isabel and Murray, including its truck plaza and merchandising divisions. Trucker Nation Corporation would own the newly proposed casino and concert venue, as well as all rights to the name, "Trucker Nation." The Highway Diner Corporation would own twenty percent of Trucker Nation in recognition of Isabel and Murray as the founders. The corporate plans would take months to finalize, but the organizers and owners were operating like the deals had already been done.

Plans for the casino were making powerful enemies in the community. Gambling was still a dirty word in much of Indiana, but Trucker Nation had already acquired the building site and bought two rundown hotels next to the diner,

The Economy Inn and The Suburban. The hotels would be demolished. Their value was in the extensive parking lots.

It was all way beyond Murray's wildest dreams. It was already March and construction was scheduled for early summer.

She was still humming when she reached the glass front doors of the diner. There was some kind of sign hung on the glass. It was dark so she couldn't read it until she shined her cell phone light. What she saw made her scream and take two steps backward to keep from falling to her knees. It was a two-foot square sign with four words on top of each other in red paint-dripping letters:

Blood.

Money.

Buys.

Death.

She looked closer and saw a bullet hole through the O in the word *money*. It had blasted through the glass and left a spider web of cracks but didn't shatter the door. She looked through the hole and saw that the bullet had also penetrated the inner glass door. She instantly regretted the decision not to install security lights and cameras at the main entrance. It had all seemed too paranoid. Until now.

Murray fumbled with her phone and called 911. She didn't want to unlock the door. It felt like pure evil. A terrible chill ran down her spine. Nothing had prepared her for the deep freeze of fear in her brain. It felt like the shooting at the diner all over again. Her mind flashed back to the bullet shattering the glass-covered photograph on the back wall.

Dispatch said police were on their way. Murray called Isabel, trying to fight back her panic.

"What's wrong, Muriel?" Isabel asked. "You sound frightened. Where are you?"

"I'm at the diner. You need to get here right away. Someone shot a hole through the front doors and put up a sign that says, 'Blood money buys death.'"

"Muriel, listen to me. Get in your car now. Don't stand in front of the door. You might be in somebody's line of fire. I'll be there in under five minutes."

Isabel arrived with tires squealing right before a lone police cruiser drove up at a leisurely pace. The first officer on scene took one look at the situation and quickly called for backup. "Looks like a hate crime to me. We might need to bring in the feds." He looked at Isabel, who was turning pale at the sight of the bullet hole and the hate sign. Her body swayed. She looked like she could fall at any moment. "Hey, I know who you are from the news," the officer said. "You're Isabel Paterson. You own this place, right?"

Murray threw a blanket around her mother's shoulders as Isabel nodded and mumbled, "That's right, I am the owner."

"Any idea who could have done this?" the officer asked.

Isabel looked frail and in shock as she motioned weakly for Murray to answer. Murray did not hesitate. "It's that stupid Cal Mavis. He's been threatening us since his brother got killed for shooting up the place a few months ago. He claims we've been making money on his brother's murder."

The officer nodded. "Well, right now we've got a crime scene on our hands, and I'm afraid you won't be opening up the restaurant any time today."

Naomi arrived, and when she saw the sign on the door, she covered her mouth in a horrified gasp. Once Naomi regained her voice, she spoke in a hushed but determined tone. "This will not throw us. Whoever did this is nothing but a coward. All this will do is make us work harder."

Murray was pleased to hear the fight in Naomi's voice. It was exactly what she and her mother needed to hear.

———

Isabel and Murray decided to keep the whole thing quiet. Bullet holes through the front door were never good advertising for a restaurant. Regardless, a photo of the threatening sign and the bullet hole was on the local morning news. Someone had taken the photo and posted it online to damage The Highway Diner, along with a written threat that the next bullet would have Isabel's name on it.

The diner was national news once again.

Isabel let out an incredulous and emotionally exhausted moan. "Why would anybody want to hurt a widow running a truck stop?"

Police authorized employees to go back into the building at 3:00 p.m. once the crime scene investigation had been completed. Cooks and servers began cleaning the restaurant and preparing to open for a maximum capacity crowd as soon as the doors could be replaced. Threatening The Highway Diner and posting it all over social media was a surefire way to create another Trucker Nation rally.

Isabel, Naomi, Murray, and Ben had an impromptu meeting at 4:00 p.m. Ben wasn't sure that Cal Mavis was the culprit. "I don't know," he said. "I only saw him getting dragged off the stage at that first rally. He didn't seem that clever. I mean, getting up in front of that crowd was nothing but stupid. He's lucky the mayor's bodyguards got to him before the truckers did."

"And calling Anita wasn't all that bright," Murray said.

"But he hasn't called her back," Isabel said. "My guess is he's getting help from the people who don't want us to build a casino. That whole mess is already headed for litigation."

Naomi sighed. "Let's not forget we've got a closed restaurant and a parking lot full of reporters. And if you haven't seen our website, the entire Trucker Nation is ready to ride to the rescue like the US Cavalry."

Chase and Leona walked into the meeting. "Did somebody call the cavalry?" Chase asked.

"Man," Ben said. "You guys are fast. You said you were coming right up, but that was only a couple hours ago."

"We're on it," Leona said. "It helps to have a jet. And hello, we got a ton of folks asking questions out there. We had to fight our way through. One reporter asked if it was true that Isabel had been shot."

"I have been shot . . . right through the heart," Isabel said. "This whole thing has been a nightmare. It puts the panic back in my head from the first shooting. We're still trying to get over that."

Leona sat down next to Isabel to comfort her.

"Let's make a statement," said Chase. "We'll keep it short and sweet. Downplay the whole thing. Let people know we'll be open for business tomorrow. Meanwhile, I've got cyber security all over the photo that was posted on social media and the text message to the local television station. So, who wants to be our spokesperson for now?"

Isabel stood up and squared her shoulders. "I can do this. People need to see I'm not dead. Would you all come out with me?"

Murray marveled at her mother's comeback. It was just like her to come out of her corner swinging. "Let's go do this, Mom. We're all right behind you."

As they walked out to meet the reporters, Murray had the feeling that something, or someone, was missing. She couldn't put her finger on it, but a nagging unease settled in as she listened to her mother shout out what had become her standard opening line:

"Greetings from the Highway Diner."

The press conference lasted nearly a half hour. Reporters knew all about the Cal Mavis situation from his brief performance at the first rally. "Let's not be blaming Mr. Mavis," Isabel said. "He's still grieving the loss of his brother. No one can blame him for that. We don't know who did this. We have no suspects at this point. It's probably just some kids being crazy. It's not that big of a deal. We'll be open tomorrow for business as usual." She paused for dramatic effect and then closed with her favorite battle cry, "Long live Trucker Nation."

Isabel had hoped her final comment would end the conference on a high note, but it only brought a flurry of questions about the proposed casino. A female reporter, wearing too much makeup, stepped out front and asked, "Is it true that opponents of the casino have issued death threats to officers of what is soon to be known as Trucker Nation Corporation?"

Chase stepped forward to answer. "That is absolutely false. And asking that question is irresponsible. You know it's not true, but you make it sound like it's already happened. Shame on you."

Once again, Chase impressed Murray and everybody else with his strong public persona and political savvy. He continued, "All of you should know that community leaders in the city and county and state are working together to make the casino and concert venue a reality. The Highway Diner has already put this section of land on the map. Now that people know where we are, we're gonna give them even more reason to come visit."

A respectful silence followed his remarks, but it was quickly replaced by a flurry of new questions. Isabel led the group back inside the diner.

Murray suddenly realized who was missing: Anita. Not only was she not there, but she hadn't called in. That could mean only two things. One, she had relapsed, which didn't seem likely since she was attending a Narcotics Anonymous meeting every day. Or two, she was in trouble. Murray had to brace herself as chills of apprehension took over her body. She could feel it in her bones that something terrible had happened.

Once inside, the television news was already reporting the press conference, broadcasting what little was known about the police investigation. The FBI had yet to get involved, reporters commented, because the hate crime didn't appear to be motivated by a bias against race, religion, or gender. That meant the search for Cal Mavis wasn't going nationwide any time soon.

It was also reported that local police had determined the bullet came from a .45 caliber pistol fired at close range, although no shell casing had been found at the scene. Photographs had been taken and the sign was being scanned for fingerprints. There were no signs of forced entry.

"Looks like a big fat nothing," Ben said.

"Come on, Ben," Murray said, grabbing him by the arm. "We've got our own investigating to do. We've got to find Anita. I think somebody's done something bad to her."

CHAPTER TWELVE

Ben and Murray arrived at Anita's small apartment on the first floor of a two-story housing complex not far from the diner. Anita's beat-up Camry was parked out front. "Looks like she's home," Murray said as she knocked on the door.

No response. Ben tried looking through the front window, but the blinds were drawn tight. He knocked on the glass. Still no response. Murray banged on the door again and yelled, "Anita, if you're in there, we need to know. Just say something and we'll go away if that's what you want."

They pounded on the door and window until the next-door neighbor opened her door and stuck her head out to say in a hoarse voice, "Hey, keep it down out there. Some of us are trying to sleep."

Murray was quick to apologize. "We're sorry to disturb you, but we think our friend might be in trouble. She's on the schedule for work, but she didn't call or come in."

"Hey," the neighbor groggily. "You're that lady from The Highway Diner, aren't you?"

"Yes, I am," Murray said as her shoulders sagged slightly in realizing she had become a public figure. "I'm worried about Anita. She's a good friend of mine. We had a little trouble at the diner, and I'm afraid she might be in danger."

The woman ducked back into her apartment but left the door open. She returned in a minute and said, "Here's a key to her apartment. I know she works for you, so I trust you. I've got her key to feed the cat when she works late. We take care of each other that way."

"Thank you so much," Murray said as she took the key and opened the door to Anita's apartment. The cat greeted them with a hungry howl. The front room smelled like a sweet-musk candle.

"Anita? You in here?" Murray called out as she and Ben walked in and did a quick search. It didn't take long to realize no one was home. The apartment had a front room with a kitchenette, a bedroom with an unmade bed, and a bathroom. The unmade bed made Murray worry. She knew Anita always made her bed as soon as she got up.

There was no sign of forced entry. The place was neat and clean, except for the bed and the cat litter in the bathroom. Murray realized Anita had not left home under normal circumstances. It was beginning to feel like Anita had been taken against her will.

Murray was in the bathroom looking for more clues to Anita's disappearance when she heard Ben call out from the living room, "Uh-oh, Murray. Come look at this. This is trouble."

Murray rushed out to see Ben pointing at Anita's cell phone in the corner, barely visible behind the television stand. "Is that what I think it is?"

Murray got down on her hands and knees and crawled to pick up the phone. She recognized it as Anita's phone from the rhinestone-bedazzled cover with the heart-shaped mirror in the middle. She knew right away that her friend had been abducted. Anita would never leave her cell phone behind. The screen was cracked, like it had been thrown against the wall.

"Look," Ben said. "Here's the dent in the wall where the phone hit."

"Yep. That's it all right." Murray inspected the dent. "She must have gotten out of bed to answer the door. Then, somebody grabbed her and got mad when she tried to call for help. Let's get the phone to Chase so he can get his people to check her calls."

"What about you?" Ben asked. "Can you check? Do you know her password?"

Murray tried to open the phone. "No, I don't know the password."

"Don't you think we should notify the police?" Ben suggested. "They might be able to find a security camera video to see who grabbed her."

"We don't need a camera to tell us who grabbed Anita," Murray said. "It's not somebody opposed to the casino. It's the only guy who's been after her all along, Cal Mavis. He put up that hateful sign last night, shot a hole through the front doors, and came here to kidnap Anita."

"We'd better notify the police," Ben suggested again. "It might make them search a little harder. This guy's committing all kinds of crimes. And he's getting bolder and more dangerous. Kidnapping is serious."

Murray closed her eyes and bowed her head. "All right. I guess you're right. We should call the police. Let's hope it's not something worse than kidnapping."

CHAPTER THIRTEEN

Anita was still missing after two weeks. Murray and Ben had been badgering the FBI about finding Anita and bringing her home. The agent in charge finally said, "Listen up, both of you. This is a highly sensitive, ongoing, high-priority investigation. It's not just about Anita. It's about domestic terrorism. Anita's kidnapping is all wrapped up in a larger investigation into a dangerously well-armed militia group. That's all I'm going to say. Except you two need to stand down and let us do our job."

The night of the FBI warning, Murray and Ben got to bed late in the RV, too tired for anything but pillow talk "I'm worried sick about Anita," Murray said. "She could be dead by now. We have no idea what this deranged idiot might do. But I don't know, something about her disappearance makes me so tired of all the drama at The Highway Diner. It makes me want to get away for a little while."

"I'm not sure we can hit the road with Anita in harm's way," Ben said.

"Ben, this trouble with The Highway Diner and Trucker Nation, the casino, and all the people who hate us for no reason is going to go on forever. First the shooting, then the death threats, and now the kidnapping, or whatever it is. I'm not sure I can take much more of this. Every time I get flustered, I hear those gunshots again. You know. How many times a night do I wake up with bad dreams? It was getting better for a while. Now it's only getting worse. I keep thinking it's going to happen again. What are we gonna do for Anita, anyway? Wait around for the FBI to find her? You drove up in your mom's RV—what—four months ago? I say it's high time we head for California. What do you think?"

Ben raised up quickly to one elbow, shocked that Murray might be ready for a road trip. "You're absolutely right. As much as we're worrying about Anita and everything else, it might be a good idea to take a couple weeks away and worry about each other for a little bit."

"It beats hanging around and feeling helpless," Murray agreed.

Ben stared at the ceiling for a moment, then mused, "Maybe it's time to name the RV. Don't you think? I mean, you can't take a trip in a vehicle with no name."

"How about the Happy Camper?" Murray giggled.

Ben laughed. "No, sounds too much like a day-care summer camp. We need something more adventurous."

"I know," Murray said, rolling herself on top of him. "How about the Intrepid?"

Ben laughed. He liked the idea, but he had to ask, "What, exactly, does *intrepid* mean?"

"Oh, Mr. Drop-Out-of-Stanford needs a truck-stop girl to explain a big word?" Murray smirked and shook her ponytail.

"I know it all." Ben shrugged. "I just can't remember it all at once."

"Well, all right then. 'Intrepid' means fearless. Like trepidation means fear, and the 'in' means 'without.'"

"Whoa," Ben said. "Where did you go to college?"

"You know I'm going to art school eventually. So, hey, we could look at some schools on our way to California."

"Good plan. I'll look right along with you."

"What? Med school?"

"No, something more to do with business and being a talent agent and manager. My time with Chase and Leona has convinced me I can be good at all that."

"You already are," Murray said. "You came up with Trucker Nation."

"We both know that was your mother's concept all the way."

Ben and Murray couldn't get out of town as quickly as they planned due to the crush of truckers and tourists that descended on The Highway Diner after the shooting and kidnapping. It was the first Trucker Nation rally all over again but without the band and the outdoor booze. The diner was much better prepared to handle the crowds. Naomi's new computerized point-of-sale system was proving its merit, all day, every day.

Media coverage of the support rally was less hysterical the second time around. Most of their attention was now focused on the search for Anita. Isabel and Murray were still worried about her. "I'm having trouble sleeping," Isabel said. "I keep thinking about all the awful things they could be doing to her. And I worry that my daughter might be next."

Naomi was concerned as well, but more practical. "We're going to have to let the government do the worrying. It sounds like they've got a plan to rescue Anita. They know she's at that compound in Newaygo, Michigan. The FBI agent let that slip a couple weeks ago, right about the time they decided she wasn't a runaway drug addict. They're calling it a kidnapping, so she's alive, at least. They must know she's not in imminent danger or they would swoop in to save her. Evidently, the militia compound is run by some super-dangerous and deranged military veteran."

Murray agreed with Naomi's assessment of Anita's situation. They had each picked up bits and pieces about the far-right militia from their conversations with law enforcement. Murray was still worried about Anita, but she was already packing for her vacation with Ben. It was obvious there was nothing she could do until law enforcement made its move.

Ben didn't need to pack. He hadn't unpacked since he drove the RV to Indiana, but he had always reserved the largest closet and two thirds of the dresser space in the Intrepid for Murray.

Isabel had immediately given her blessing to the proposed voyage. "Nobody deserves a vacation more than you two. Don't worry about Anita. We're all pretty sure the FBI knows where she is, and they're watching her somehow. Don't worry about work, either. Naomi and I can handle the diner."

At least, that was what she said when Ben was in the room.

Later that afternoon, Isabel cornered Murray in the kitchen. "You do realize what it means when a man takes his girlfriend home to meet his mother?"

Murray had not thought about the trip in terms of Ben getting down on one knee and asking her to marry him. The visual image terrified her. Getting married was not something she was ready to do. She had just turned twenty-one on April 4. Ben had just turned twenty-five in March. They'd been too busy for birthday parties, except for splitting several bottles of champagne on each occasion. *We're way too young to get married*, she thought. *He wouldn't be ready either, would he?*

"Let's not get ahead of ourselves here, Mom," she said. "We're taking a vacation, not a honeymoon. And I really want to meet his mother. I've seen so many photos of her, I feel like I already know her. She's an artist, like me. I'm sure we'll get along just fine."

Isabel smiled knowingly. "Your father took me home to meet his mother and that was it. We were married six months later. And, by the way, I was twenty years old."

Murray shook her head. "You know I love Ben with all my heart, but that doesn't mean I'm ready to settle down and have kids."

"I know you're not," Isabel said with an understanding shake of her head. "Let him know you're not ready. Work it into the conversation somewhere in Iowa, or wherever."

"How do I do that?"

Isabel looked her in the eye. "Just mention something about how you want to finish college before you get married."

"How subtle would that be?"

Isabel laughed. "You'll know what to say. Just make sure he gets the idea before you meet his mother. She'll ask him when you're not around."

"You know it's not all about marriage like it used to be."

"I know, Murray. Blake and I talk about that all the time."

"You and Blake are talking about marriage? Oh, good one, Mom. I can see my no-dating rule went out the window. Now I've got to say no getting married to a musician?"

"No, honey," Isabel said. "We talk about *not* getting married, not about getting married."

"It sounds like the same thing to me."

Isabel's eyes twinkled and she raised her eyebrows to crinkle her forehead like she always did before making a joke. "I know what. Let's get married together," Isabel teased. "We could have a joint ceremony at the new casino."

"Very funny, Mom."

Isabel hugged her. "I love you so much, Muriel Paterson, daughter of my beloved Brodie. I see him in your eyes all the time, you know." Isabel blinked back tears. "Anyway, have a great trip, my dear. I know you're going to have the time of your life."

———————

It was 8:00 p.m. before Murray and Ben headed west on Highway 30 to check out the School of the Art Institute of Chicago, one of the best arts and design universities in the nation. The river of headlights and taillights lulled them into reflective moods. As they waited through stoplights in every small town along the way, Murray thought about her mother and how good their relationship was. It hadn't always been that way.

Isabel had been the tough parent. She made Murray help with the dishes, the vacuuming, and cleaning her own room. Murray was thirteen and working at the diner after school when she first called her mother an "evil witch." Isabel had come down hard on her. No television or cell phone for a week, a punishment worse than death.

Murray was always daddy's little Tomboy, especially after her younger sister died at the age of six from a rare case of pneumonia. Murray was eight years old at the time, too young to understand the terrible loss her parents were feeling. She did realize how lonely and confused she felt without her little sister. They had shared a bedroom with two single beds. Murray couldn't bring herself to look at her sister's empty bed. Nighttime was the worst. She often whispered her sister's name, asking where she had gone.

One night she woke up standing between the beds, expecting her sister to return at any moment from the bathroom. She thought she heard someone running the water, but when she opened the door, there was no one there. Murray ran back to her bed and flung herself face down into the pillow, sobbing at the realization that her sister was never coming back.

The loss of her sister changed Murray forever, although she wouldn't realize it until later losses forced her to understand. She looked at people differently from then on, wondering how long each person had to live. She was cautious about making friends, fearful about what suffering another loss could bring.

Once Murray became an only child, Isabel constantly chastised her husband about spending too much time with his daughter and not enough time with his wife. By the time Murray was sixteen and learning from her father how to drive a big rig, Isabel started riding along for the lessons. "If you can't beat 'em, join 'em," she had said every time she climbed into the truck.

Murray's world came crashing down for the second time at the age of seventeen when her daddy died. She wouldn't eat and she couldn't sleep. Her grief turned into anger. Problems with fighting at school, sometimes with boys, got her expelled. Isabel had to home school her for a time. Murray learned most of her lessons at the diner her mother was desperately trying to manage on her own. She lashed out mercilessly at her mother. "There's no way Daddy would let you take me out of school. Now, I don't have any friends. What's even worse, you're violating child labor laws by making me work all the time at your stupid restaurant."

Isabel was never one to take guff from anyone, least of all from her sassy daughter. "Don't talk to me about child labor. I was in labor for eighteen hours giving birth to you. So, here's what we're doing. You're going back to school, and you're not getting kicked out again. If you do, I won't have you living in my house."

Isabel's tone had turned from angry to sad. "It's not my

fault your father died. It's nobody's fault. Neither one of us is ever going to get over it. We're just not. So, we better try getting along, because I'm all you've got and you're all I've got."

Murray remembered how her mother had broken down and sobbed. For the first time in her young mind, Murray had realized that she wasn't the only one grieving. She didn't want to cry, but she couldn't help it. Her mother took her in her arms. They felt each other's pain. From then on, they gradually began working together instead of against each other.

"What are you thinking about?" Ben asked as they stopped for the fifth red light in Warsaw, Indiana.

"The day my mother and I stopped fighting each other over Daddy's death."

The light turned green, and Ben accelerated smoothly to get up to speed. He didn't speak. Murray looked at him to see if he was waiting for her to continue or if he had something on his mind. His lips were pursed, and he wouldn't look at her. She waited for him to speak.

Once they were cruising at sixty-five miles per hour, Ben finally said, "You know, Mom and I lost my father too. It might have been easier if he died. Running off with your nurse is a horrible way to say goodbye to your wife and two children. It sent my mother into a terrible depression. She stopped painting. She cried all the time. She wouldn't cook or clean or even take care of herself. I was thirteen and my sister was fifteen. Mom wouldn't even drive us to school or anywhere. We had to start riding the bus."

Murray knew about Ben's parents' divorce, but he had never gone into the gory details. She placed her hand on his shoulder. He looked at her and smiled weakly.

"Thanks, Murray. Hard times, tough to talk about. It took us all a couple of years to regain our footing. Not that I'll probably ever get over it. I never see my father. I tried for years to keep up with him. He gradually disappeared from my life. He was too busy with his new family. Two new kids. Can you believe that? My half-brother and half-sister, and I never see them."

Murray couldn't help herself. "Cheaters always pay the price. I'll bet that sweet young thing had him changing diapers for years."

Ben slapped the steering wheel and cackled in laughter. Murray was glad to see him loosening up. It occurred to her that their shared grief over the loss of their fathers had been a bond between them. She couldn't wait to see if he was as close to his mother as she was to hers.

CHAPTER FOURTEEN

Murray and Ben spent the night in a budget hotel in Valparaiso. They got naked and played together in the reflections of the many mirrors in the room. They finally drifted into an exhausted sleep after midnight and didn't awaken until 9:30 a.m. By noon, they were in Chicago. It was a sunny day in late April. Glass skyscrapers shimmered as high as their expectations.

They left downtown to find an RV lot near Humboldt Park, packed overnight backpacks, and took an Uber downtown to the Art Institute of Chicago on Michigan Avenue. By 2:00 p.m., they were asking a stranger to take their photo next to one of the two massive bronze lions out front. "These big boys have been here since 1894," Ben said as he checked his phone. "Edward Kemeys and his wife, Laura, created them. Whoa! She was a sculptor too."

Murray laughed. "Anyone with a cell phone can be an art historian."

Once inside the museum, Murray convinced Ben to take a guided tour, and off they went with a young docent named Tyra Cooper and a group of ten people. Tyra was an African American woman with cinnamon-brown skin, a bushy Afro hairstyle, and long legs that kept a brisk pace. Murray was impressed with her knowledge of art history as she led them on a dazzling and dizzying tour of original works by Picasso, Chagall, Warhol, Hopper, and many more.

Ben was overloaded by all the art in an hour, but Murray convinced him to hang in there and complete the two-hour tour. Meanwhile, she got to know Tyra by asking good questions about the paintings. When Murray asked about the relationship between color and values, the docent stopped dead in her tracks.

She adjusted her horned-rimmed glasses. "Let's talk about values for a minute," Tyra said. Then she turned to Murray and added, "You must be a painter."

Murray nodded and Tyra addressed the group. "So, values. What are we talking about? American values? Christian values? No, there's a thing called the value scale in art, referring to the range of darkness to lightness within a painting. A bright reflection, for example, has a value of one. A shadow might have a value of nine, or maybe no value at all if it's dark enough." She turned to Murray. "So, what do we say about the relationship between value and color?"

Murray was embarrassed to be singled out, but she answered, "Color gets all the credit, but values do all the work."

"Oh, my goodness," Tyra said. "We have a professional in the group. Does everybody understand why color gets all the credit?"

A man with a white beard in need of a trim spoke barely loud enough to be heard. "Color is more obvious. Values deal in contrast."

"Does everybody get that?" Tyra asked.

People nodded their heads, but they didn't really seem to understand.

Near the end of the tour, Murray asked Tyra about the connection between the museum and the arts and design school. "Great question," Tyra said. "The school and the museum have a symbiotic relationship. In fact, I'm a student at the School of the Art Institute. And you, my dear, look like you're thinking about enrolling there. Am I right?"

"You are a mind reader," Murray said.

Tyra wrapped up the tour by thanking her guests, accepting their tips, including a twenty from Ben, and wishing them happy viewing on the art trail. She took Murray aside. "I don't know why, but I keep thinking I know you from somewhere." Murray shook her head and shrugged her shoulders. Tyra continued, "Anyway, today must be your lucky day. I'm headed for my drawing class right now. You and your friend can come along and maybe even sit in."

After a short walk, Ben and Murray were sitting in a drawing class at the Art Institute. Twenty artists encircled a nude female posing as the Statue of Liberty. Tyra whispered that the instructor had secured the model's permission to have guests. The floor of the room was sloped downward to the small stage in the middle so everyone got a good view.

The teacher was a middle-aged Asian woman with a big smile wearing jeans covered in paint stains. When Tyra introduced Murray as a prospective student, the teacher surprised everybody by saying, "Tyra, perhaps your friend would like to sit in and draw with us this afternoon?"

Murray looked quickly at Ben, her eyes searching for his encouragement.

"Go get 'em, Mur," said Ben, grinning. He understood what a tremendous opportunity this was for Murray. "I'll take a walk to the lake and the park. Call me when you're ready."

Tyra shared her pencils and paper. Murray was rendering, shading, highlighting, and cross-hatching before she had a chance to pinch herself. She had never drawn a live nude before, much less sat in a college class. The feeling was so electric she thought every hair on her body must be standing on end.

A half hour later, the teacher looked over Murray's shoulder and said, "Nice work, so nice. Now, loosen up her hanging arm. You've got the raised arm right, but the hanging arm looks a little stiff. Maybe it's too short."

Murray looked at her drawing. The teacher was correct. Murray was quietly delighted. "Thank you," was all she said, but her artist heart was soaring. With practical instruction like this, she could get better in a hurry. Even the shooting, death threats, and kidnapping wouldn't stop her.

The teacher's encouragement was a revelation. Her dreams of becoming an artist could come true. She didn't have to look at any other art schools. This was the place for her. She knew it as soon as she walked in the door and smelled the oil paint and tasted clay dust in the air. Tyra's helpfulness, the teacher's kindness, and the nude model in the college class all combined to feel like destiny. A genuine camaraderie of artistry prevailed. Murray desperately wanted to be part of it.

She called Ben after class. When he arrived, she was still chatting with a group of five art students. They all encouraged her to enroll. Tyra followed Murray and Ben out the door. "I realized who you are about halfway through the class. You're Murray from The Highway Diner. I can't believe I didn't put it together as soon as you told me your name."

"Thanks for not saying anything," Murray said. "I really needed to just blend in. It was so perfect." She took Ben by the hand. "And this is Ben, also from The Highway Diner."

"Oh my God, you two. I've been following you for months. I love Trucker Nation and everything you're trying to do. It's about time somebody stood up against all the hate."

"Thank you, Tyra. That's good to hear. And I can't thank you enough for changing my life forever. This drawing class was so good for me, I can't believe it."

"Yay," Tyra said. "That's good because you've got real talent. I knew you'd be good from talking to you on the tour. So, okay, I don't want to sound like a groupie, but could you both sign my drawing? No one will believe me if I don't get it in writing."

Murray and Ben signed her drawing. "Looks like you've got some serious skills of your own," Ben said. "I've got a feeling we'll be seeing you again."

Tyra rolled up her drawing and hugged them both. "See you in September," she said. Then she looked lost for words until her face brightened and she raised her voice, "Long live Trucker Nation."

Murray and Ben walked out of the building in a bit of daze. "I can't believe we're getting asked for autographs in Chicago," Murray said. "Is that a good thing?"

"It's good if we don't let it go to our head," Ben said. Murray nodded in complete understanding as she unrolled her drawing for Ben on a picnic table. A ray of late afternoon sun illuminated the artwork like a stage light.

"Oh my God! It's beautiful," he said. "You just did this? In what? Under two hours? This is truly impressive. She doesn't even need a torch. You've captured the essence of Lady Liberty. She's bold and beautiful. But you did leave out something."

"What?" Murray became immediately defensive. Her eyes narrowed slightly.

Ben waved his hands to show he wasn't being critical. In fact, he decided to keep his mouth shut.

"What?" Murray demanded.

Ben laughed at himself. "Here the author pauses, realizing he's written himself into an untenable corner."

Murray wasn't letting him off the hook. She crossed her arms, furrowed her brow, and waited.

"All right, all right," Ben relented. "You left out the under-arm hair."

"Ben," Murray pushed him on the shoulder. "You're not supposed to notice."

"Hard to miss," Ben said. "That girl was hairy. And what about that huge bush? You left that out too. Did the instructor critique your work?"

"As a matter of fact, she did, and she was very helpful. And no, she didn't mention the lack of hair in my drawing. Women don't focus on 'the bush,' as you call it."

"Well, wait. Look. You gave her a nice patch of pubic hair. So much sexier than the real thing. Come on, you can admit it to me. The armpit hair made you gag just a little."

Murray looked to the sky for relief from Ben's teasing. He changed his approach. "No, all I'm saying is that it's a beautiful drawing. We need to frame it. It's your first college drawing. It looks like you've already enrolled."

Murray decided to give him a pass on the pubic hair. She threw her arms around his neck and hugged him. "Oh Ben, I had the most wonderful time. This is the place for me. The teacher was so perfect, and the students were all part of this thing. I can't explain it. It's like an art club, but it's not snooty. Everybody wants to help. And you were so good to wait and then come get me."

Ben squeezed her and said, "To tell the truth, I was glad to get out of there. I was feeling a little uncomfortable doing nothing but staring at a naked lady."

"The model was a total pro," Murray said. "She held her arm up like that for two hours with only two five-minute breaks. I wanted to talk to her at the end, but she got dressed and left before I had a chance."

Ben rolled up the drawing carefully. "I hope you don't

mind, my queen, but I've taken the liberty, as in Lady Liberty, of booking you a room with a skyline view of Lake Michigan, a pool, and a full-service spa at the Fairmont Hotel."

Murray jumped up and down on the sidewalk. "Perfect, perfect, perfect. Lucky thing I packed my swimsuit. Did you bring yours?"

Ben slapped himself on the forehead. "Damn, I forgot it." Then he recovered. "No problem. I'll just skinny dip. Nobody notices once you're in the water."

Murray couldn't help but chuckle. "You'll do no such thing."

"What? You don't think I look good naked? You said I looked great last night."

"That is hardly the point. We'll have to buy you a swimsuit."

Ben interrupted her. "No. Don't worry. I've got a pair of shorts that'll do just fine. Come on, we can walk over there and check in. Perhaps a bottle of champagne would be in order."

⸻

They didn't leave the hotel all night. The room was luxury large with a thirty-fifth-floor view of the Chicago skyline and the vastness of Lake Michigan. The watery horizon provided a tranquil contrast to the metropolitan chaos. Ben popped the champagne with a flourish. "Here's to your first college drawing. May it be followed by a thousand more."

Murray danced in front of the glass window wall with her champagne. "That classroom was so magical. Didn't you love the way it all sloped to the center? And the smell. That was the best. Like we walked into an oil painting."

"What I loved was the look on your face when the teacher invited you to sit in and draw. Like you hit the jackpot in Vegas."

"That's what this whole day has been. Hitting the jackpot. And the biggest prize is you."

Ben clinked glasses with her. "Thanks, Murray," he said. "How did I get so lucky?"

Murray gave him a champagne kiss. "Don't you mean *we* got so lucky." They embraced in the dazzling moment as the setting sun disappeared behind clouds and lights of the city began to glow in the growing darkness.

"Let's hit the spa," Murray said after she drained the last of the champagne from the bottle and set it on the counter. She walked to a closet and opened the sliding door. "Oh, look, his and her robes."

They almost got sidetracked into bed as they got naked and put on their swimming attire, Murray in her floral bikini and Ben in his workout shorts. But even the warmth of each other's skin couldn't delay them from exploring the amenities of the five-star hotel.

First stop was the pool. Murray kicked off her sandals, took off her robe, and dove in right over the "No Diving" sign.

Ben laughed as he took his time and waded down the steps. "Water's a little chilly," he said.

"That's because you're getting in too slow," Murray said as she splashed him.

Ben ducked underwater, pushed off the bottom step, and glided to grab her by the ankles. He tried to drag her under, but she danced away. When he came up for air, she caught him off guard and jumped into his chest with such force that they both went underwater.

They played in the water like children. Their world was so simple in that pool. Being together was everything they needed. They thought it would last forever.

Ben was gentle with her until he grabbed her under the

arms and threw her across the water. Murray was surprised by his strength. The only other man who had been able to do that was her daddy. And she was a lot smaller in those days. Even so, she let out the shriek of a delighted little girl. Her shrill voice echoed throughout the pool area. The only other people at the pool were a couple wearing robes who pretended not to notice.

After the pool, they hit the hot tub, sauna, and steam room. They would have gotten a massage had the masseuse been on duty. Instead, they drank lots of citrus water from the cooler.

After the spa, they got dressed and went downstairs to the Columbus Tap restaurant for craft beers and fancy burgers. Every beer on tap tasted better than the one before. After four or five rounds, all they could do was stumble back to the room and collapse into bed. They were asleep before they could kiss goodnight.

CHAPTER FIFTEEN

Wake-up sex in the high-rise hotel room was as inspiring as the rising sun. Murray was the playful instigator. "Last night was perfect, but we forgot our favorite part."

"More like we saved the best for first thing in the morning," said Ben, easing into action. They were both naked in a flash. "Come dance with me," he said as he stood up and waltzed her to the window. The view was outrageous. Lake Michigan stretched out blue and green as far as the eye could see, relentless waves shimmering in the sun. He turned her around to face the morning as he held her from behind.

Murray could feel his excitement as he caressed her. She leaned forward with her hands on the glass as he eased his way inside her with a move that felt smooth and powerful. Murray felt the sexual rush of his heat as he held her tightly by the hips. "Ben, Ben, Ben," she moaned as she looked out at the lake and felt one with all the water in the world.

She made the mistake of looking all the way down to the street filled with tiny people and cars running around like toys. It felt like she was already floating. A mild dizziness quickly became full-blown vertigo. "Oh, God, Ben. Stop. Stop!"

Ben pulled himself out, turned her around, and held her as she tried to regain her balance. "What's the matter? Did I hurt you?"

"No," Murray said. "You were perfect. But I looked down and got so dizzy I thought we were falling."

Once Murray felt steady on her feet, she had to take deep breaths to regain her mental balance. "That's definitely not something you write home about," she said as the humor of the situation began to reveal itself. "I guess falling in love is much better than plain old falling."

They fell back into bed laughing. "Doctor," Ben said, "I'm afraid the experiment went horribly wrong."

"You saved me from certain death," Murray said. "You're my hero."

"Let's stay in bed where it's safe," he whispered as he kissed her earlobes.

Murray had no trouble convincing Ben to stay an extra day in Chicago. They walked to the lake through Millennium Park and explored the shoreline all the way to Navy Pier. Despite her morning vertigo scare, Murray agreed to ride the Centennial Wheel so they could get a view of Chicago and their hotel from the water's edge.

"This is so romantic," Murray said as she clung to Ben to stay warm. "People wouldn't believe it if they saw it in a movie."

Murray hadn't been on a Ferris Wheel since she was a little girl. She loved the feeling of floating high above the water. It wasn't frightening at all. "So, Ben," she asked, knowing he would have an answer, "why do we call it a Ferris wheel?"

Ben threw his head back and laughed. "I knew you would ask. That's so funny. I already looked it up. Some guy named Ferris constructed one for the Chicago World's Fair in 1893. We're right here, where history was made."

Murray kissed him gratefully.

———

After two unforgettable days in Chicago, Murray was driving the Intrepid on Interstate 90 toward Rockford, Illinois. The vehicle handled like an SUV. It hugged the road and had power to spare. Ben proudly pointed out the vehicle's electrical and mechanical features.

"I'm glad we're taking I-90," he said. "I drove I-80 from San Francisco to Chicago more times than I'd like to remember. It's a straight shot, but it got boring after a while. And I never had a beautiful woman to share the ride."

I-90 was the more northerly route. They took it because Murray wanted to see two places along the way: the Badlands and Yellowstone National Park. The itinerary was exciting. The highway felt magical. Little did they know, a billboard was about to change everything.

Murray saw it before Ben. They were coming into Rockford, Illinois. The sign was big and red with black letters. It read, "Trucker Nation Is a Lie."

Murray felt the heat of rage rising inside as she pointed out the sign. "Ben, look. That big red billboard. Does it say what I think it says?"

"Oh, damn," Ben said. "That's not good. Who would do that? And why?"

Murray kept driving as she and Ben fell into a shocked silence. "Here's the problem," Murray finally spoke. "Trucker Nation has always been more of a dream than a reality. It's not one big, happy family like we want it to be. Look at the truckers who blockaded the Ambassador Bridge between Detroit and Canada. They shut it down for six days. And for what? To protest mandatory COVID vaccinations. How crazy is that? It wasn't Trucker Nation that shut that bridge down. It was right-wing truckers who didn't want the government telling them what to do."

"Those blockade truckers are the far-right militia on wheels," Ben said.

"I wouldn't think those fringe people would have enough money to put up a billboard," Murray thought out loud. "Those things aren't cheap, you know. And why put one in Rockford?"

"Maybe it's not just one," Ben said. "That board could be part of some campaign. This is the first one we've seen, right? I mean, it would be hard to miss."

"No," Murray said. "We didn't miss one. This is the first one since Chicago. That's almost ninety miles. We should stop and ask who put it up."

"I can find out faster on the phone," Ben said. "But I think we both know who's got the money to put up a bunch of hateful billboards."

"That idiot who's got Anita in his compound," she said as she pounded the driving wheel like an angry drummer. "We know she's up there. That's why the feds won't rescue her. They've got the entire compound under investigation. An FBI agent told me there are nearly one hundred men and some women living in a fortified military compound with enough weapons to start a war. It doesn't have a name, just Michigan militia with some number behind it."

"I think you got that right," Ben said. "She's stuck in the middle of an undercover operation. She's in the wrong place at the wrong time."

They drove in silence, each pondering the troubles they couldn't seem to leave behind. "Here comes Beloit, Wisconsin, and the state border," Murray announced. "Look, there's the Welcome to Wisconsin sign."

"Let's hold our breath for good luck as we cross the border," Ben said. He was getting back into the spirit of the trip until another big red billboard appeared. "Oh no. There's another sign north of the border."

"And can you believe that?" Murray raised her voice when she saw the billboard that read, "The Highway Diner Is a Lie."

"Oh man," Ben said. "Now they're getting personal. The next one will probably say, 'Isabel Paterson is a witch.'"

"These signs remind me of the stories my father used to tell about the Burma-Shave posters along the road that told stories, one sign at a time, so you had to keep driving to get the joke. Daddy's favorite was, 'Within this vale, of toil and sin, your head grows bald, but not your chin, Burma-Shave.'"

Ben chuckled, but Murray could tell he was much more disturbed by the second sign than the first. He got out a pad of paper and a pen. "We'd better make notes on where these things are posted and what they say. This is beginning to look like a campaign that leads to no good."

By Janesville, Wisconsin, they saw the third sign. This one read, "Trucker Nation Is Communism."

"Shit, shit, shit," Ben said. "Looks like the honeymoon is over."

"Not for us?" Murray whined. "We're not going to let a few crazy signs turn us around, are we?"

"No, no. Of course not." Ben put his hand on her shoulder. "I'm not talking about us. I'm talking about Trucker Nation being this righteous force for national unity. Looks like some people with money aren't ready for one nation, under God, with a smooth supply line for all."

"We better call Mom."

"Yes, we'll call Isabel, but first, we need to call Chase Marshall and see what's happening."

Chase picked up immediately and the call came through the Intrepid sound system on speakerphone. "Hey, Ben. Hey, Murray," Chase said. "Where are you?"

"Fifty miles from Madison, Wisconsin, on I-90," Ben said.

"We just saw three big red billboards, miles apart on the highway. One says 'Trucker Nation Is a Lie.' The second one says, 'The Highway Diner Is a Lie.' And the third one says—are you ready for this—'Trucker Nation Is Communism.'"

"Damn," Chase said. "They're going way overboard, calling us communists. But here's the really bad news. These boards are popping up on all the east-west interstates. Whoever put 'em up has plenty of money, and I've got a bad feeling they're not going to stop at billboards."

"What do you mean?" Murray asked. Her voice had a high tone that sounded anxious.

Chase backtracked. "I'm not saying there's anything to worry about. Probably another truck blockade is coming. That's all I'm saying."

"Why would anyone do this?" Murray asked.

Chase thought about the question for a moment, then said, "All you gotta do to bring out the hate is start talking about love. Look what they did to Jesus Christ. Or Martin Luther King Jr. Or John Lennon."

"I never thought about it like that," Ben pondered. "I'm afraid you might be right. Why is that?"

"Some people get nervous when somebody starts talking about a brotherhood of man," Murray explained. "Like that somebody is going to take something away from them. Those people want to keep what they have, and they're afraid change won't work for them."

"Whoa, Murray," Chase said. "That's some profound stuff for right off the cuff. Well said, my friend, well said."

Ben asked, "Since when does anybody have money for a national billboard campaign?"

"I'm getting word from my sources that the money's coming from that militia group around Newaygo, Michigan," Chase said. "They've got a highly profitable marijuana operation up there. It's river country. It's remote. They're selling guns and ammo too. That guy who calls himself 'the Commander' has more money than he can spend."

"Where is Newaygo?" Ben asked.

"It's east of Muskegon, about fifty miles from Lake Michigan. I'm told they've got a small army of heavily armed men guarding the operation. Maybe even tanks and artillery. And here's the kicker."

Murray and Ben waited for him to continue.

"It looks like Cal Mavis and Anita are shacking up together."

"We've been thinking that for a while now," Murray said. "But what do you mean by shacking up?"

Chase hesitated again, then decided to plow ahead. "The FBI already has an undercover agent embedded in the operation. Initial reports say Anita's fallen under Mavis' control, physically and emotionally. It might be Stockholm syndrome, where the hostage begins to trust the kidnapper. Or maybe she just likes the Mavis touch."

"So, she's relapsed?" Murray asked.

"We don't know that. But we do know this militia group wants to make an example of The Highway Diner."

"Why would they want to do that?" Murray asked. "What did we ever do to them?"

"We could make a big mistake trying to make sense out of these folks," Chase said. "The good news is we don't have word on any kind of violence. It's pretty much a media campaign to let the world know that truckers have power and not all of them are ready for business as usual. There's a whole new idea gathering steam that says gas prices must come down or truckers will strike."

"I'm all for cheaper gas," Ben said. "But what makes any-body think a strike would make that happen?"

Murray leaned forward on the steering wheel and shook her ponytail hard. "Who do these people think they are? I'm about to drive up to Newaygo, or wherever they are, and give them a piece of my mind. Maybe rescue Anita while I'm at it. And by the way, if they know where she is, why don't they go get her? She was kidnapped. We can prove it."

Chase sighed. "The problem with that is Anita's the star witness in that case. And if she says she wasn't kidnapped, then she wasn't kidnapped. But it's trickier than that. The feds don't want to move in yet. They want to see how this thing develops so maybe they can take down the whole militia unit."

"How do you know so much about all this?" Ben asked.

Chase responded slowly and carefully, "You know I trust you or I wouldn't be telling you this, but the undercover agent in Newaygo used to work security for me in Nashville."

"Ah, Chase," Ben said. "You do cover all the bases."

"Should we come home now?" Murray asked.

"No. No need for that. This harassment will be going on for a long time. You two go ahead with your trip. I'm sure you'll be back before anything else happens. Murray, you do need to call your mother. She needs to know you're safe."

CHAPTER SIXTEEN

By the time they reached Madison, Wisconsin, they saw an uplifting sight. A billboard that read "The Highway Diner Is a Lie" had been defaced by a thick, black X painted from corner to corner.

Murray bounced up and down in the passenger seat. "Looks like the local artists have taken sides already. I love it. And I'm so excited we're here. It's the University of Wisconsin. They've got a great art department and a big museum."

Ben pulled off at the first Madison exit and stopped to search for an RV park on his phone. "There's one in Mendota County Park, right on Mendota Lake, north of Madison and the campus. They've got openings. Let's go."

"Let's cruise the campus on our way," Murray said.

Ben grabbed Murray's hand and raised it to his lips for a kiss. "Campus central, here we come."

"I need to call my mom," Murray said. "I don't want her to worry."

Isabel answered on the second ring. "Murray, thank God. You're all right?"

"Yes, Mom, what's wrong?"

"Chase and Leona told me you're seeing these horrible signs along the interstate. Is that right?"

"Hi, Isabel. You're on speaker," Ben said. "Is that okay?"

"Yes, of course, Ben. I'm so glad you're there with my baby

girl. This sign business has me worked up. I heard one says 'The Highway Diner Is a Lie.'"

"The last sign we saw had a big black X painted over it," Ben said.

"The University of Wisconsin students are definitely on our side," Murray said. "You don't have to worry."

"Tell that to Chase," Isabel said. "He's got two undercover guys guarding the diner. They try to blend in, but they don't. There's talk they'll start searching vehicles, but that hasn't happened yet."

"Oh no," Murray said. "He didn't tell us that. Maybe we should come home."

"No, Chase says he's overreacting just in case. You two go on with your trip. I'll call if I need you."

Murray told her mother all about her experience at the Chicago art school and how they were going to check out the Wisconsin campus. They talked for fifty miles. Ben didn't say a word until it was time to say goodbye. Once Isabel hung up, Ben looked at Murray and said, "She doesn't sound too bad."

Murray nodded, but she didn't look convinced. Both she and Ben were aware of the horrible threats and accusations being posted on social media. A small percentage of truckers were mad about everything from inflation and the price of fuel to regulation and taxation.

"So why do we call the militia 'far right'?" Murray asked.

"Well, the left is the Democrats," Ben explained. "They're for more government. The right is Republicans who want less government. The far right is opposed to the government in general. Not only do they want less government, but they want to overthrow the government we have."

"Can they do that?" Murray asked. "I mean, are there enough of them to start a civil war?"

"I've heard people say the militia is like gasoline spilling all over the country," Ben said. "All it's gonna take is one charismatic leader with a big enough match to send the whole thing up in flames."

Murray pondered his assessment but did not continue the conversation. It was 5:00 p.m. on Thursday, and the weekend had already begun in Madison at campus bars like The Kollege Klub, Wando's and The Double U. "Oh my," Murray said. "Going to college looks like so much fun, Ben. Just think, we could do it together."

"It looks pretty crowded to me," Ben said as he drove through the party district and onto the main campus and residence halls along University Bay on Lake Mendota. They stopped at a liquor store and picked up two six packs of local craft beer. By the time they found the RV park and paid for a campsite, they'd each had a couple beers. They were more than ready to get out of the RV, stretch their legs, and hit the public restroom.

Murray came out of the women's room and Ben looked like he'd seen a ghost.

"I didn't want to tell you this because I didn't want you to worry. But a black Ford 150 pickup truck pulled into the park while you were in the bathroom. I'd seen that same vehicle a couple times since we left Chicago. It has a slightly damaged right front fender. It drove to the end of the road and parked at a trailer site in a wooded area. The pickup wasn't pulling a trailer. I think we're being followed. Or maybe those billboards are making me paranoid."

Murray's eyes widened. "How would anybody know where we are?"

Ben looked at her with a wry grin. "It's not like we're traveling undercover in the Intrepid. We stick out like a sore thumb. They could have easily followed us from the diner."

"Why would anyone want to follow us?" Murray asked. Then she gasped and put her hand over her mouth. "Maybe they want to kidnap us like they did Anita?"

"I don't know," Ben said, "but we'll see what we can find out tonight. We'll take the Intrepid into town. I saw lots of big, empty parking lots. We'll get something to eat and come back after dark. I'll get out of the van just before we get to the trailer park and sneak up on whoever's driving that pickup. You stay with the van, and I'll keep watch on the outside. We'll see what happens."

Murray could hardly eat once they got into town, found a parking spot, and got into a bar that served food. Her stomach was churning from the thought of Ben going commando on the driver of the pickup truck. "Maybe we should call the police."

"Not yet, Mur. I'm not sure we're even being followed. There's a million black Ford F 150s on the road. Besides, I'm more than sick of calling the police and watching them do nothing. Even the FBI has done nothing but sit around and wait. So relax. Have a couple beers. We'll be fine. I'm not going to play hero. I'll feel it out. If the opportunity presents itself, I confront the driver and ask if he's following us."

"Are you trying to make me feel better or worse?" Murray wondered out loud.

They ate a quick dinner, mostly in silence. Murray only had two bites of her cheeseburger. Afterward, she drove the Intrepid back toward the park. Ben prepared for his mission. He holstered his Glock before they reached the park entrance.

"Won't he be able to see it's just me driving back?" Murray asked.

"Not if we turn down like so," Ben said as he darkened the interior and dashboard lights. "Okay, here's my spot. It's 9:00 p.m. I'll be back in the Intrepid by 10:00 p.m. You know what to do."

"I know what to do, but I'm not sure I want to do it. Why does it feel like you're using me as bait?"

"Don't worry," Ben said as she stopped the RV for him to make a quick exit. "I'll be keeping a close watch on you."

Murray parked the RV and drew the curtains so no one could see there was only one person in the van. Then she turned the inside lights off like they'd gone to sleep. Once the waiting began, time slowed to a near standstill. By 10:30 p.m. she was hearing every sound the night wind had to offer. She kept her pistol at the ready and watched the clock in a state of heightened awareness. *This is stupid,* she tried to reassure herself. *Nobody's following us. Why would anyone even do that?*

Then, she heard Ben slamming someone against the passenger side of the Intrepid. She leaped up to open the side door. Her heart was pounding. Sure enough, Ben had a hostage pinned against the Intrepid with his gun at the man's throat. Ben had a hunting rifle strapped over his back. Murray wondered where he'd gotten the rifle.

"Get in," Ben growled at the man, who was short and bald, heavyset, wearing glasses and at least sixty years old.

"Who are you and why are you following us?" Ben demanded as he forced the man at gunpoint to sit down at the table. Murray had never seen Ben like this, but under the circumstances, she was grateful for his gangster approach.

"Don't shoot, please, don't shoot," the man cried. "I was just following orders."

"You might want to fix your fender if you don't want to get spotted tailing someone. And what's with the rifle?" Ben unstrapped the rifle and shook it in the man's face. "Planning to follow us out in the country and ambush us?"

"No, no, no." The man held up trembling hands. "It's a Winchester 70. It's a deer rifle. Nobody told me to shoot anybody. I wouldn't kill anybody. I've got grandchildren, for Christ's sake. The rifle's always on the rack in my truck. It goes wherever I go. Look, it's not even loaded."

Ben checked to make sure the gun was not loaded, then turned to Murray. "I surprised him, opened his driver's side door, and stuck my gun in his face. He confessed right away. He was following us. I grabbed the rifle off the rack before he got out."

"Who sent you?" Murray was now in the stalker's face with her pistol as well. She surprised herself by how angry she suddenly became. The thought of being followed infuriated the peaceful art lover right out of her. A fury emerged from a dark place in her soul she didn't know existed. "Who sent you?" she snarled.

The man gasped for air and looked like he might be passing out from fright. He didn't answer right away. Ben set the rifle down and put the man in a one-handed choke hold until he blurted out, "Michigan Militia, unit 714."

"Who the hell is that?" Murray raised her voice, shocked to learn the militia had a number like it was one of many. The man looked at Ben for protection from the crazy woman. The panic in his eyes told Murray and Ben the man was not a threat. He was nothing but terrified. They holstered their Glocks as Ben released his hold.

"Answer the question," Ben said in a more diplomatic tone. "Who runs 714?"

The man gulped and tried to talk, but all that came out was a hoarse croak.

Murray opened the refrigerator under the sink and got out three beers. She twisted off the tops and handed one to Ben and one to the man, taking a big swig out of the third one. "Let's try this nice and friendly like," she said. "What's your name and where do you live?"

The man's eyes bugged out, seemingly shocked that he was being given a beer. He took a drink and let out a long "aah," as if he were beginning to think he could get out of this situation alive.

"I'm Dean Worthington, and I live at the Newaygo militia compound by the river in Michigan. I'm a retired truck driver. I do some carpentry around the place. My wife left me when I joined the 714. Said we were a bunch of delusional lunatics. I'm beginning to think she might have been right. This isn't me, following people around the country. I feel like a fool. I'm obviously not very good at it. I'm sorry."

"Why are you following us?" Ben asked.

"I guess to see where you were going," Dean said. "They saw you leaving Fort Wayne and they told me to follow you. That's all I know. I'm not sure they had a reason other than to keep tabs on you. Or maybe they see you as some kind of threat. I really have no idea."

Murray and Ben looked at each other to decide who would continue the questioning. Murray took the lead. "Tell us about this compound. Who's in charge and how many people live there?"

Dean took another long pull on the beer. He was beginning to loosen up. "A guy named Andrew Gibson is in charge. And, man, is he in charge. He's almost like one of those guys who runs a—what do you call it—a cult. Yeah, he's the absolute leader. He's retired military, decorated Afghanistan war hero, purple hearts, and something like the Service Cross medal. Worse thing about him, though—he's got a bad case of PTSD. He's mad at the world all going to hell. And now he's got six hundred men, more than a hundred living on site, and lots of heavy firepower. He's even got a tank."

"A tank?" Ben raised his voice in surprise. "What kind of tank? How'd he get it? What's he going to do with it?"

"I don't know any of that," Dean said. "All I know is that it's a big, modern one from the Army."

"What's he got against Trucker Nation?" Murray demanded.

Dean cleared his throat. "I don't really know that, either, to tell the truth. All I know is the 714 doesn't like the federal government or the teamsters' union."

"What about you, Dean?" Murray asked in a softer tone. "What you got against The Highway Diner? Don't you know it's just me and my mom trying to run a restaurant and feed as many truckers and tourists as we can?"

"I'm not gonna lie," Dean said. "I saw the rally, and I thought it was pretty cool. I even saw Cal Mavis get up and say y'all murdered his brother."

"Have you seen Mavis at the compound?" Ben asked.

"Oh yeah." Dean grinned for the first time since his capture. "He's up there with us, all right. Him and that little Anita that's all over the news for getting kidnapped. I got news for you. I figure she's your friend, right?" he asked Murray. "She's not looking like a victim. No sir. strutting around the camp like she and Mavis own the place, or they're on a honeymoon, or both."

Murray got out some drawing paper and a pencil and handed them to Dean. "Here, draw us a picture of the compound from the top, like you are a bird looking down."

"I can't draw," Dean said with an embarrassed frown.

"Don't worry about that," Murray said. "You tell me about it, and I'll draw the picture. What's in the middle of the compound? An office?"

Dean shook his head. "It's a bunker—a military bunker. The school he originally bought is right next to it, but the whole place is military all the way." He went on to describe the compound like it was an impregnable fortress.

"Where does he keep the tank?" Ben asked.

Dean put his finger on the map between the central bunker and another bunker in the north at the twelve o'clock position. "Right there. In the middle, between those two bunkers. It's in a buried steel building."

"Is it operational?" Murray asked.

"Oh, hell yes." Dean took another swig of beer. "That tank's his pride and joy. The Commander and his crew take it out for target practice all the time."

"Good lord," Murray said. "What's he going to do with a tank?"

"You tell me," Dean said as he finished his beer and held up the empty bottle as if he was ready for another.

"All right, Dean," Ben said. "That's more than enough. So, Murray, what do you say we fire this RV up and drive out of here nice and peaceful like?"

Murray got behind the wheel and started the engine.

"What you gonna do with me?" Dean asked with renewed fear in his voice.

"Nobody's going to hurt you," Ben said. "We're just going to drive off into the night together. Here, give me your cell phone. You can keep your wallet. About ten miles down the road, we'll throw this phone into the river. Then twenty more miles we're going to drop you off in the middle of nowhere. Nobody's going to get hurt. With any luck at all, you'll find your way back to civilization before dawn."

Murray drove out of the park and headed north on Highway 12 into the rural darkness. Ben pretended to throw the cell phone into the river at Sauk City. He threw a beer bottle to make a splash and kept the phone for Chase and his people to analyze. "There," he said to Dean. "Serves you right for being such a creepy little spy."

Dean didn't say a word. He was still praying they wouldn't shoot him when they dropped him off.

Midway between Baraboo, Wisconsin, and Wisconsin Dells, Ben shouted for Murray to pull to the side of the road. He was standing in the back of the van near the side door with Dean. "I ought to shoot you in the leg to teach you a lesson, but we're gonna let you off easy this time. In fact, take your rifle for good measure. But do yourself a favor: get out of the 714 while the getting's good."

"Thank you, thank you, thank you," Dean said as he walked down the steps and out of the Intrepid.

CHAPTER SEVENTEEN

Murray drove north after they dropped off an unharmed but shaken Dean Worthington along a deserted stretch of Highway 12 in pitch-black darkness. There were no streetlights, lights from distant residences, oncoming headlights, or light from the moon and stars. The night was deeply overcast. Dean hung his head and disappeared like a magic trick as Murray drove away.

Her mood was troubled. "I don't think we should go back to the campground. We need to put some miles on before they send more people after us."

"What about seeing the Wisconsin art school?"

"As much as I want to see that school, we'll be safer on the move," Murray said. "That bastard just ruined my entire vacation."

Ben nodded. "I don't feel right running from a guy like Dean, but you never know who they might send next."

They reached I-90 and started heading west. For Murray, the shock of being followed by a far-right militia member morphed into a cold, clammy mix of fear and anger and sadness. They drove in silence around Wisconsin Dells. As the lights of the small city faded in the oversized rearview mirrors of the Intrepid, Murray said, "It's good you didn't hurt him."

Ben let out a heavy sigh of relief. "He was too pathetic. I can still see his chubby cheeks trembling. One thing for sure: these militia guys aren't all as tough as they'd like people to believe."

"We know they're not all like Dean," Murray said. "They've

got billboards all over the country, and they've still got Anita. Even the FBI hasn't been able to get to them."

"No doubt," Ben said as he got up to grab a couple of beers. "You good to keep driving for a while? I say we keep moving till we hit the Badlands."

"That's all the way to South Dakota," Murray said. "We need to check in with some folks. Are we even sure we're going to California? We better call Chase."

Ben handed her a beer and took his seat. Murray managed a slight laugh as she brought the conversation back to Dean. "I can't believe you gave him back his rifle."

Ben took a long pull on his beer and chuckled. "It'll make hitchhiking impossible."

"Unless he gets picked up by another hunter," Murray said.

"Oh man." Ben slapped his thigh. "I hadn't thought about that. But anyway, I don't need to hurt someone or steal from him just because he did a terrible job of tailing us."

"My guess is our boy, Dean, will be fine. He's got his wallet anyway," Murray said. "But here's what I don't understand. What makes a guy like that join a militia? Is it just boys playing with guns?"

Ben took another swig of beer. He was beginning to come down from the adrenaline high of capturing and interrogating Dean. "I don't know," he said. "I guess it's a club-joining thing. Some people go to church, others play sports. My guess is he joined because he didn't have much else to do after he stopped driving trucks. And because things weren't going well with his wife. She was probably a lot happier when he was on the road making money."

Murray thought about that for a minute. "But why all the hate? They're so mad at the world, I wonder if they're just mad at their own lives for not turning out like they planned."

"You're on to something there," Ben said.

"I suppose they're mad about being overtaxed and seeing their money go to people who they think don't deserve it," Murray said. "I feel sorry for them. I really do. Problem is, I find myself getting mad a lot lately. People shooting up our restaurant, threatening to kill us, kidnapping my friend, having military compounds. And that asshole, Dean, ruined our visit to the University of Wisconsin. It's all starting to turn me into an angry woman. I don't want to be that person, but these billboards and the whole mess are about to push me over the edge."

The two of them lapsed into a mournful silence. Murray was deeply saddened that all the high hopes of The Highway Diner and Trucker Nation had attracted such bewildering opposition. The billboards had been slaps in the face. *Who could possibly be opposed to one distribution system working together for the good of everybody?*

"Let's call Chase," Ben suggested. "We need to find out everything we can about this Andrew Gibson character."

It was the middle of the night, but Chase picked up after the fourth ring. He sounded sleepy at first but perked up when Ben told him they'd been followed by a member of Militia 714. He listened carefully as Ben told him about catching the guy parked in his truck and dropping him off on a dark, deserted road north of Baraboo, Wisconsin.

"Never heard of Baraboo," Chase responded. "Who names a town Baraboo? You can't make this stuff up. This surveillance on you two is really their first overt act of aggression. They didn't kidnap Anita, you know. Mavis did that on his own and ran to hide out with them. We're still not sure what connection he has to the 714."

"If they're holding Anita and following us, "there's no

telling what they'll do next," Ben said. "The leader up there is a guy named Andrew Gibson. We need to find out everything we can about that guy."

"I'm already on it," Chase said. "The guy's a war hero, you know."

"He's a war wacko, more like it," Murray said. "Some of those guys who make it back from Afghanistan are totally damaged units."

Chase responded, "We've got to plan for the worst and hope for the best. I've got the diner under heavy security—six special-force types in plain clothes on premises at all times."

Murray did not like the sound of special forces. "My God, Chase! It sounds like we're at war. Is my mom even safe there?"

"Oh yeah, Murray." Chase tried to tone it down. "She's more than safe. Blake Dawson's off the road for a couple of weeks, and he's keeping a close watch on her. And you know your mother. She'd keep that diner going if there was a war on. But no, the undercover guys are mainly there to protect the building site for the new casino. We've got concrete coming in soon."

Murray wasn't sure if his explanation helped or not. She wondered why concrete needed special-forces protection. Then again, she knew the casino construction would make an excellent target for the militia to make a statement against Trucker Nation. She wanted her anxiety to go away. She wanted to feel like she felt in that college drawing class. Free, creative, and inspired. Instead, her sense of dread was only getting worse. Every nasty billboard she saw, the little creep who'd followed them, and every security guard they had to hire made her feel like something truly terrible was about to happen.

"Do you think we should head home?" Murray asked.

"I don't see how you two cutting short your trip will help

anything," Chase said. "This bull crap is going to go on for a long time. We're taking precautions against something that's probably never going to happen. So, no. Y'all keep going. We can talk on the phone."

Murray didn't say a word for a long time after the phone call. Ben finally asked, "What's up, Mur?"

"I don't know, Ben," she said. "Now that all the excitement of catching Dean Worthington is winding down, this doesn't feel like much of a vacation. It feels like we're running away from something we should be going after."

"I feel the same way," Ben said. "But going after a militia unit is asking for trouble. These are crazy people. We could get shot going after Anita. They're not all made of Jello like Dean. We're gonna have to wait and see. Everything's gonna be fine."

"I don't know, Ben. I hope you're right."

———

Murray and Ben stayed on course to begin the nearly eight-hundred-mile drive to Badlands National Park. Rochester rolled by in the night, as did towns named Austin, Albert Lee, and Fairmont. They appeared in the night as surreal and lonely clusters of light. Murray drove all the way to Worthington, where they stopped for gas and supplies. "Look, Ben," she said. "Here we are in Worthington. This must be Dean Worthington's hometown."

Ben laughed as he took the wheel. "He'd be better off here than at the militia compound in Newaygo, or wherever he ends up."

"How much was the gas?" Murray asked.

"Almost three hundred dollars. Can you believe that? If gas gets much higher, the whole economy's gonna break down. The Intrepid's got a one-hundred-gallon gas tank, but it gets less than ten miles per gallon. I don't even want to do the math on what this trip's gonna cost in gas alone."

Murray was too tired to respond. She shuffled to the rear of the Intrepid as Ben took off on the highway. She collapsed on the queen-sized bed without taking off her clothes or getting under the covers and fell into an exhausted slumber. An hour later, she woke up as they stopped in Chamberlain, South Dakota. Ben kissed her on the forehead and told her he was off for a bathroom break and a fast walk to loosen up his legs.

She had to shield her eyes from the morning sunshine once she stepped outside. Adjusting to the light, she found herself dwarfed by a fifty-foot stainless-steel statue of a Native American woman. The giant size frightened her at first. It was more than thirty feet wide. But the more she looked at the incredible work of art, the more intriguing it became.

The woman wore a two-hide, full-length dress from the middle of the nineteenth century. Her face was stoic and resolute. She looked like a warrior. Her hair was braided. She held an outstretched quilt behind her with her hands just above shoulder height. The quilt was slightly billowed and covered with diamond shapes that sparkled in the sunlight. Murray was spellbound. The title of the piece was *Dignity*. It was a monument to female determination on the Great Plains and a tribute to the Native American Dakota tribes.

Murray looked up and pondered the statue. It seemed to come alive as she studied every detail. There was no doubt the Native American woman had a message for her. "Am I dreaming?" she whispered. "What is she trying to tell me?" She listened intently, but all she heard was a gentle whistling of the wind.

An inexplicable sadness enveloped her, though not because she wasn't communicating with the sculpture. Murray began to feel her recent emotional traumas reflecting in the shimmering, diamond-shaped patterns of the quilt. The heavy sorrow of conflict surrounding The Highway Diner brought tears to her eyes. Being followed by the militia was almost as traumatic as the shooting at the diner. She was so tired of dealing with people who hated her for no good reason. It made her feel defeated.

A flash of bright light reflected from one of the diamond shapes on the quilt, refracted through her tears, and plunged deeply into her internal turmoil. The meaning of the moment rang into her mind louder than church bells in a tower. Murray suddenly understood what the woman was trying to tell her.

This woman suffered more than I ever will. And she never had the time or energy to feel sorry for herself. That's it. That's what she's telling me. Suffering is part of survival. It's something to be embraced and nurtured into a stronger will.

Murray contemplated the revelation as she walked around to the back of the sculpture, only to be dazzled once again by an eight-pointed star of gleaming diamond shapes. It looked more like a shield than a quilt. Murray bowed her head gratefully as she realized the protection the woman carried was a symbol of her own bravery.

In full-blown epiphany, she felt the fearless grit of the Native American woman flowing into her soul. Her heart was filling up with ambition. No more falling apart at the seams of indecision. No more dreams of alibis. Something inside straightened her posture and quickened her pulse. She chanted softly as she slowly raised both arms to unfurl her own quilt of valor.

Murray's transformation took her by complete emotional surprise. She felt the strength of her own inner warrior for the first time. It was more powerful than her strongest athletic move, more stimulating than her most perfect brushstroke. It was a thrilling confidence, an answer to her trials and tribulations, a serenity she knew she would need in the days ahead.

———

Back on the road, Ben was driving again when Isabel called Murray in a worried huff. "What's this I hear about you and Ben getting followed by some militia clown and having to dump him out on a back-country road at night?"

"Hi, Mom. We've been meaning to call and tell you about that, but—"

"And why do I have to hear about all this third hand from my boyfriend, Blake, who heard it from our agent, Chase, who heard it from your boyfriend, Ben? What's the deal? I'm out of the loop with the good old boys' network?"

"Mom, don't be mad."

"Murray, what's wrong?" Isabel said. "You sound different. Here I am getting all worked up, and you're staying cool, calm, and collected. I'm not saying it's a bad thing; it just doesn't sound like you."

"Nothing's wrong, Mom. This trip is making me grow up in a hurry, I guess. It's making me realize we've got a whole lot of trouble to get through before we come out the other side."

Isabel continued in a more respectful tone. "One thing for sure is that we're not running from these fools. Don't even think about coming home. Go on to California. Believe me, we've got plenty of protection here. Chase has a private army on duty, and Blake is here to protect me."

"Is he staying at our house?" Murray asked, wondering why she hated the idea of her mother shacking up.

"Of course he is. And he's packing a .45 everywhere, even when he plays guitar at the diner every afternoon. You should hear him. He's got a little PA setup and a small stage about a foot high. People love it. Even the songs they've never heard before. You do know he's got one of his songs on the country charts."

Murray laughed at her mother's exuberance. It eased her mind to hear the happiness in her voice. "Yes, Mom, we know all about what a big deal your boyfriend is."

"But you do need to know." Isabel lowered her voice. "It must be the devil himself who introduced Cal Mavis to that so-called commander, Andrew Gibson. Those two believe in all that deep state, Q-Anon conspiracy bullshit, and they think we're part of it. From what Chase hears, they're plotting truck blockades and publicity campaigns. They're heavily armed. And here's the worst part."

"Like that's not bad enough?" Murray said.

"No, the worst part is that Anita's right in the thick of it, egging them on, all drugged up on we don't know what. Their latest plan is to sober her up for a minute so they can put her on television and say that she wasn't kidnapped and how Trucker Nation is making a fortune off the murder of Red Mavis."

"How do you know all this?" Murray asked.

"You know how. Chase said he told you."

"Oh, God," Murray moaned. "This is all sounding like some bad series on Netflix."

"Sorry, honey," Isabel said. "It's our life now. And it's not changing anytime soon. We're not making money on the death of Red Mavis. We never wanted him to get killed in our parking lot. We're successful despite Red Mavis, not because of him. So, don't put your life on hold, waiting for a happy ending. Don't worry about us. We'll be waiting for you when you get back. We miss you already."

"I miss you, too, Mom. Okay, I'll call you from the Badlands."

"Please call me every day, Muriel," Isabel said. "This whole militia thing has me spooked. And you know I worry about my baby girl."

"I'll call, Mom. I promise. And remember, I love you."

"I love you more than you'll ever know. Take care of yourself. And take care of Ben, too."

Ben joined the conversation to say goodbye. "We'll take care of each other. And I'm gonna show her California in all its glory."

Once they hung up, Ben turned to Murray and asked, "What's with you? You seem—I don't know—less worried, or more confident, or something."

Murray threw back her head and laughed more freely than she had in months. "Okay, Ben. You're the only one I'm telling this to, so please don't repeat it."

Ben nodded.

"So, here's what happened," Murray continued. "I had a big talk with that giant statue of the Native American woman, and she changed my life forever. Sounds crazy, doesn't it?"

"Crazy in a good way," Ben said. "What did she say?"

"She didn't really say anything. She showed me a side of myself I wasn't sure I had. My warrior. The fighter in me. The one who counts on courage to make it through suffering. The one who stays tough when things get rough."

Ben drove in silence for several miles. Murray waited for his response. Finally, he looked at Murray with a knowing grin and said, "I knew I liked that statue."

CHAPTER EIGHTEEN

Andrew Gibson, the commander of Michigan Militia 714, had a bushy horseshoe mustache that almost covered the bullet scars on both sides of his mouth. His Special Forces patrol had been ambushed in northern Afghanistan in 2006. He lost half his teeth, two fingers on his right hand, and too much blood from the bullet wounds in his left thigh and right side. The firefight had lasted all afternoon. It was a savage slaughter. Captain Gibson killed more enemy fighters than he could count, most of them at close range after he'd been severely wounded. Only at the end of a horrific day, what was left of the mangled patrol had managed to escape down the mountain in the darkness.

Gibson had been a handsome boy in high school. His reddish-brown hair, prominent forehead and chin, blue eyes, and hawk nose gave him the appearance of a Viking conqueror. He was a star linebacker on the high school football team, but at five-eleven, one hundred eighty pounds, he was too small and too slow for college ball. Life lost a lot of its luster when the crowds stopped cheering for him.

After the 911 terrorist attacks in 2001, he dropped out of Michigan State in his junior year and joined the army to "cap a Qaeda." Three tours of duty in Afghanistan convinced him he was fighting for the wrong side. He left the Army with a permanent limp, demoralized, traumatized, and completely disillusioned with his country. Turning to booze and pills to ease the physical and emotional pain, he became a drug-addicted monster of a man. His wife left him for good one night after he'd beaten her half to death.

In 2009, he got sober long enough to purchase an abandoned elementary school near Newaygo, Michigan, for next to nothing. He had saved money from years of military pay, and a couple of Army buddies loaned him their savings to invest in his plans. It took Gibson six years of his own hard labor to turn the school playgrounds and baseball diamonds into the most popular shooting range in the region. Once the range started selling weapons and ammunition, Gibson had more money coming in than he knew what to do with. He purchased nearby farms and developed a secret marijuana grow operation in a vast complex of camouflaged greenhouses and defensive bunkers, connected by tunnels and storage facilities. In case of emergency, he kept the mayor and the sheriff on his payroll.

Captain Andrew Gibson evolved into Commander Gibson, better known to his followers as the Commander. The larger his compound became, and the more people he recruited and hired, the more he started believing in his own delusional worldview. He began seeing himself as destined to save America from the dark forces of totalitarianism. The more money he made, the more contemptuous he became of an economy he saw as hopelessly mired in political paralysis. By 2023, he was looking to teach the world a lesson.

The Commander knew Cal and Red Mavis from their youthful days of giving boat tours on the Newaygo and Muskegon rivers. The three young men were inseparable. They swam in fast currents, dove off high cliffs, and swung from ropes into deep pools, confident that individual greatness was in store for each one of them. Who could doubt it? Girls loved them, their boats and cars were fast, and they always had plenty of booze and pot to share.

"It's murder, plain and simple," the Commander had screamed at the television when he saw the news of Red's death. "Red wouldn't kill a squirrel. They shot him in the back, for Christ's sake." The fact that no one from The Highway Diner had anything to do with the shooting did not mean a thing to the Commander. He came to hate The Highway Diner for what he called "the diner bitches getting rich and famous off Red's death."

It was the Commander who encouraged Cal Mavis to kidnap Anita and bring her to the compound. "We'll figure out what to do with her once you get her here."

———

Anita was lounging in a lawn chair in the Commander's compound when she thought about how she had arrived at the militia hideout. A shiver crawled down her spine.

She had been confused at first when Cal Mavis appeared at the door of her apartment. He looked so much like his brother, it felt like Red Mavis had come back from the dead. Once she realized Cal had come to abduct her, she fought him and tried to call for help. He'd slapped her hard across the face. She fell to the floor and kicked him until he threw himself over her legs and landed on her chest and face, knocking the wind out of her. He grabbed her phone and threw it against the wall. She tried to wiggle out from underneath him until he choked her into submission and threatened to kill her if she screamed.

She thought he was going to rape her. She stopped struggling so he would loosen his grip and allow her to breathe. "That's more like it," he said as he stood her up and handcuffed her.

He pulled out his handgun and held the barrel to the back of her head. "Now, we're going to take a little walk. Don't act up and you won't get hurt." With that, he walked her to his car, then cuffed her ankles as he shoved her into the back seat. "One word out of you and I'll put you in the trunk."

Anita kept her mouth shut. It felt like the man was going to murder her. Deathly afraid of being locked in the trunk, she practically held her breath until they reached the Michigan State line. At that point, she'd broken the silence and said, "I gotta pee."

"You'll be pissing in the woods," Cal grumbled without turning around, making angry eye contact with her in the rearview mirror. Anita shook her head and looked away.

He drove off the main road and stopped in a wooded area. He uncuffed her ankles and hands and led her behind a massive maple tree, watching carefully as she pulled down her jeans and panties.

"What are you? Some kind of pervert?" Anita snapped. "At least have the decency to turn around."

Much to her surprise, Cal did turn around. At that moment, Anita knew he had no intention of hurting her any more than he already had. She was furious at feeling so powerless. She thought about trying to run, but she knew he would catch her and beat her up before throwing her in the trunk.

"Where are you taking me?" she asked as she pulled up her jeans.

"I'm taking you to meet an old friend of mine. A man who's been interested in you for quite some time."

———

The Commander had greeted Anita sarcastically as Mavis unshackled her ankles and hauled her out of the car. He was sitting at a picnic table outside his central bunker when he jumped up and pretended to come to the military position of attention. "Well, well. Isn't this an occasion?" he said. "So nice of you to pay us a visit, Little Miss Highway Diner. I've been looking forward to meeting you since you got my friend, Red, killed for no good reason."

Anita could see demons dancing in the Commander's twitching eyes as he gave her a twisted smile. Against her better judgment, she blurted, "I loved Red. Don't you dare say I got him killed." The handcuffs cut into her wrists as she shook her shoulders in anger. "I tried to save him by stealing his drugs, and then he went and shot up a diner full of innocent people."

The Commander looked startled that someone was talking back to him. It took a moment before he snarled back.

"And then you went to work at the diner while they made a fortune on Red's death and the big trucker support rallies."

"People love The Highway Diner," Anita said. "Red loved the diner. You would love the diner too if you gave it half a chance."

The Commander stared hard at Anita with anger in his eyes. "I don't give people chances when they shoot my friend in the back and act like heroes because they're selling burgers to truckers."

"Nobody in the diner shot Red," Anita argued. "It was a trucker outside the diner who shot him."

"You might as well have shot him yourself, you ungrateful bitch."

Anita glared at the Commander, but she was no match for the intense hatred in his eyes. She looked away. There was no point in continuing any stare down or argument. The man was deranged. She could feel his rage in her bones. Cal Mavis was so afraid of him he didn't say a word.

The Commander took a breath and allowed the red in his face to lighten a couple shades. He pulled out a fat joint and lit it with a wooden match. "Now, now. Let's not get off on the wrong foot. I got some wonderful home-grown reefer here, laced with a little something special just for you." He held the joint up to her lips.

Anita shook her head and pursed her lips tightly. "No way I'm smoking that. I've been clean for months."

He took it back, inhaled deeply himself, and exhaled into Anita's face. "Come on, girl. We know what you are. You're a drug-addicted, truck-stop hooker. The sooner you play ball, the better off you'll be."

Anita lowered her head so she didn't have to look into the Commander's face. It felt like she was bowing to the devil himself. "All righty then," he said as he patted her head. "Take her away, Cal. We'll lock her up in apartment seven. Give her time to think things through."

Cal walked her down the highly shined linoleum floors of the school hallway and into apartment seven. "See here," he said. "It's nice. Got a bathroom and a kitchenette, like your place in Fort Wayne." He uncuffed her and paused. "I'll be back with food three times a day till you come around. You know, we could have a lot of fun here once you decide to get with the program."

"If you think you're going to have fun with me, "you got another thing coming," she seethed.

"We'll see about that," Cal said as he slammed the door and locked it from the outside. Anita quickly checked the windows. They had bars. She was in a prison cell. Her anger melted into despair. She collapsed to the floor and sobbed.

Anita held out against Cal for nearly a week. She couldn't believe no one was coming to rescue her. How could Isabel and

Murray let this happen? What about the police? She had no radio or television to see if she was on every news station as a kidnap victim or if a search was on.

Cal brought her food three times a day, and three times a day he retrieved the uneaten meals. Anita dreaded being held captive, but she was stubborn about wanting to stay clean. She was afraid that taking food would lead to taking drugs. Allowing herself to be fed would open emotional doors that needed to remain closed.

Hunger and her survival instinct eventually prevailed. On the morning of the fourth day, she picked up a bowl of beef stew Cal had left the night before. She ate it as slowly as she could. It tasted better than anything she'd ever eaten.

"Well, well, well," Cal said as he came in about an hour later and picked up the empty bowl. "I see we're making progress. What else can I get you?"

"You can get me the hell out of here," Anita snapped.

Cal smiled and left the room without saying another word. Anita couldn't help herself. She loved that smile. Cal Mavis looked like his brother, Red, when he smiled. *No, no,* she thought. *I can't let him get away with kidnapping and holding me hostage. He's nothing but a criminal. Then again, getting next to him might be the only way I'm getting out of this mess.*

Loneliness eventually got the best of her. She found herself looking forward to his visits and not wanting him to leave once he had arrived. Anita started chattering to him about anything and everything, like someone who'd spent too much time alone in a Michigan winter. She needed to talk, and once she started, she couldn't stop. Solitary confinement had taken its toll.

Cal kept bringing her food. He was sweet as Red, but more gentle and kind. By the eighth day, they were eating together in the prison-cell apartment.

Cal Mavis was patient. He seduced Anita mainly by being a good listener. She began to think of him as her therapist. Eventually, she let him hold her when she cried out her guilt and shame about slipping into prostitution and drug addiction.

Anita was still constantly thinking about how she could escape, or at least get to a phone. But on the ninth night, they slept together. She was desperate for any kind of human touch. Their first kiss was surprisingly tender. Cal was worshipful. He was every bit as much fun as his brother had been, without the jagged edges of drug addiction. Anita relaxed to the point of almost forgetting she was being held prisoner.

On the twelfth day, Cal took Anita to Gibson to show what progress he had made with his ward. The Commander was impressed. Anita held Cal's' hand as she smiled and did a slight curtsy to say hello.

"Whoa, Cal, you do have a way with the ladies," he said. "Now, let's see, where were we before we got so rudely interrupted?"

She took him up on his offer of getting high, nodding her head as he took out a joint. It seemed like the only thing to do. She desperately wanted out of her cell. She needed to get to a phone. The joint was a test she clearly needed to pass. He lit the number and took a huge hit before passing it on to her.

The Commander gurgled up a mischievous chortle as she took her first hit. She couldn't avoid looking into his dangerous eyes as she exhaled. The rush nearly collapsed her knees. She knew right away it was killer weed, laced with something from the poppy plant.

One of the strongest revelations in her life occurred to Anita the instant she got high. She could feel the Commander's pain. She could see it. The opium united them on several levels. She realized his anger came from fear. Fear that combat had ruined his mind forever. Fear that the world would never understand how helpless he felt in the face of his own insanity. The fear that everything he once held dear had been ripped from his soul.

She closed her eyes and let the golden glow of opium flow through her veins and into her brain, holding her arms up to the sky. Even as she realized the Commander's pain, she could feel her own evaporating.

"Look at you, Hollywood," he chuckled as he took a hit, relaxed, and smiled like the happy young man he had once been. "You see, we're not all bad around here."

Anita took a second hit and then a third. She was flying high as Cal walked her away and gave her a tour of the compound. "Oh, man," she said once she recovered her ability to speak. "I was afraid the Commander was going to have his way with me."

"No, no," Cal said. "We talked about it. He wanted to, but I said no. You're my girl, nobody else's. The Commander has his own girlfriend. You've met her. Her name's Gina. She works in the cafeteria. She only comes and goes late at night. Anyway, you're free to go anywhere you want now, as long as you're with me."

"So, I'm still your prisoner."

Cal stopped walking and looked her in the eye. "Did you feel like my prisoner last night?"

"Actually, no," Anita said as her voice trembled in a mix of fear and mischief. "It felt more like you were my prisoner."

CHAPTER NINETEEN

Ben's mother, Julia Sorenson, lived alone in a light-filled home in Sausalito, California. She had restored her maiden name of Sorenson after her divorce. The house was halfway up the coastal mountain city, with an inspirational view to the east of Angel Island State Park. From her broad sundeck, Alcatraz Island and the cities of San Francisco and Oakland looked like a dreamscape across Richardson Bay.

Julia was bouncing up and down with excitement as Ben drove the Intrepid up her steep and winding driveway and came to a stop. He set the emergency brake and leaped out to sweep his mother off her feet in a bear hug. "Oh, my beautiful Benjamin," she cried as she squeezed him tight. Then she pulled out of their embrace to run around the Intrepid and greet Murray as she got out.

"Murray," she gushed as she embraced her guest. "At long last we meet in person."

Murray had tears of joy in her eyes as Julia continued. "How long have we waited for this moment? Six months? How was your trip?"

"The trip was wonderful," Murray said. "But I must say, you look even better than Ben told me. You look so young and tan and fit."

Julia looked at her son with approval in her eyes. Then she returned her smile to Murray. "You're gonna go far in this world. I'm so happy you're finally here. Come on in, you two.

We'll get your things later. I've got lunch ready and cold Double Daddy beer in the fridge. It's May Day and the sun is shining."

She led them into the modern, split-level home and straight out to the deck. Murray was not prepared for the startling majesty of the view. "Oh my goodness! It looks like a fairy tale come true." She turned to Julia. "Now I see where you get inspiration for your wonderful oil paintings."

"Thank you, my dear. If you can't paint here, you can't paint anywhere."

Ben and Murray laughed with Julia. "I'm so excited you're an artist too," Julia said. "I don't know how you can sit in on a drawing class in Chicago and come up with what you did. Ben sent me the cell phone snap. I am truly impressed. We're going to have so much fun. I've got paints and canvases galore, so maybe we can paint together."

"That would be more than wonderful," Murray said as her shoulders sagged. "But all the bad vibes surrounding the diner are bringing me down to the point I'm not sure I can paint anymore." Murray's gaze wandered sadly over the bay view.

"That's exactly how I felt after my ex-husband left me with two kids to raise on my own," Julia tried to reassure her. "It took me too long to realize that painting is the best therapy. It felt impossible at first, but it eventually brought me back."

"Oh, I do hope it works out that way for me," Murray said. "But I know you're right."

Julia changed gears to serving lunch. Ben and Murray chatted happily about their trip. After a few beers, Murray opened up about the Badlands. "We had the best time there. I always wanted to go. We got a great camping site and there weren't many people. We hiked through canyons and mountains with spires and pinnacles and buttes and even some jagged ones with stripes of yellow and purple. You would have loved painting what we saw there."

Ben chimed in before Julia could respond. "We saw bison and big horn sheep up close, and maybe some prairie dogs in the distance. The place is like a journey back in time. Way back. Back to before Native Americans. The fossils there are millions of years old. The landscape is like something from another world."

Julia was energized by their enthusiasm. Once they were done raving about the Badlands, she asked, "So, what about Montana? I've been meaning to go there for some time."

"We stayed on I-90 West until we came to Bozeman, Montana," Ben said. "That town you wouldn't believe. It's not that big—fifty thousand people, maybe—surrounded by snow-capped mountain ranges. It's got great restaurants and a historic-building main drag. There's a gun shop with a neon rifle hanging over the front door. Another store has a sculpture of a rearing horse lit up at night on its balcony. It's the Wild West."

"But the best part," Murray added, "was the Bozeman Hot Springs near a town called Gallatin, a little south of Bozeman. You pay twelve dollars, get a towel and a locker, and jump into one-hundred-degree water in a huge outdoor pool that's fed by a hot spring. From there, you bathe in the indoor steam and sauna rooms and then do laps in a big swimming pool."

Julia smiled. "It sounds like you two had the time of your lives. And you got to Yellowstone National Park?"

"Yes, we did," Ben said. "That was high on Murray's list. We drove south on 191 from Gallatin. There were rock cliffs and snowy peaks in the distance as the road wound back and forth over the Gallatin River."

"The river was shining in the sun and splashing over rocks," Murray said, bouncing on her chair in excitement. "We drove by The Big Sky ski resort. It's on a mountain that looks like the Matterhorn in Switzerland. Thirty more miles or so and we were in Yellowstone. So magnificent. So pristine."

"It was spooky not seeing any development along the road," Ben said. "No houses or barns, pure and untouched. And so big. We drove for miles without seeing another car. We stopped for lunch in West Yellowstone and tried to get to Old Faithful, but the roads were still snowed over."

Julia got up to clear their plates and returned with small dishes of strawberry sherbet on a serving tray. "What's this I hear about you two being followed in Wisconsin by a member of one of those awful militia groups?"

Ben and Murray looked at each other like they'd been caught hiding in a closet. "How'd you know about that?" Ben asked.

Julia laughed so hard she almost lost one of the sherbets off the tray. "Never underestimate the power of mothers. I talk to Murray's mom on a regular basis. Isabel and I talk about you two and compare designs for all the building projects you've got going on. You know my biggest claim to fame was designing the logos for The Highway Diner and Trucker Nation. You might not realize how big that whole deal is out here. All my artist friends are dying to meet you, Murray."

"So, how much did Isabel tell you?" Ben asked.

"Mothers tell each other everything, my dear boy," Julia said as she handed him a sherbet. "We're both worried sick about this Andrew Gibson guy who calls himself 'the Commander.' And that Mavis man who kidnapped Anita. And all those awful billboards."

Ben and Murray shook their heads, embarrassed to be caught trying to whitewash their trip.

"I was waiting to see what you wouldn't tell me," Julia continued with a big smile. "Don't feel bad. I know you don't want me to worry. But let me tell you, it's way too late for that."

"Now I do feel bad," Murray said.

"Don't," Julia said as she patted her shoulder. "I want to hear your version of how you two captured that militia guy, and interrogated him, and gave him back his rifle, and dropped him off in the dark near some town called Baraboo, Wisconsin. Believe me, I looked that one up. And you won't believe what I found."

Ben looked at Murray quizzically. "What's up with Baraboo? Other than the funny name."

Julia took a deep breath and straightened her back and neck like she was about to give an oral book report. "It's famous for being known as Circus City. The Ringling brothers gave their first circus performance there in 1884. They called Baraboo home and had their winter quarters there until 1918. Then they joined forces with Barnum and Bailey."

"And the rest is circus history," said Ben.

The three of them laughed in the sunshine. Murray was stunned they had stumbled onto the home of the circus. "What do you think it means that we dropped old Dean Worthington off at Circus City?" she asked.

"He was kind of a clown," Ben said.

Julia and Murray chuckled politely at the all too obvious joke. "No," Julia said. "It's significant in ways we don't quite understand. It feels to me like—I don't know—we're all getting caught up in a big circus."

Murray marveled at Julia's thought process. She reminded

Murray so much of her own mother it made her homesick. Julia and Isabel had much in common: two strong women in their forties who'd lost husbands and still worried about their grown-up babies. Yet, each had surprised herself by the liberated spirit that emerged once she was on her own.

Maybe Ben's attracted to me because I'm an artist, like his mother. And maybe I'm attracted to him because of how much he loves his mother. It might be more about loving our mothers than losing our fathers.

Ben and Murray told Julia the whole story about nabbing the militia man, except for the part where Ben held a gun to his neck and threatened to kill him.

"You two are so brave," Julia said. "He could have used that rifle to shoot you."

"That's pretty much what we were afraid of," Ben said.

"I thought he might try to kidnap us like they did Anita," Murray added.

"I'm glad you didn't hurt him," Julia said.

"He was pretty pathetic, Mom."

"What about Anita?" Julia said. "Aren't you worried sick about her? Isn't anyone going to rescue her? It seems like everybody knows she's with the militia."

Murray sighed. "I think about Anita all the time. Most of the time I get the feeling she's going to be all right. But other times, I imagine all the horrible things those men might be doing to her."

"The FBI has her under surveillance," Ben said. "They've got some undercover guy imbedded in the militia. They told us to back off on trying to save her until their investigation is complete and they can take down the whole compound."

"Does that really make sense when a woman is in danger?" Julia asked.

"My sentiments exactly," Murray said. "But, for now, we wait and see what happens with the FBI. They told us she's not being mistreated."

Once they reassured Julia about Anita, the conversation turned to family stories. Julia had tales to tell about Ben. "When he was a little boy," she began as if they were sitting around a campfire. "He hated the training wheels on his bicycle. Said the older boys were making fun of him. He begged his father to take them off, but Daddy was always too busy. So, he asked me.

"When I told Benjamin he wasn't ready, he threw a terrible tantrum, crying and pounding the garage door with his little fists and even throwing toys at the bike. Next thing I know, he's trying to take them off himself with a crescent wrench. I let him go until, much to my surprise, he finally succeeded. He threw those wheels as hard as he could into the garbage can, looked at me with a pouty lip, got on that bike, rode it ten feet, and fell and skinned his knee so bad it was dripping blood. When I tried to help him, he shouted, 'No!' Then he got back on his little bike like a television cowboy on a horse and didn't fall again as far as I could see."

Murray loved the story. It was so Ben. He was laughing at the retelling. She looked at him, so handsome and happy to be with his mother. She realized the cross-country trip had brought them closer together. *And, oh my God*, she thought, *if he asked me in this moment to marry him, I would say yes.*

"You know Ben was always quite the athlete," Julia continued. "He played basketball and football in high school. Before that, he learned how to box at the YMCA and got a karate belt. What was that one, Ben?"

"It wasn't that big a deal, Mom," Ben said. "I never got past a blue belt."

Murray was surprised. "I can't believe we never talked about your athletic background," she said. "All we ever talked about was my volleyball. I knew you must have been a sports guy by how strong you are. But karate? That is impressive."

"All the better to protect you from the bad guys, my dear," Ben said.

"Now, Murray," Julia said, clearly on a roll. "I must tell you our Benjamin was never much of a ladies' man. I think his big sister scared it out of him. And I'm not lying when I say you are the first woman he's brought home to meet me. Except for his date for the senior prom. And that didn't go very well, did it, honey?"

"Aw, Mom, now you're just trying to embarrass me."

"Come on, Ben, I gotta hear this," Murray said.

Ben shifted in his seat and hemmed and hawed a little before he finally said, "Okay, if you must know. Her name was Danielle, and she drank way too much and puked all over me and my tuxedo and her dress and Mom's car."

"I never did get the smell out of that car," Julia said. "I had to trade it in."

They laughed so hard they decided it might be a good idea to have another beer. As the sun began to set, Julia announced, "I've got an exciting tour of the Bay Area planned, starting after sunset with dinner at Tadich Grill, the oldest restaurant in California."

"My favorite restaurant in the world," Ben said. "Besides The Highway Diner, of course."

"We better take my car," Julia said. "It's a BMW, but we can squeeze in. It's got a sunroof. Ben, you drive. Murray's got to sit up front for maximum viewing. I'll direct from the back seat."

—————

Thus began four whirlwind days of touring San Francisco with Julia. Murray was becoming truly torn between two pathways for her future. On one side, there was the School of the Art Institute of Chicago and being near her mother and The Highway Diner. On the other side, the artistic royalty of the San Francisco Art Institute and cable cars, Fisherman's Wharf, Chinatown, Nob Hill, and the Pacific Ocean. Julia introduced Murray to all kinds of people, from French painting instructors to Chinese chefs to architects and gallery owners.

Murray was shocked that everyone she met knew so much about her and Isabel and The Highway Diner. For the first time, she realized her life had become a television reality show. So much news coverage from back home in Indiana was causing some important people on the West Coast to ask for her autograph. Even Ben was being treated like a celebrity.

Julia was extremely well connected. She not only knew art professors but also the donors who kept the school afloat. Her paintings had sold in prestigious art galleries before her divorce. She loved introducing Murray and Ben around the city. "Yes, this is my son, Benjamin, and his partner, Murray. They're taking a break from saving the national supply chain to pay us a visit."

Murray and Ben had fun with it. When asked for her autograph, Murray took to saying, "Only if I can get one from you."

They weren't mobbed on the street like rock stars, but they were often recognized. Julia steered them into intimate introductions in quiet places with highly successful people who valued their own privacy. Invariably, the militia situation came up in conversation. "What are you going to do about all those gun-crazy people out there in Michigan?" one of Julia's painting friends asked.

Ben couldn't help but laugh at the question as he responded, "Don't look now, but there's way too many gun-crazies in California. All over the country, in fact. The far-right militia is everywhere. And yes, they are dangerous, but we're not letting them scare us away. We're trying to bring this country back together with peace and love, diesel fuel, and all-day breakfast."

A colorfully dressed Chinese woman named Min Zhang, a community leader on the San Francisco Board of Supervisors, asked Murray much too bluntly, "What did you do to make the radical right hate you so much?"

"We really have no idea," Murray said, trying not to flinch at the woman's total lack of tact. "My mother and I were surprised by all the support we got from truckers and travelers. But what really shocked us was the hate coming at us from these militia groups. They say we're part of some government plan to take away their guns."

"You know," Ms. Zhang said, "you could turn all this into a successful political career."

Ben and Murray laughed so hard at this suggestion that Min Zhang frowned and seemed genuinely offended. Julia quickly tried to smooth things over. "Not that politics is a bad thing," she said. "And we love what you've been doing on the board. It's just not for Murray and Ben. Me either, for that matter. We wouldn't last a minute in your political arena."

At the end of their second day, Murray and Ben collapsed into bed. "What are we gonna do, Ben?" Murray asked.

Ben sighed. "I'm glad it's what are *we* gonna do instead of what am *I* gonna do."

Murray looked up at him. "We really are in all this together, even if we didn't see any of it coming. I absolutely love your mother and San Francisco. But I love my mother and Chicago too. The college decision gets tougher every time I think about it."

"Don't worry," Ben said. "Decisions have a way of making themselves. We don't have to make any of them today."

Murray rolled over and put her head on his chest. "That's what I love about you, Ben. You don't let any of it worry you or get you down. I should say that's one of the many things I love about you." She nuzzled his neck.

———

Julia made sure she and Murray had time to paint together. In fact, it was Julia's down-to-earth love of painting that really attracted Murray. "It's so much fun to think of layering," Julia said as they painted on her deck while Ben was off servicing the Intrepid. "Sure, flat-space composition is valid. So is abstract art. But the real action is in the depth of a painting. It doesn't matter how much paint you put on a canvas. What matters is how layers create emotion with color combinations and contrasting values."

It amazed Murray that she understood most of what Julia was talking about, as if she'd heard it all before in a former life. It was the same with the basic skills of painting. She'd never used a palette knife to put paint on a canvas, but it felt doable right away.

"Look at you," Julia cooed. "You're a natural. Now, use the knife to scrape away paint so the underlayer shows through. It's called *sgraffito*, the Italian word for 'scratch.'"

Murray squealed in delight. "This is so cool I can't stand it."

After a couple hours, Murray's painting looked a little muddy. Too much paint on too many layers. It looked like she felt: overwhelmed. "Don't worry about it," Julia said. "Let's have an iced tea with lemon. We'll let it dry. Acrylic paint dries much faster than oil. We'll come back to it with fresh eyes."

Ben came bounding onto the deck, out of breath. "Mom, quick, turn on the television. Fox News is interviewing Anita Montgomery. I heard it on the radio. She's saying she was never kidnapped and that The Highway Diner and Trucker Nation are one big teamster-government lie to take over the country."

Julia and Murray rushed into the den and turned on the TV. There was Anita, larger than life, looking slightly haunted even in her professionally done makeup and hair. "Isabel Paterson and her daughter, Murray, own The Highway Diner. They lied to the world and said I was kidnapped. Why? To promote their business and the new casino they're building. Like they always do. All they care about is money. I'm here to tell you I was never kidnapped. I'm not being held prisoner. Nobody's forcing me to say anything. Look at me. I'm fine. And I'm telling you, Isabel and Murray are liars. Don't believe a word they say," Anita said.

Murray sat down on the sofa, feeling like she'd been punched hard in the gut. Anita was her friend. It was a relief to see her alive and relatively unscathed, but how could she say such terrible things? Ben sat down next to her, but he didn't put his arm around her. He, too, was in shock. Julia's cell phone rang. She didn't answer it.

"She's high as a kite," Murray said. "They got her back on something. Look how tired she looks. Her eyes are glazed. It's so sad to see her this way. And notice they're not showing where she is or who she's with."

"She's in a television studio," Julia said. "That's pro makeup and hair. And look at her eyes, moving side to side. She's reading from a teleprompter."

The coverage shifted to a wide shot of The Highway Diner

and the truck plaza. The camera zoomed in to a closeup of Isabel and Blake with a cluster of microphones in their faces.

"Let 'em have it, Mom," Murray yelled at the television as she pumped her fists in the air.

Isabel and Blake looked calm and camera-ready. "Yes, we're very worried about Anita," Isabel said. "She didn't show up for work one day a couple weeks ago. That's not like her. She's a hard worker and quite responsible. My daughter, Murray, and her boyfriend, Benjamin, went to Anita's apartment. Anita was gone, but her cell phone was left behind. She never went anywhere without her phone. There were obvious signs of a struggle. We called the police. Everybody knows she was kidnapped. She's been all over the news for weeks, and now she suddenly shows up from some unknown location like nothing's wrong. It's kind of like she's got that . . . what do you call it, Blake?"

"Stockholm syndrome," Blake answered. "It's when a hostage starts having positive thoughts about her captor. And I'll tell you one thing for sure. That's not Anita up there calling us liars. She's a good woman. She would never say such things if she was in her right mind."

Ben hit the mute button as the news took a commercial break. Julia let out a shriek. "Yay, Isabel. And Blake too. That's what I call a first-rate comeback. Taking the high road. And I love the way she calls you Benjamin instead of Ben."

"This is going to backfire so big on the Commander," Murray said.

Julia was thinking ahead. "I suppose this means we'll have to postpone our trip to Yosemite."

Murray and Ben looked at each other. Words did not need to be spoken. Ben nodded. "I'm afraid we've got to get back as fast as possible. If the militia is putting Anita on television, there's no telling what they're planning next."

Julia stuck out a pretend pouty lip in disappointment. "I was so looking forward to a road trip with the two of you in the Intrepid. But, honestly, I'm more worried than disappointed. It does feel like something bad is going to happen."

"Nothing we can't handle, Mom," Ben soothed. "From what we've seen of the militia, they're more bark than bite."

"Who puts a drugged-out kidnap victim on television to do their talking for them?" Murray said.

The next morning, Julia cried saying goodbye. "I wish you could have met Benjamin's sister, Stephanie. I'm glad you at least got to talk to her on the phone. Please, please, call me every day. I need to hear you're all safe and sound."

Murray could see her waving as they turned onto the road at the end of the driveway.

CHAPTER TWENTY

Murray and Ben made it back to The Highway Diner from Sausalito, California, in two days. They drove eighty miles an hour, alternating drivers, stopping only for gas and snacks and one scenic break in the mountains east of Salt Lake City. Anita's television interview made them feel they had to get back in a hurry. Trouble with the militia was brewing.

Isabel was excited to see them. "I'm so happy to have you honeys back home," she said as she hugged them both. "We've all been worried about you. How long has it been? Almost a month? Come on in. Everyone's waiting to see you."

Naomi, the new manager, beamed as she hugged them. "Ah, the heroes of Baraboo. We want to hear all the road stories."

"You won't believe what the Commander is up to now," Isabel said as they walked into the diner kitchen to a rousing welcome from the cooks and wait staff.

Murray and Ben accepted the celebrity treatment gratefully by hugging everyone they could get their hands on. Then they sat down at the round table in the corner of the diner to feast on the special of the day: stuffed cabbage rolls with a vegetable medley and loaded mashed potatoes. "Nothing ever smelled so good as this diner," Ben said as Isabel and Naomi joined them.

"I'm starving," Murray said. "All we've had are road snacks all the way from California. I'm ready for some real food."

"We've got the best cooks in the business now," Naomi said. "Everybody wants to work here. We're paying top dollar."

"I see you're busier than ever," Ben said. "I almost felt guilty cutting in front of that line. The place is humming. Nobody seems too afraid of a militia attack."

"That's because they don't know what's been going on," Isabel said.

Naomi caught Murray's eye and changed the topic. "Food sales are up almost three times since we expanded into the store. Construction starts in a week on the new building for the upgraded shopping and driver services center."

"Beer and wine sales are through the roof," Isabel said. "And our hard liquor license has been purchased and approved. We'll be serving margaritas and Manhattans by May fourteenth."

"Wow, we're faster than ever on the service," Murray said, looking around at all the activity in the restaurant.

"Naomi's new point-of-sale system," Isabel said.

Naomi held up her right hand. "Stop it, Isabel. It's The Highway Diner's new system."

Halfway through dinner, Murray managed to stop eating long enough to ask, "So, what about the Commander? And has anybody heard from Anita?"

Isabel placed her fork on the table carefully and for emphasis. "Nothing from Anita, that little traitor. I want to be loving toward her, but I feel so betrayed. Maybe they've got her so doped up she doesn't know what she's doing. As for the Commander, he is planning a truck blockade this weekend at the state capitol building in Lansing, Michigan. Not a rally, mind you—a blockade."

"I'm surprised he'd telegraph his battle plan like that," Ben said. "The governor will have the National Guard on hand with two hundred tow trucks on standby. What's he protesting now?"

"The Commander thinks he's bigger than the governor," Naomi said. "He's been surrounded by yes-men so long that he's starting to believe his own bullshit. You know he's paying a private army to live at the compound."

"What's the blockade for?" Murray asked.

"Something about too much tax on truckers," Isabel said. "I'm not sure. Nobody is. Maybe the high price of gas. I might even get behind that. But we've already put out word to Trucker Nation that we want nothing to do with the militia or its blockade."

"Next thing you know, the Commander will do a blockade on The Highway Diner to protest the high price of hamburgers," Naomi said.

"So, what are we gonna do to rescue Anita?" Murray asked. "I'm about ready to go up there and drag her home."

Isabel straightened up in her chair. "You'll do no such thing," she said before softening her approach. "I mean, I can't tell you what to do, but I don't think that's a good idea. We can all talk about it tomorrow when Chase and Leona get here. Now that you and Ben are back, they want to have a joint meeting between Trucker Nation and The Highway Diner to talk about the casino. From what I understand, things are moving faster than anyone thought possible."

After dinner, Murray and Ben bowed out gracefully. They were exhausted from the road and from the nagging fear of what was coming next. Murray hugged her mother. "We'll still sleep in the Intrepid," she said, "but can we use the walk-in shower at your house?"

Isabel grinned. "You know I'll always be your mother. I put fresh towels and extra shampoo in the shower for you."

The next day, Chase and Leona showed up looking uncharacteristically tired and twenty minutes late for the 10:00 a.m. meeting. Something was terribly wrong. The two of them were never late. Chase had his arm around Leona. He was tightlipped and shaking his head sadly. Leona's makeup was running. She'd been crying. They were leaning on each other for support as they approached the roundtable. Chase's hair wasn't blonde anymore; he was letting it go gray.

Ben and Murray were on their feet to help them take their seats.

"What's wrong? It looks like you two just got some bad news," Isabel asked.

"We did," Chase said as he sat down. "Got a call on the plane that Neil Vorderman was killed yesterday at the shooting range on the militia compound in Newaygo. Local police did a half-ass investigation. They're calling it an accident, but the feds know better. It was murder, for sure."

Nobody said a word. News that the militia was killing people was sinking in fast and hard.

"Who's Neil Vorderman?" Isabel asked. "I'm sorry, should I know this person?"

Leona put her hand on Isabel's arm. "No, no. I don't think we ever told you his name. He was a very dear friend of ours for many years. He used to run security for us in Nashville."

Chase looked around to make sure no one outside the table was listening. "He was working undercover for the FBI and feeding me information on the side. I told you about him, just never his name. Problem is, the people who killed him probably know he was still reporting to me."

"How would they know that?" Murray asked.

Chase furrowed his brow. "Same way they found out he was

working for the FBI. Hacked into his phone or his computer, or both."

"He went down range to retrieve a target, and the guy who shot him said he didn't see him," Leona said as she broke into tears. "That's all we know so far. I can't believe he's gone."

Murray grabbed tissues for Leona and refilled coffee and water for the table.

"This is bad news for us," Ben said. "If the Commander knows the heat is on him, and he orders a kill on a federal informant, there's no telling what he might do next."

Chase put his elbows on the table and held his head in his hands. "Neil was careful. I'm pretty sure he had a safe phone somewhere. He was always outside the compound when I heard from him. The last time we talked must have been two days ago, and he said somebody was watching him. I told him to get out of there, and he said he would."

"Neil leaves behind his ex-wife, Darlene, and two teenaged boys in Nashville," Leona said. "They're gonna be devastated. Darlene still loved him. Told me herself many times. She left because he wouldn't quit working undercover. She always said something like this was gonna happen."

"He felt strongly that guys like the Commander are a real threat to the country," Chase said.

"We'd better hope the feds get to the Commander before he gets to us," Ben said.

"Please don't talk like that." Murray dragged out every word for emphasis.

"The so-called accident at the shooting range was murder," Chase said. "I don't know how they talked the cops into not filing charges. Some people up there must be damn good actors. Then again, they've got the whole county on the take."

"We need to get to Anita," Murray said. "It's time to turn her head around so she's working for us again. I know she is feeling guilty for siding with the militia, even if they made her say those terrible things about us. She's probably planning her escape now. I know if I could just talk to her everything would be different."

CHAPTER TWENTY-ONE

Anita slipped further down the marijuana and opioid rabbit hole after she gave the news interview saying that she had never been kidnapped. She had started using drugs again to ingratiate herself with the Commander and get out of her private jail. Predictably, once she got started, she couldn't stop. The guilt she felt for publicly betraying Murray and Isabel accelerated her downhill slide. She realized that Cal Mavis and the Commander were only keeping her on drugs to fog her mind and ensure her cooperation.

Late one night, the two men were drinking shots of whiskey in the living room of the apartment Anita now shared with Cal. Anita had been passed out in the bedroom, but she was beginning to regain consciousness. She scratched her scalp and pulled on her ears, trying to remember where she was.

The Commander got up to get another bottle of whiskey from the kitchen cupboard. He was forty-three years old and forty pounds overweight. He carried the weight well with his broad hips and muscular shoulders. Staying in shape was nearly as high a priority for him as overeating and getting high. He was well trained in karate and Jiu-Jitsu.

"The reason our truck blockades don't work is because that goddamned Trucker Nation is convincing drivers not to participate," the Commander seethed.

"No doubt about it," Cal agreed as he poured two more shots. "Trucker Nation and The Highway Diner are doing everything they can to stick it to us. And they're in bed with the federal government."

"They're one and the same," the Commander spit out his words. "All they want to talk about is the big, happy supply chain. What they're supplying is totalitarian control. I'd love to see the day when all the trucks are electric and driverless. No one to buy their food and gas and cute little hats and T-shirts. Trucker Nation's gonna be robot nation."

The Commander's post-traumatic stress had manifested itself into a progressive case of obsessive-compulsive disorder. His attention to detail was well known to anyone who stood at attention for daily room and weapon inspections. The only aspect of his life left to its own device was the length of his hair and beard. People joked behind his back that the longer his hair grew, the more insane he became.

"We're the only ones who can save the country," he shouted. "And we're not going to do it with a bunch of phony, rigged elections. The only ballot we need is a bullet."

Then, the harangue took a surprising twist. The Commander tried to lower his voice, but he was still whiskey-loud. "Let me tell you how we got rid of that slime ball undercover agent, Neil Vorderman."

Anita was now hearing every word they said. The faint voices of Cal and the Commander reminded her that she was still a prisoner in the compound of Michigan Militia 714. Her drug haze and the bedroom wall made voices sound like they were coming through the squawk box at a fast-food drive-through. But there was no mistaking that the conversation was turning into a confession of murder. She got up and tiptoed to the bedroom door. She opened it a crack so she could see the two men.

The two men downed their shots. "Did you really have to kill him?" Cal complained. "You never told me you shot him in the back That's as bad as what they did to my brother at The Highway Diner. Couldn't you just tell him you knew what he was doing and get the hell out?"

The Commander poured himself a shot of whiskey and drained his glass before trying to speak. "He was a . . ." He had to cough through the whiskey to continue. "He was a traitor, plain and simple. Traitors get shot. It doesn't matter if you shoot 'em in the back or hang 'em. Traitors got to die."

"So, it was just you and Vorderman and Josh Nelson at the range when it happened?" Cal asked.

"Right. I was running the range, and Josh pulled the trigger. I told the sheriff we never sounded the bell for the 'all clear' to change targets. Told him Vorderman never should have been down range."

"So why did Vorderman go down range? He knows better than that."

The Commander gave Cal a crooked look of sarcastic sympathy. His head tilted, and his right eye closed in a pronounced wink. His mouth snarled.

Cal's eyes widened. "Oh, I get it. You did sound the bell. That's why he went downrange. Sorry. Took me a while. But what about Josh?"

"Josh said he didn't see him. Perfect accident."

Cal wasn't satisfied. "You'd think Josh could have seen him at one hundred yards."

"Not at night. Josh didn't have a scope on his AR-15, and he said he wasn't wearing his glasses."

"How did he hit him?" Cal asked.

"You ask more questions than the sheriff," the Commander

complained. "But for your information, Josh *was* wearing his glasses and Vorderman was right in front of Josh's target. He was changing targets for both of them."

"Can we trust Josh?"

"Oh yeah," the Commander chortled. "He knows what happens to traitors. And you both should know what I learned from Vladimir Putin."

"What's that?"

The Commander smiled like an evil clown. "You gotta kill somebody every once in a while to instill respect and inspire loyalty."

Cal couldn't keep his mouth shut. "I just wish you'd talked to me before you did it," he said. "I never thought you'd kill somebody without at least talking it over."

"Spoken like another innocent soul who never did a combat tour," the Commander hissed. His eyes had been dancing in the whiskey moments earlier. Now they froze in place like a predator stalking his prey. A chill crawled up Anita's spine as she watched Cal cower. She wanted to flee for her life, but she knew it was much too late to run.

Anita could tell the Commander was lost in the nightmare of close and deadly mountain combat exploding in his brain as he started shouting to people who were not in the room. Cal tried to bring the Commander back to reality.

"How did you even know he was an informant?" Cal asked.

Anita opened the bedroom door just enough to see the Commander close his eyes and shake his head like a wet dog shaking itself dry. "Whoa, Cal, sorry man. Left the ranch for a minute there. I get these spells where I want to kill everything. Kill the Qaeda, kill the pain. Kill what they did to us. Kill what we did to them. The whiskey helps . . . sometimes. Other times it makes it worse. Anyway, what was your question?"

Anita could see that Cal felt engulfed by the horror. He'd pulled his feet up on the couch and was hugging his knees. Cal's voice was barely above a whisper when he managed to repeat his question. "I was wondering how you found out Vorderman was an informant."

The Commander slammed his empty shot glass down on the table in triumph. His eyes were dancing again. "Oh, that Vorderman. He thought he was so clever. Had himself a secret phone wired up in his truck. Every time he drove to the liquor store, the phone charged up and he made his calls. Bart Tritch, our liquor lookout, noticed him always on the phone and looking around like he was afraid someone might be watching. We rigged up an intercept on his phone. Hacked into his phone records, got the number of his iPhone, and used a remote access app. Or something like that. I don't really know how they did it. But guess what we found?"

"Talking to the feds?" Cal guessed.

The Commander stood up and bowed as if to congratulate himself. "Not only that. The bastard was talking to that Chase Marshall talent manager guy from The Highway Diner. Telling him all about Anita and you and our operations up here. How about that? FBI agents reporting to goddamned Mr. Trucker Nation, Chase Marshall."

By this point in the conversation, Anita was wide awake and listening intently. The Commander's attitude about getting away with murder shocked her into temporary mental clarity. An emotional flood of guilt swept over her for cooperating with her captors. It was replaced by bone-chilling fear in the next instant.

———

Cal unfolded his legs and got up off the couch to come check on her, as though he could feel her regaining consciousness. He and Anita had developed a symbiotic relationship, despite her drug usage and confinement. Anita clicked the door shut and scrambled back into bed with no time to spare. Cal opened the door and took a couple steps toward her bed. He was so drunk he could barely walk. She closed her eyes and tried to breathe normally.

"How's the diner girl?" the Commander yelled from the living room.

"She's out like a light," Cal said as he left the room, shut the door, and stumbled back to the drinking table.

The Commander put his hands behind his head to stretch. He spoke clearly, as if he hadn't had a drink all night. "Those Highway Diner folks, with that new casino they're building, are putting the heat on me. I'm starting to feel surrounded by all this Trucker Nation bullshit. And the feds will be all over me soon. They're holding back for now. They don't want to admit that Vorderman was undercover."

Cal was five-eight and weighed maybe one hundred fifty pounds after a big meal. He was no match for the Commander, physically or emotionally. Still, he managed to remain in the conversation. "It can't be a coincidence that the FBI undercover agent was also working for Chase Marshall," he said.

The Commander laughed. "It's no coincidence. The Highway Diner is out to get us. So, guess what?"

"What?"

"We're going to ruin them before they can ruin us."

"How so?"

"For starters, we're going to blow up that casino before it ever opens. We're gonna take out The Highway Diner, too, along with the bitches who run it. In case you haven't heard the test explosions lately, I've got demolition guys working on a plan to take their buildings down and make it look like a gas leak accident."

CHAPTER TWENTY-TWO

Murray was happy to be back from California and working with her mother and Naomi at The Highway Diner. The three women made a powerful team. Besides handling the skyrocketing food and beverage business, they supervised construction of the truck plaza shopping and services building. The new building would be connected to the upgraded diner and sports bar. It would be a shopping mecca and high-end health club for truckers, complete with spacious restrooms and showers, sauna, fitness center, and laundry service.

"Drivers are making a lot more money than they used to," Isabel said. "They expect more from us, and we are gonna provide it. And we're not forgetting that a lot more women are getting into the trucking business."

"Like us," Murray said. Isabel and Naomi looked at each other and smiled.

"Women's wear is selling better than men's," Naomi said. "Course, lots of men are buying gifts for women. We can't keep the custom T-shirts, caps, and sweatshirts in stock. Imagine how we'll do if we sell boots, jeans, and leather jackets."

"And paintings," Murray added. Her trip with Ben and the time she spent painting with Julia had begun to restore her creativity after the trauma of gun violence, death threats, kidnapping, hate billboards, and being stalked. She had started painting trucks and soon had more commissions than she could handle. The Highway Diner opened a small shipping department so drivers could buy her artwork and have it shipped home. The process was an instant success since it worked well for all merchandise. Truckers could buy as much as they wanted without having excess baggage.

Ben was happily swamped with his duties overseeing construction at Trucker Nation Casino. Four twelve-story towers for elevators were nearly completed by July Fourth, and the rest of the building was rushing to catch up.

Meanwhile, Isabel had become an endorsement celebrity in her own right. She made big money for herself and Trucker Nation with television commercials for truck tires to credit cards. Most of the spots were shot on location at The Highway Diner. Murray appeared in a few ad campaigns, but she left most of the product modeling to her mother. Having her picture taken over and over was not Murray's idea of personal fulfillment.

Unfortunately for Isabel, Blake Dawson's success with The Long Road Band was leading to the inevitable excesses of sudden stardom. The band's drummer was arrested for drunk driving in St. Louis, too many shows started late or were canceled altogether, and Blake was photographed with a fashion model draped all over him in a Kansas City hotel.

Murray found her mother in the office one night after work, crying over a tabloid story about Blake. She hugged her from behind and whispered in her ear, "Mom, you can't believe what you read in those entertainment publications."

Isabel looked up at her with a sadness Murray hadn't seen since her younger sister died. "It's not the magazines," she began sobbing. Murray took her into her arms. "He hasn't called in eight days. You know what that means. He always calls at least once a day."

"Have you called him?"

"Yes," Isabel whined as she backed out of the embrace. "That's the worst part. He's not even answering my calls. I don't know what to do. I still love him. But I can't be treated like this. I just won't."

Murray comforted Isabel as best she could, but she was furious with Blake for making her mother cry. She took the matter to Ben, who was not surprised by Blake's behavior. Ben had seen it coming. "His head's so big he can't use the elevator," he said as he set up a conference call with Murray, Leona, and Chase.

"Tell you what," Chase said after he got the lowdown from Murray. "The Long Road Band are in Denver tomorrow night. I'll drop in on Blake unannounced and see what he's up to. It doesn't sound like him to do this to your mother. Then again, that tour's collapsing under the weight of too much booze and drugs."

———

Ten days later, Isabel finally got a phone call from a sober Blake.

"I'm so sorry, honey," Blake began. "I know I let you down. I got so caught up in the drugs and alcohol I didn't know what I was doing. The whole band did. We got so messed up we couldn't even make it to our own shows."

"You should be sorry, Blake. In fact, you're a sorry excuse for a musician. What happened to the music being the most important thing? And by the way, it's not just me you need to apologize to. It's all your fans and the folks here at The Highway Diner who love you and used to believe in you, and now you're throwing us all under the bus you're probably calling 'addiction.'"

"It is addiction, Isabel. And it's a disease. I'm learning a lot here in rehab."

"Where are you?"

Blake paused. "I'm at the Hazelden Betty Ford Foundation in Rancho Mirage, California. Chase checked the whole band in, but we're all in separate units."

"Well, isn't that handy?" Isabel said. "You celebrities all go hide in rehab like that's going to make everything all right. What about me? I lose my husband and finally find it in my heart to love another man and then you . . ." Isabel trailed off into tears.

Blake let her cry for a short while then spoke through his own tears. "I'm not going to say I'm sorry anymore, Isabel. I'm going to get clean and finish rehab and come out and prove myself all over again, to you and the rest of the world, that I'm a good man."

Isabel couldn't help but chuckle as she heard the old Blake bluster coming out again. "You got some fancy dancing to do to get that done, mister."

"I'll pay the fiddler, darlin'. You wait and see."

"Don't count on any back up from my daughter, Murray. She hasn't said 'I told you so' yet, but she's been thinking it all along."

"Please tell Murray I say hello. She might understand a little bit about addiction from being friends with Anita. I saw Anita say on television that she wasn't kidnapped. She looked stoned as hell. Don't give up on her. She'll come around once she's twelve steppin' with her higher power."

"I don't know what all that means, Blake. But I will say this: I'm proud of you for admitting you have a problem and for doing something about it. Good luck to you. Come see us when you get back on your feet. I'll talk to you later. The diner's slammed."

She hung up as Blake was trying to get a few more words in.

Isabel took the rehab news from Blake stoically as a woman who had already suffered terrible losses in life. All the articles and photos of The Long Road Band's exploits had already made her feel foolish for falling in love with Blake and for getting a big head about her own celebrity status. She resolved to lose herself in The Highway Diner and see how things turned out. She knew that she and Blake would never be the same. Fame had turned out to be more than a pain in the ass.

Isabel found fortune to be quite a different story. The money was liberating and empowering. She was free from years of worrying about making ends meet while trying to raise a daughter and run a truck plaza on her own. Her share of huge endorsement paychecks went into well-managed accounts. She was able to donate to good causes and promote Trucker Nation.

The best part of Isabel's good fortune, by far, was meeting Diamond Lil, her favorite country singer. Chase and Leona were longtime friends of Lil's. They'd known her since she was singing for tips in funky Nashville bars, well before she added "Diamond" to her name.

Leona brought Isabel to see the superstar singer, actress, and businesswoman at her concert in Indianapolis. Leona knew Lil wanted to meet Isabel, and she knew Isabel needed some cheering up after the Blake heartbreak. The show was uplifting and perfectly produced. Diamond Lil sang all her hits, including Isabel's favorite. Leona and Isabel had front-row seats and cheered their heads off. The superstar acknowledged their exuberance with a wave to Leona. Isabel was starstruck.

Diamond Lil greeted them backstage and gave each of them a warm hug. Isabel had to bend over a little to get down to Lil's five-foot height. It felt like she was dreaming. Meeting her idol was so overwhelming that all Isabel could say was, "I love you, Diamond Lil."

"Just call me Lil. Leona here knows I'm still just good old Lil. And I love you. Don't think I don't know who you are. You're Isabel from the Highway Diner and Trucker Nation. I see you on television more than me. Ain't it great Leona got us together?"

The legendary singer-songwriter was even more dynamic and charming in person than she had been onstage. "I'm a huge fan of bringing the country back together from all the hate. I love what y'all are doing," she bubbled. "Count me in as your first big show at the new casino. We'll donate half the proceeds to wherever you want it to go. But right now, let's go eat. I'm starving. I never eat before a show."

Isabel and Lil got along right away. "I can't believe I'm sitting here talking to Diamond Lil," Isabel said. "It feels like I've known you all my life. How do you stay so down to earth?"

Lil didn't hesitate to answer. "It's all about rememberin' where you come from. And I know you know that. You're still feeding truckers, gassin' up their rigs, and giving them a place to sleep. That's God's work, far as I know."

Leona and Lil listened with interest as Isabel gave a quick construction update on the truck plaza and casino. "You know, there's a lot more women driving semis these days," she said.

"You know what I say to that," Lil chimed in. "It's about high time for women to get in the driver's seat."

The conversational energy elevated as they shared stories about navigating their careers through the stormy waters of a man's world.

Isabel decided to ask Lil for some practical advice. "You've had a lot more experience with fame and fortune than me. I'm finding it all quite overwhelming."

"Well, it is that," Lil said. "No gettin' around it. You just can't let yourself be blinded by the bright lights. I've had my times gettin' a big head, that's for sure. But mainly I remind myself the good Lord's giving me a chance to help people. That's what's saved me. Keeping my good intentions. Long as I worry more about helping others than about myself, I know I'll be just fine."

Lil's words of wisdom rang true to Isabel. *It really is that simple,* she thought.

"By the way," said Lil, shifting gears. "I love your rhinestone cowgirl outfit on that new credit card ad. You look better than Loretta Lynn." Then she gasped and put both hands over her mouth. "Oh goodness! Do not tell anyone I said that." The three women laughed so hard they almost cried.

Once they caught their breath, Leona surprised even herself by bringing up a sensitive topic. "You know, you two have a friend in common who's gotten himself into trouble lately."

A long conversational pause lasted until Lil asked Isabel, "How is Blake doin'? I mean, I know it's hard on you going through all this. Obviously, I've been following the story. And I know how horrible it is to see your picture on those stupid magazines, not to mention all over social media. I've known Blake for a while from his songwriting. He's big talent. We're going to record one of his tunes for my next project.

"Yes, he is," Isabel began slowly. "But I haven't heard from Blake since he went into rehab. I wish him well, but I'm not holding my breath."

Lil gave Isabel a heartfelt hug. "I'm sorry to hear you haven't heard from him. But good for you on not holding your breath. Musicians and drugs are a big problem. Drugs and anybody are a big problem. I do pray Blake gets clean and stays clean. I know he can do it just by how much he loves his children. If he does, he'll be a better man than ever. If not, he'll be no good to anybody."

Leona jumped in to change the topic, trying to recover from bringing it up in the first place. "So, what about Diamond World? Your theme park outside of Nashville keeps getting bigger and bigger. We're kind of headed that way with Trucker Nation."

Lil responded cautiously, "The thing about branding and selling products is that it's good business. You've got a big name now, and you can use it. Money's not a bad thing if you use it to help people. Leona and I do a lot of charity work, and I know Trucker Nation supports good causes. I been keeping up on you."

"We're all about ending the hate," Isabel said. "But it seems the more we try, the more hate comes our way."

"What do you mean?" Lil asked.

Isabel and Leona explained their problems with the Michigan militia. "The strangest part was the billboards that said, 'The Highway Diner is a lie,'" Isabel said. "I don't know why anybody would even think that."

"Well now," Lil said. "Tough girls like us can't let the bad boys stand in our way. These militia groups are everywhere. They're all over Tennessee and the rest of the country. They're dangerous. You got the federal government watching out for you?"

Isabel nodded. "I just don't understand why they hate us so much. We've never done one thing to them or even said a bad word."

Lil nodded her head in sympathy. "One thing I've learned is that unhappy people don't like happy people. It's that basic. I ought to know. I've had a lot of folks mad at me because of my success. The worst part was feeling like maybe I deserved it. I do hope you're over that."

Isabel sighed. "For the most part. I keep reminding myself."

Lil raised her hand for a high-five with Isabel. "You stay strong, girl. The world is in desperate need of women like us."

CHAPTER TWENTY-THREE

Anita cut down on the marijuana and pills once she realized how truly insane and dangerous the Commander had become. She needed to escape and warn her friends at The Highway Diner. The drug fog was no longer insulating her from reality; it was amplifying the violence around her, as if she was trapped in a loud video game she never learned how to play. She began praying to whatever was out there, asking for help to get clean.

The militia compound sounded like a war zone. The shooting range was packed at all hours of the day and night. Automatic weapons were firing hundreds of rounds at a time. Men in combat gear were marching in and out of the compound to conduct military maneuvers in surrounding fields. Ground-shaking explosions were becoming commonplace and sounding much too close to home.

"What are those loud booming noises?" she asked Cal.

Cal looked at her suspiciously. "Nothing to worry about. Just some of the boys playing with mortars."

"Don't mortars shoot bombs into the air that come down and kill people? Why would anybody around here need mortars?"

Cal shrugged his shoulders and rubbed his eyes with the palms of his hands like he was trying to make a bad feeling go away. He wasn't about to answer her question. For one thing, he didn't know the answer. He looked at Anita with tears in his eyes, then lowered his gaze to the ground.

Anita knew she shouldn't ask any more questions. But she suspected Cal was becoming fearful of the Commander and his intentions. She asked, "Do you think he knows what he's doing?"

Cal let out a growl of annoyance. "Anita, you know I love you. And you know you can't ask questions like this. But you're smart as hell. And you know me too well. I can see you looking right through me. So, I'll tell you straight out. I'm scared."

Anita took his hands in hers, encouraging him to continue.

"I'm scared about what the man is capable of doing. He thinks he can take on the whole federal government. But that's not what really scares me. What I'm afraid of is the feds coming in here and busting the whole marijuana operation and seizing all the illegal weapons."

"Would we go to jail?" Anita asked.

"You might wiggle out of it since you could say you were kidnapped. But I would go down with the ship. Worse yet, we could get caught in the middle of a major gun battle. The Commander won't surrender peacefully. It's like he built this place so he could go out in a blaze of glory."

Anita covered her mouth with her hands in horror. "He'll shoot me before anybody so I won't be a witness against him."

Cal nodded as it suddenly occurred to him that might be a real possibility. Anita was emboldened as she saw the confusion and concern in his face. "Oh, Cal, can't we both just get out of this mess?"

Cal grabbed her firmly by the shoulders. "Don't even think like that. Talking like that makes you a traitor. And we both know what happens to traitors."

Anita was tired of Cal quoting the Commander. "Did you help him kill that undercover guy, Vorderman?"

Cal looked hard at her, shocked to see in her eyes that she knew the truth. "What did you hear?" he barked in her face.

Anita did not back down one inch. "Was there something to hear?"

Cal backed up a step and stared at her, dumbfounded by her ability to outwit him.

"No, I didn't hear anything," she lied. "You don't need to be Sherlock Holmes to know that it was no accident at the shooting range. You told me yourself he was undercover. Everybody in the compound knows that. And traitors get shot, remember?"

Cal did a double-take and opened his eyes wide until he squinted in an unsuccessful attempt to hide his surprise. "I didn't tell you anything about Vorderman."

"Come on, Cal," she said. "If we stay here, we'll be just as guilty of murder as the Commander. You are many things, but you're not a murderer. Remember how upset you got about your brother?"

"He'll track us down and kill us if we run," Cal said as he looked over his shoulder.

Anita was surprised to hear him even considering leaving the compound. "Not if we tell the feds he's guilty of murder. The Commander will go to jail for life."

"He's not the only one," Cal said. "There's militia all over this country. And they're all connected."

Anita didn't say a word. Cal was obviously spooked and not about to get over it any time soon. She took him by the hand, led him back into their apartment, and had sex with him like that would make everything all right.

Later that night, Cal was passed out on the sleeping meds Anita had slipped into his last few drinks. He hadn't noticed she stayed sober the entire day and night. That would have tipped him off. She pretended to drink vodka tonics, but they were only tonic. Her plan required a clear head. She took a long last look at Cal and began her escape.

She wore running shoes, wool socks, long jeans, a warm shirt, and a hoodie sweatshirt to hide her blonde hair. It was the only jacket she had, and she would need it. Even in August, Michigan got cold at night. She took nothing with her, not even a flashlight. She knew the half-moon would be mostly cloud-free.

She crawled out the first-floor window of their apartment in the Commander's renovated schoolhouse. The bars had been removed. Her path was dictated by the surveillance camera location. She'd been scoping out the cameras every time she took a walk with Mavis. Most of the cameras covered the front sides of buildings. She was pretty sure there was a camera-free path almost all the way to the shooting ranges. The only two cameras on that route were mainly in the shadows.

She crawled on her hands and knees beneath the windows on the backsides of several apartment buildings clustered around the schoolhouse, moving carefully from shadow to shadow. The compound had night guards around the perimeter. They rarely patrolled the interior of the compound. She could avoid detection if nobody was watching the monitors too closely. And they wouldn't be at this time of night.

She hid behind a dumpster when she saw a man approaching with his dog on a leash. The dog barked and pulled on its leash in her direction. She wanted to run but resisted the urge. The dog was so strong it pulled its owner toward her. The man looked directly at her but didn't see her in the shadows. She remained motionless. He yanked the dog back on course and kept walking. The dog continued barking and trying to turn around, but the owner dragged it away. Anita breathed a deep sigh of relief. *Thank God dogs can't talk*, she thought.

It was nearly midnight by the time she made it through the housing and to the edge of the shooting range. It was lit up like a night baseball game. Two men were still shooting targets. Their rifles were making a faint snapping noise. *Silencers*, she thought. *What kind of weirdo puts a silencer on a rifle?*

Nobody was running the range. The office was dark.

She stayed low and slow as she snuck up behind them, close enough to hear them talk as she hid behind a fence. They were drinking beer and arguing about who should quarterback the Detroit Lions in the upcoming football season. Anita had always been mystified by men and their sports obsessions. Tonight was no different. Except now she was forced to listen while she waited them out.

The only safe way for her to get out of the compound was through the range and out behind the back-stop earthen mounds. She knew the fence was under repair from mortar fire damage. She'd seen the hole the day before while she was checking her target.

The conversation of the shooters shifted to how Blacks, Latinos, and Asians were taking over the country. "When the whole mess collapses," the man with a cigar said, "we'll pick off the urban flight with these rifles before they ever reach our water."

"Motherfuckers be better off dead, anyway," said the second man. "And with these silencers, they'll never know what hit 'em. They won't even hear it coming."

Anita could not believe the stupidity and bigotry as she

listened for at least half an hour. *What's the matter with these guys? What went so horribly wrong in their lives that they hate people they don't even know?*

She began to worry about how long the escape attempt was taking. Without a watch, the time she had to wait felt twice as long. If Mavis woke up, he'd have the whole compound looking for her. Finally, the two men walked downrange a hundred yards to change their targets. Once they were occupied with checking bullet holes, she hustled past the darkened office and made it to the earthen mounds behind the fifty-yard targets before the men turned around.

As the two shooters walked back to their firing positions, Anita sprinted from behind the fifty-yard back-up mounds and ducked behind the hundred-yard mounds. Nobody heard or saw her. And, yes, the fence had not been repaired. She slipped through and found herself standing on the edge of freedom. From there, she knew it would be nothing but farmers' fields until she hit the county highway. There was just enough moon to cast a dim light on her escape route. The loose soil under her feet felt liberating. Outside the compound lights, she had a fighting chance of making a clean getaway.

Anita ran hard for a quarter mile, falling twice on the uneven ground and rolling in the dirt without stalling her forward progress. Then she had to stop, hands on her knees, as she fought to regain her breath. After more than a month as a captive, smoking and drinking and laying around, she was woefully out of shape. But she was young and terrified.

Back on the run, Anita kept a slower and steadier pace. She set her course by a low-hanging planet to keep going due west. She ran another half mile without stopping. Finding the road was her only hope. She knew it would be out there. Mavis had all kinds of maps in their apartment. She'd studied them when he was out with the Commander.

Leaving Cal Mavis was not as easy as she thought it would be. He looked so sweet and peaceful sleeping. After the kidnapping, he had been mostly kind to her. She picked up with him where she left off with his brother, Red. What trouble would Cal be in if she escaped? Probably a lot. *Not my problem*, she thought as she stumbled and hit the dirt once again. *If he's too chickenshit to leave, he can go down in flames with the Commander.*

She saw the road in the distance. It shined in the moonlight like the inner tube of a tire. In a few hundred yards, she climbed up a slight embankment and felt herself on solid asphalt. The road was deserted. It had to be after 1:00 a.m. What if nobody came along?

Hitchhiking would be a gamble, but it was one she had to take. And she wasn't going to just stick out her thumb. She would have to get lucky to escape in time to warn Isabel and Murray of the Commander's plan to blow them up.

Suddenly, a pickup truck came over the hill in the distance. *Please, please, keep coming,* she pleaded to any good spirit that might be listening. *And please don't be anyone from the compound.*

The truck kept coming. When it got within fifty yards, she jumped in front of the headlights and waved her arms in distress. Her hair was a mess; she was sweaty and dirty.

The pickup had no choice but to stop. Amazingly, the bright lights blinked for her to come around and get in. The driver was a middle-aged man wearing overalls. He looked amazed at his dumb luck to find a young woman in his path.

Anita checked his face before she got in. Thank God she did not recognize him from the compound.

"What's a pretty little filly like you doing out here in the middle of nowhere?" He slurred his words. Anita smelled booze on his breath as she buckled her seatbelt.

"Oh, thank you so much for stopping." She pretended to break down in tears. "My boyfriend and I had a fight, and he beat me bad and pushed me out of his truck."

"You don't look hurt."

"It's my head," she sobbed hard and wailed. "He always hits me where my hair will hide the bruising. I think I have a concussion. Everything is blurry. I need to get to the hospital."

"Okay, okay. I'll help you if you just settle down a little. I can get you to the edge of Newaygo, but you're on your own from there. I'm too drunk to be driving around a bunch of cops. You'll have to get somebody in town to take you to a doctor."

The farmer drove her five miles to the edge of town. He made a halfhearted effort for her to come home with him and put some ice on her head. Anita started moaning and crying again, holding her head in both hands. He dropped her off without further flirtation. "Good luck," was all he said.

Anita walked into town, found an open bar, and marched straight back to the ladies' room to wash her face and fix her hair as best she could without a comb. Then she walked out and hopped onto the middle stool of a mostly empty bar. "Mr. Bartender," she said, batting her eyes at the young man. "I lost my cell phone, and I was wondering if I could borrow yours to make just one little call."

The man fell all over himself to lend her his phone.

"Thank you so much, kind sir," she said as she dialed Murray's number.

Murray picked up on the third ring. "You won't believe where I am," Anita said in hushed tones as she lowered her head.

"Anita?" Murray squealed. "I knew you'd come back. Thank God and praise the stars. Where are you?"

"I'm on the run. I'm in Newaygo on West State Road at the Antler Bar. Get it? The horniest bar in town?"

"Ben and I are on the way right now."

"Better hurry," Anita whispered. "I ran away about an hour ago. They're probably after me by now. And oh—don't come in your big, fancy van. It's way too conspicuous."

"Wait, Anita, don't hang up. Should we call the police?"

"No," she whispered fiercely. "All the cops around here are with the militia. The Sheriff deputies and city police use the shooting range at the compound like it's their own private club. Even the state cops come and shoot."

"Okay, okay. But listen. It's one o'clock and we're three hours away. The bar will be closed by the time we get there."

Anita paused, then said, "Tell you what, I'll hide down by the river and meet you in front of the bar at 4:00 a.m. You'll know the place from the giant rack of moose antlers over the front door."

"Won't you be cold?"

"I'm too scared to be cold."

CHAPTER TWENTY-FOUR

Anita handed the phone back to the bartender and smiled. He asked what she wanted to drink. "Could I please have just a big water with a lemon?" she asked. "And I have to apologize in advance. I lost my purse, which is how I lost my cell phone, so I won't be able to give you a tip."

The bartender nodded his head like he had no problem with that and brought her a tall glass of ice water with two lemon slices on the rim. Anita drank the water quickly and ate the lemons, rinds and all. "Thank you so much," she said as she was leaving. "I'll be back with your tip."

Anita heard someone get up in a hurry as she walked out the front door. Something about the way the chair banged against the wall made her think that someone—probably a man—got up suddenly to follow her. He was too drunk to be catlike in his quickness.

She didn't turn around to see who it was. Instead, she walked out the door and headed slowly and obviously to her right, past the front windows. Once no one in the bar could see her, she sprinted down the side of the building, around the back corner, and around a second corner to hide and see if she was being followed. She got low and peeked around the concrete foundation.

Anita thought no one had recognized her in the Antler Bar, but someone had. None other than Josh Nelson, close confidant and trigger man for the Commander, drowning his late-night sorrows and regrets alone at a shadowy table in the back corner of the bar.

And there he was, already at a trot toward the river as he got beyond the bar building. She saw it was Josh Nelson. An electric shock of fear sizzled up her spine. He was the man who had murdered the undercover agent.

She got up carefully, ran back to the street, turned left, slowed to a walk for at least seven buildings, and ducked back into the shadows between two houses. She scampered to the back of the building and took a careful peek. She could see Josh searching from tree to tree, using the light from his cell phone. He even called out her name. "Anita. Come on out, honey. I'm only trying to help. Anita, come on out now."

In less than ten minutes, three men with flashlights and rifles ran to the river to join Josh. He pointed at the water as if he thought maybe she'd hit the river to escape. Two of the flashlights doubled back toward the bar. She knew more men would be coming once the Commander learned she hadn't been found.

What to do? What to do? Ben and Murray could be driving into real danger. She had no way to warn them. But first she had to make sure she couldn't be found. They'd be searching the whole town soon. She was at the side of a two-story house. It didn't look like anyone was home, but who could tell at this hour? There was a metal rail around a stairway down to a basement door. She started down the stairs, wondering what little chance there was of the door being unlocked.

The stairway had not been used in some time. Deep piles of dry leaves made too much noise under her feet. The spiderwebs were thick and stuck to her hands. If the door were unlocked, it would be a miracle. No one had been down these stairs in months.

She held her breath and turned the doorknob. The knob turned, but the door didn't open. She leaned into it. It didn't budge. She placed both hands on the door and used her legs to jolt it open, but the door was stuck shut. She could hear men shouting on the street nearby to begin a door-to-door search. She thought about breaking the dusty window on the top third of the door. No, that would lead them right to her. She was already making too much noise. If the door didn't open, she'd have to bury herself in leaves and hope for the best.

She braced her feet against the stairwell and pushed with all her might, fully extending herself until she was suspended between the door and the concrete wall. She fell into the leaves and banged her hands and knees when the door opened suddenly with a long, loud creaking and shrieking from its rusty hinges. A Siamese cat in heat could not have attracted more attention.

Anita brushed off the leaves and stepped into the darkness of the basement, closing the door with an unavoidable thunder rumble back into its frame. She felt for a deadbolt turner. There it was. She locked the door and sat down behind it, amazed at her luck. The basement smelled like musty mold and mildew. It was quiet as a morgue, but her heart was beating like a jungle drum.

Relief at finding a hiding place did not last long. In a very short time, being alone in the dark began to convince her that something evil was lurking in the basement. She fought the fear as it rose inside her to near panic.

No point in trying to find a light switch. As much as she needed to see what she felt was all around her, a light would be a bad idea. She hugged her knees and tried not to cry. *It's gonna take a miracle to get out of this mess.* She heard voices in the space between her house and the next. She froze in fear.

A flashlight shined through the dirty window at the top of the basement door. For an instant, she could see the large room was filled with nothing but boxes and old furniture.

A man came down the outside basement stairs and checked the door. She could hear him breathing heavily and cursing what was left of the spiderwebs. "Locked up tight," he yelled as he went back up the stairs. Once he was gone, Anita was left alone in the darkness.

Good thing I wasn't hiding under the leaves, she thought. *Thankfully, he was in too much of a hurry to notice the doorknob had recently been dusted. And thank God there's just junk in this cold, clammy place.* She thought about feeling her way to the upstairs of the house so she could find a clock. How else could she be on time for the pickup? But no, she felt safe by the door. There was no light in the basement for her eyes to adjust. *Blind burglars make too much noise.*

Anita began to shiver from the cold and damp as she resolved to wait an hour for the searchers to be gone. All she had to do was count to sixty—sixty times.

Murray had driven Isabel's red Mercedes SUV almost to Angola, Indiana, when she got a call on her cell phone. Ben answered the call. It was the bartender at the Antler Bar. "I don't know who I'm talking to, and I don't need to know. But you need to know that the lady who called you about an hour ago on this phone, borrowed from me, is the target of a big manhunt up here. Guess you'd have to call it a woman hunt. Anyway, it's the militia, and they are the law in these parts. Don't call the cops."

"Have they found her?" Murray asked.

"No, they haven't found her. But there are still lots of men with rifles roaming the streets. I hate those militia guys. They worship guns, and they don't tip worth a damn. The young lady seemed like a good person. Hope you can help her. Anyway, that's all I know. Please don't call me back."

"What do we do now?" Ben asked Murray after the anonymous caller hung up. "We can't just drive into the middle of an ambush."

Murray kept driving. Her brow furrowed, and she looked angry like she always did when she was lost in thought. A calming confidence took over. She remembered the giant statue of the Native American woman. "Whatever we do, it's not going to be at night. We've got to let that town wake up before we make any kind of move. Anita's smart enough to know we'll wait for plenty of witnesses on the street before we roll into town. Then, we drive back and forth past the Antler Bar until she knows it's us."

"Then what? She jumps in the car, and they shoot all three of us?"

Murray had to laugh at the desperation in Ben's voice. "No, no. Sorry for laughing," she said. "I know this is scary. But think about it. Nobody's going to shoot up a car in the middle of the day. Yes, that's it. We'll wait until high noon. Like in the cowboy movies. But we'll be looking for the lunch crowd instead of a shootout at the O.K. Corral."

"Murray, cut it out. We should call the FBI and let them handle it."

Murray thought about his suggestion for a short time and concluded, "Actually, you're right. They've been looking for her since she got kidnapped."

"Not once she told them she wasn't kidnapped," Ben said.

"They'll change their attitude when we tell them she's on the run and being chased by an armed militia posse. Let's call them.

What's their number? They've got to be about ready to raid the compound, anyway."

Ben's cell phone search came up with several numbers. Nobody answered on any line. He left the same message every time. "Missing person Anita Montgomery located in Newaygo, Michigan, in imminent danger, being chased by militia group 714."

He left a phone number, but there was no call back by the time they reached Grand Rapids, Michigan. "Let's stop and get breakfast at the next truck stop," Ben suggested. "It's three in the morning. We're less than an hour away from Newaygo. We're way too early. Even the FBI is sleeping."

———

Anita fell asleep in the basement blackness, trying to count out the minutes. She was exhausted. Once the adrenaline wore off, she passed out as she tried to count the seconds.

When she awoke, light was glowing through the basement window. She knew it was way past the 4:00 a.m. pickup. Shivering turned into uncontrollable shaking from the cold and fear as her imagination ran amuck. Ben and Murray would have assumed the worst when they got to the Antler Bar and she wasn't there. Hopefully, they didn't let the search party know who they were. The militia might have taken them hostage. If anything bad happened to them, it would be all her fault.

She listened intently for any sounds coming from the house above. She thought she heard voices, but they could have been coming from the street. The inside steps up to the house were now vaguely visible. One thing for sure, she had to get to a phone.

She waited and listened. Were those voices she was barely hearing or just her imagination? Then, she heard a man and a woman coming down from the second floor and into a room just above her. They were bickering about being late for a doctor's appointment. Their voices were shaky. They sounded elderly. The woman was taking the man in for chemotherapy. They were late and blaming each other. It sounded like they grabbed something from a refrigerator and hurried out the door. She heard the car start in the driveway next to the house and drive away.

Creeping up the squeaky stairs as quietly as possible, Anita was keenly aware there could be more than two people living in the house. She waited after the creaking noise of each stair and listened. Nothing.

The door at the top of the stairs opened smoothly. She was in the kitchen. The telephone was a landline hanging on the wall. Mail with the couple's address was on the table.

Anita walked around the first floor carefully and listened at the bottom of the staircase for several minutes. No sounds of life. Walking back into the kitchen, she looked at the clock on the wall over the sink. It was 7:30 a.m. She picked up the phone and dialed Murray's number.

Murray and Ben awoke from napping in the car to the sound of the phone, thinking the FBI was finally calling them back. Murray thought she might be dreaming when she heard Anita talking almost too fast to be understood.

"I'm so, so sorry I missed the pickup. Are you guys all right? I was hiding in a dark basement, and I fell asleep. The people who live here just left for a doctor's appointment. I snuck in from the basement. I'm using their phone."

"No, you didn't miss anything," Murray said. "Calm down. We're fine. We haven't been to Newaygo yet. I'm so glad to hear your voice. The bartender—the man who let you use his phone—called us and told us the militia was searching all over for you. We decided to wait until noon to come into town. We called the FBI, but they haven't gotten back to us."

"No need for the FBI," Anita said. "Here's where I am." She gave Murray the address and waited for Murray to write it down and read it back to her.

"Just get here as fast as you can and pull in the driveway on the left of the house," she said. "It's between two houses so you won't be seen once you pull in. I'm looking out the front windows now, and I don't see anybody on the lookout. I'll be watching for you."

CHAPTER TWENTY-FIVE

Murray called Isabel at 9:00 a.m. "Oh, thank goodness," Isabel said once she heard Murray's voice on the phone. "Are you and Ben okay? Is Anita still alive?"

Murray laughed. "We're all more than fine. We've got the little old lady in the car with us, and we're headed home."

"What?"

"It's Anita. She dressed up like an older woman so no one could recognize her. You should have seen her, all hunched over, having trouble getting down the stairs. Ben and I thought we were at the wrong house for a minute."

"Hallelujah," Isabel sang into the phone. "I can't wait to see that crazy little girl again. You can tell me all about it once you get here. Come straight to the diner. We've got four FBI agents waiting to talk to her. They said you called them. They won't tell me anything. You sure no one's following you?"

"No, we're good, Mom. Clean getaway. The FBI finally called us back almost an hour ago. They tried to talk us out of getting involved, but the pickup was already underway. They've got a helicopter overhead as we speak. Anita looks pretty good. She's been sober, going on two days now."

"Wow! Two days," Isabel chuckled. "My, my. Well, I guess that's a good start." She knew Anita probably heard what she said, so she added, "Way to go, Nita. You gotta start somewhere."

"Okay, Mom," Murray interrupted. She didn't want Isabel

and Anita to get started. "Love you. Talk to you soon." She ended the call. She smiled at Ben.

Anita couldn't stop talking once she got started. "The Commander is even more evil than you think. I heard him confess, with my own two ears, to killing the undercover agent. And here's the worst part: he has plans to blow up the casino and the diner."

"What?" Murray cried out in disbelief. "Why does the Commander want to blow up the diner? What did we ever do to him?"

"Do you want me to answer that?" Anita asked.

"No, thank you," Murray said. "I've heard it all before, and it will never make sense to me. So, tell us everything, Nita. How you were captured, why you relapsed, how you escaped. We're ready to hear it all."

Anita leaned forward and put her head between Ben and Murray in their bucket seats. Ben and Murray listened intently as she talked about Cal Mavis handcuffing her and kidnapping her, living in the compound with him, target shooting AR-15s with Cal and the Commander, getting back into drugs to get out of her private prison, and making her escape. She didn't stop talking for sixty miles.

"You know I didn't mean what I said on television," she said. "I had to say it. They wrote it out and made me read it. They had me so doped up, and I knew the only way out was to cooperate."

"We knew that," Murray said. "But I'm glad to hear you say it."

Once they arrived at the diner, they sat down with the four FBI agents. Anita was ravenous. They hadn't stopped to eat. She finished most of the breakfast special and three cups of black coffee, then left with the agents to tell them everything she knew in an on-camera statement.

"Ben, you'd better call your mother," Isabel said. "She called this morning. I told her you were out of town on business and you'd call her back, probably before noon. She wondered why you weren't answering your phone. I didn't tell her anything. Didn't want her to worry—"

Suddenly, a monstrous explosion shook The Highway Diner with a blast wave that felt like an earthquake. The deep, low boom was so loud it left a ringing in the ears. It morphed into a jagged ripping sound that seemed to last much longer than mere seconds. Walls shook, the floor heaved up and down, and parts of the ceiling fell onto diners and their food. Two large windows shattered at the front of the new convenience center next to the diner. Murray thought part of the diner had blown up.

Everyone hit the ground instinctively, inside and outside the diner. Panic set in before the dust began to settle. People started screaming and crying and reaching out for each other. No one knew what to do. Ben ran outside to see what had exploded. Murray followed him out.

A massive mushroom cloud of smoke and dirt shrouded the entire construction site of the half-built Trucker Nation Casino. Flames were rising thirty feet high through the smoke. Murray ran toward the devastation, but she couldn't catch up with Ben. At least seventy workers were on site that morning, people she and Ben had hired and cared about. It looked like no one could have survived the blast.

Ben had reached the edge of the dust and debris. He was winded after a fifty-yard sprint and bent down, with his hands on his knees, panting. Thick, black smoke made it difficult to breathe. Screams of the wounded could barely be heard over the roar of the blast blaze.

"Ben!" Murray shouted as she raced toward him.

A second explosion rocked what was left of the site. It had even more force than the first. Murray felt a blast of fiery air as her body flew backward and slammed into the pavement. Her vision blurred. A high-pitched ringing filled her ears. She opened her eyes, trying to figure out what had just happened.

"Ben!" Murray tried to scream, but only a hoarse whisper croaked out of her throat. She couldn't sit up. Her body was paralyzed in shock until she managed to roll over on her stomach. Her brain was fogged by a bruising confusion as she struggled to her knees. She began breathing deeply until her mind came slowly into focus. A pulsating image of Ben being blasted off his feet energized her with the panic of desperation. He was flying through the air backwards when she lost sight of him as she herself fell. She rose cautiously to her feet and realized she had somehow avoided serious injury. Everything hurt but nothing felt broken. She began stumbling toward the spot she had last seen him, shielding her eyes from the dust.

She finally reached him. He was on his back, unconscious. Trickles of blood ran out of his mouth and ears. She grabbed his arms and shook him, fighting back hysteria as she barely heard herself yelling his name. "Ben, Ben, can you hear me? Oh, Ben, please, say you hear me."

Murray's ears felt muffled, and she was having trouble hearing. Smoke burned her eyes. She let go of Ben as she realized shaking would not wake him and might cause further injury.

Isabel and Naomi ran over, their faces etched with fear. Naomi said ambulances were on the way.

"Mom, Mom, look at him," Murray howled. "I'm afraid

he's dying. What can we do?" She held his limp right hand and gently squeezed it as she rocked back and forth and sobbed and moaned his name.

Isabel tried to console her. "He's still breathing. The blast knocked him out. He'll come to." Murray could barely hear what her mother was saying.

Naomi was first to notice blood beginning to puddle beneath his head. "He's got a head wound," she said. She took off her apron and wrapped it around his head so that the cloth cradled him in a sling when she lifted it slightly and applied pressure to the wound. "Hold it just like this," she showed Murray. "Just so his head is barely off the pavement. We don't know what we're dealing with, but we need pressure on the wound. I'm going to get blankets and bandages."

Murray held Ben's head up as she looked into her mother's eyes. What she saw was not comforting. Isabel was crying. Murray looked down at Ben. The color had drained from his lips.

Isabel maintained a brave front. "He's going to make it, Muriel. Look, he's breathing. Don't worry about the blood. Head wounds always bleed too much."

Ben remained motionless. His breathing was shallow. His face looked like it had been sandblasted. Even his eyelids were raw and red from the exploding particulate. Murray checked his body. There were no visible shrapnel wounds, but his legs and arms looked flat and broken.

The horrors of war were all around them. The air smelled like burning electrical components and an oil fire. It was hard to breathe. Murray pulled her sweatshirt up and over her nose and mouth, but it did no good. Smoke got in her eyes and she could barely see.

A man with a severed right arm, pulsating blood, staggered

out of the bomb site. Half his face had been blown off. Murray and Isabel watched in helpless horror as he collapsed not twenty feet from where they huddled over Ben.

Screams of the wounded and dying filled the air. Lifeless bodies lay in crumpled heaps near the ruins of the casino. Dust blew over the entire area, suffocating everyone in soot and particulate on their hair and clothing.

Murray felt herself being sucked into the whirlpool of chaos that surrounded her. Nothing looked real. A woman wearing a hard hat stumbled out of the destruction, covered in dust but somehow unscathed. The woman walked toward Murray with outstretched arms like she was sleepwalking in slow motion and unaware of her circumstance. A short man wearing big boots took the woman's arm and escorted her away from the surreal scene.

People were shouting and running toward the explosion site to help. Isabel stood up and waved her arms for them to stop. "There could be more bombs. Get back. Stay back." Two thirds of the enormous casino had been turned into a heap of rubble. Victims were buried, dead or alive. Burn victims who survived the blast were stumbling around like zombies.

Naomi came running back with supplies and a young woman in tow. "I can help," the woman said. "I'm an ER nurse at Parkview Hospital." She looked down at Ben. "He's in shock. Let's lift his feet up and put this blanket under them. Now, hand me another blanket so we can keep him warm."

She took the apron cradle from Murray and lowered Ben's head to the ground. Then she let the apron loose, got down low to the pavement, and raised his head slightly so she could assess the wound. Murray did not like the sudden grimace the nurse tried to hide. The nurse said nothing as she removed the apron, folded a towel, and gingerly placed it beneath Ben's head.

Murray took one look at the blood-soaked apron and collapsed into her mother's arms, sobbing uncontrollably as sirens wailed in the distance.

The nurse said there was nothing more to be done for Ben at the moment. She sprang up and ran to help a bearded man who had a spear of metal stuck through his chest and out through his back. He staggered in circles until she got him to sit down on a large chunk of concrete.

Three men in hard hats walked out from under the corner of the casino that was still standing. They were covered in dust and holding on to each other for support, both physical and emotional. One man fell to his knees when he saw the extent of the damage. The other two took off their hard hats out of respect for the dead.

Paramedics began flooding into the blast zone with stretchers and medical gear. A team of EMTs gathered around Ben to assess his injuries and load him onto a stretcher. As they were organizing the lift, two black FBI sedans came speeding into the parking lot, sirens blaring. They screeched to a halt in front of The Highway Diner. Out jumped the four agents who had been at the diner earlier.

"Everybody out of the diner!" the lead agent screamed as three other agents charged inside to clear it out. Anita had told them, only minutes before the explosions, that The Highway Diner and the Trucker Nation Casino were both bomb targets.

Customers began filing out of the diner, along with waitresses, cooks, dishwashers, shoppers, and cashiers from the store. The diner's private security team joined federal agents and scores of local police and firefighters as they began escorting the shocked and frightened citizens across the street to parking lots that were, hopefully, out of harm's way. The bomb squad, clad in protective gear that made them look like deep-sea divers and astronauts, arrived. People began running away from the scene as fast as they could.

Isabel said to Murray, "You stay with Ben. Naomi and I are going back to the diner to see what we can do." They would have charged back into the diner had they not been stopped by emergency personnel. "You need to let us in," Isabel shouted. "We own the place. We can show you where things are."

"No need for that, ma'am," a fire captain said. "What you both need to do is clear out of here for your own safety."

Murray climbed into an ambulance with Ben on a stretcher. She knew it wasn't a good sign when the ambulance turned on its lights and siren and sped out of the parking lot.

Murray sat next to Ben in the ambulance with one medic on his other side, a second medic driving, and a third riding in the front passenger seat. She lowered her head and sobbed as she felt herself slipping into despair. Then she sat up straight in a sudden motion as a voice inside rallied her back into action. She grabbed Ben's hand and leaned down to shout in his face, "Don't give up on us, Ben. Don't give up. We're all going to make it."

Halfway to the hospital, Ben suddenly stopped breathing, and his body shook uncontrollably. Murray scooted over as the two medics tried to hold him still and administer CPR while they held an oxygen mask over his mouth and nose. Ben's body fought back instinctively. Murray had to help hold him down. As she held him with both hands and all her might to keep him in her world, she could feel him slipping away.

By the time they reached the hospital, the medics and Murray were covered in Ben's blood.

Murray was unable to speak as they rushed him into the emergency room. The horrible thought of losing Ben was more than she could bear. He had become more important to her than she thought any man could ever be. He was the one she turned to in happiness and sadness. She thought he would always be there for her to love, no matter what. A flash of vengeful anger shook through her body and nearly knocked her down. She had never felt such violent thoughts. She wanted to kill whoever did this to Ben.

The world began spinning inside Murray's head. Delirium made her dizzy. Her knees got weak. She collapsed onto the sidewalk and had to be carried into the emergency room. Ten minutes later, she regained consciousness in her own hospital bed. She was frantic as she struggled with the nurses, screaming at them to let her go so she could find Ben. She punched and kicked until one of them managed to inject a sedative into her leg.

Murray had terrible nightmares under sedation. She and Ben were in the Intrepid being chased by militiamen. She was driving, and Ben was returning fire. He took a bullet in the chest and slumped over as he bled all over everything. She had to keep driving. She couldn't stop to help him.

CHAPTER TWENTY-SIX

While Murray was in the hospital with Ben, Isabel and Naomi watched and waited from fifty yards away as the search continued for explosives in The Highway Diner. The two traumatized women clasped each other's hands and held each breath they took. Every minute that passed made them more afraid the building would explode into nothingness like the casino an hour earlier.

Isabel could not believe her diner, which had transformed from just another roadside attraction to national prominence, was about to be destroyed. She could still feel herself, not so long ago, in Brodie's arms as he carried her across the threshold of their new business. She saw Murray and her sister playing kickball in the parking lot as the diner evolved into a formidable truck plaza. She remembered trying to keep the business afloat after Brodie died. And the unprecedented success as The Highway Diner came to symbolize a unified distribution system.

Her worry turned to anger. *How dare anyone try to take away everything I worked so hard to build*, she fumed. *I'm going to destroy that evil bastard who calls himself the Commander, even if it kills me. I've suffered terrible losses before, but never at the hands of a murderous maniac. How many people did he kill today?*

At this terrifying crossroads of her life, the woman who had been preaching peace and love was now ready to kill. The shock of bone-shaking explosions and seeing Ben bleeding on the ground had flipped a primal switch in her brain. She shook her head in disbelief as dark emotions boiled. The anger and violent thoughts frightened her. She had never felt anything close to bloodlust. It confused her. How could anything so wrong feel so righteous?

Thoughts of revenge slowly melted down into helpless frustration. There was nothing she could do now but watch and await the fate of her beloved diner.

"I know it's gonna blow," Isabel murmured to Naomi. "There is no way they would bomb the casino and not the diner. There's got to be a bomb in there. The clock is ticking and so is that bomb. There is an evil presence in our diner. I can feel it. It makes me cold. I'm shaking. So are you. Please, God, help them find it."

Naomi squeezed Isabel's hand. "You know what this is? This is an exorcism, plain and simple. Like something out of *The Exorcist*. They ought to bring in the priests."

"It's definitely evil," Isabel said.

Naomi stomped her feet on the pavement. "We have done nothing to deserve this. Nothing. All we've done is work our asses off to keep truckers moving down the road. Now, I'm crying and shaking and about to wet my pants. I'm gonna explode myself."

"I know, I know," Isabel said. "I've gotta pee so bad I can't stand it. Come on, let's run over to the truck wash and hit the ladies' room. If we're fast enough, they won't even try to stop us. It's either that or squat down right here."

"Right behind you," Naomi said as they took off slowly and then sprinted across the street in fine running form to the truck wash. The cops who were guarding the off-limits area yelled, "Stop," but no one tried to catch them.

"Ah," Naomi said afterward as she and Isabel took the time to wash up in the sinks and rinse some of the soot from their hair. "The world does slow down once you take a good long pee."

"Yes, it does," Isabel said. "Yes, it does, indeed, slow down. But I'm still expecting to hear that terrible explosion sound any moment. I don't think I can take much more of this."

"I hear you, Isabel, I hear you," Naomi said. "But I've got a feeling everything's gonna be all right. The FBI is all over this."

As they walked out of the truck wash, they heard excited yelling from inside the diner. Then the FBI agent in charge came out of the diner, dusting off his tight-fitting suit as he walked. The two frantic women ran up and begged him to tell them what was happening.

He was all business, but he smiled broadly when he recognized the owners. "I should kick you out of this restricted area, but you know I won't. We're no longer standing in a danger zone."

Isabel and Naomi threw their arms around him in appreciation. "Our hero," Naomi squealed. The girly outburst was completely out of character for her. She always tried to maintain an exquisite self-control.

The agent hugged them back momentarily and then peeled them off to return to professionalism. "Don't call me your hero. I'm just doing my duty. We got lucky today. Another half hour and none of us would be alive."

Naomi and Isabel became instantly subdued as the agent continued. "So, here's what we've got. And I'll tell you this only if you promise to keep the information confidential." Isabel and Naomi nodded. "The bomb squad located and defused a blast bomb in the diner at 11:52 a.m. It was the size of a compact refrigerator. It was a big one. Maybe even bigger than the two at the casino. It was on wheels and rolled into the crawl space beneath the kitchen, probably from a truck posing as a delivery vehicle. Our dogs sniffed it out and started scratching the floor near the coolers. The timer had been set for 12:30 p.m., clearly designed to kill as many people as possible."

"And now you've got the bomb that didn't explode and all its elements to use as evidence," Naomi said. "I'm assuming you'll run fingerprints and get DNA."

"Exactly," the agent said. "That's the problem with the casino bombing. Most of the evidence blew up."

"I don't need any evidence to know who did all this," Isabel said. "We all know it's that fool up in Michigan who calls himself the Commander. What I don't understand is how anybody can hate everything so much that he wants to kill innocent people. It makes me feel so . . ."

Isabel broke down crying. She was still in shock from the casino bombing. While she was happy to hear the good news about the diner, the defused bomb weighed heavy on her heart. Her precious diner had been targeted for mass murder. The Commander had tried to kill her and everyone she held dear. And he was still on the loose.

———

Isabel arrived at her daughter's bedside two and a half hours after the explosions to find her moaning and thrashing off blankets and sheets. She couldn't grab Murray's legs for fear of getting kicked herself. No nurses were available to assist. The emergency room was so overcrowded that even burn victims were sitting in chairs in the hallways. The hospital had been completely overwhelmed by victims of the explosions.

Isabel screamed for help until nurses came and strapped Murray to her bed with restraints. Murray eventually settled down and into a fitful slumber. About a half hour later, Isabel left Murray's curtained corner of a room to inquire at the nurses' station about Ben's status. All they told her was that Ben had been taken into emergency surgery.

Isabel called Ben's mother. Julia picked up after the first ring. "Oh Isabel, please tell me my Benjamin is all right. I'm watching this awful thing on television right now. They showed a photo of Benjamin and said he was seriously injured. Please tell me he's going to make it."

Isabel fought to keep from blubbering into the phone. "Julia, it's bad. You need to get here right away. He's got a serious head injury, and all I know is they've taken him into surgery. He ran out of the diner after the first explosion and was trying to help at the casino when the second explosion knocked him back quite a way and he hit his head. Murray and I were there with him right away. He was unconscious."

Julia cried and moaned, "No, no, no. This can't be."

"Julia, we don't know what's going to happen at this point. He might come out of the surgery quite well. Nobody seems to know."

Julia regained her composure well enough to ask, "How's Murray holding up?"

"Murray collapsed on the sidewalk outside the emergency room. She's been admitted to the hospital herself—not from the blast. From seeing Ben get hurt."

"Oh no," Julia cried. "So it is that bad." She tried to catch her breath and calm down. She was finally able to say, "All right, hang in there, Isabel. I'll be flying in as soon as I can. I can't believe this is happening to us."

Isabel tried to say goodbye and offer some words of encouragement, but Julia had already hung up.

Murray came out of her sedation just after midnight and

was released by 6:00 a.m. the day after the blast. Her release was expedited to make room for other bombing victims.

Murray and Isabel pestered medical personnel for hours about Ben's status. It was 2:00 p.m. before an exhausted female surgeon finally sat them down in a private room to deliver the diagnosis. She looked up from a medical chart and said, "Benjamin suffered a serious brain bleed from his head injury. Then, he had a massive hemorrhagic stroke in the ambulance. Doctors in the emergency room and neurosurgeons in the operating room worked for hours, and they did bring him back to life. Believe me, we're doing everything we can. The head wound was . . ."

Her voice trailed off as Murray and Isabel burst into tears. The doctor was too tired to provide much comfort. She closed her eyes, sighed deeply, and got up to leave. Isabel stopped her. "Wait, please. We know you tried. Thank you so much. This is so hard for us. We don't want to sound ungrateful. Can you tell us what's going to happen with him?"

"The prognosis is grim, I'm afraid to say." The doctor hung her head and continued in a softer tone. "Benjamin is now on a ventilator because he can't breathe on his own. He's in a coma. It was not medically induced. Being thrown to the ground and hitting his head caused him to bleed profusely, then he went into a seizure and a coma. Brain scans show severe traumatic injury. His skull was badly fractured. I'm sorry, but we cannot say if he will regain consciousness."

———

The day after the bombings, Chase and Leona flew up from Nashville. The diner was sad and empty. It still smelled like fallout from the bombs. Isabel hadn't even made coffee. She hugged Chase and Leona with all her might. They cried together. "It doesn't look good for Ben," she said. "The doctor said he might never regain consciousness."

Chase and Leona gasped in disbelief.

"Oh my God, Isabel. Not our Ben," Leona moaned. "What are we gonna do? What are you gonna do? How is Murray handling all this?"

Isabel looked to the sky as if for guidance. "I don't know how any of us is gonna handle this. The news says thirty-three people were killed at the casino, but they're still finding bodies in the rubble. Worst of all, and I hate to say it, Ben is probably gone."

She bubbled up and started sobbing bitterly. Her knees began to buckle. Chase and Leona grabbed her arms and held her up.

"I know I should be thankful to be alive," Isabel choked on her words. "But I'm not. This whole mess is my fault. All we did was give the world a big target to attack. I should have been killed. It would have been easier."

Chase and Leona helped Isabel take a seat at the round table in the corner of the diner. They didn't say a word. Isabel wasn't finished. "Ben went into harm's way to rescue Anita," Isabel stammered. "He and Murray were both so happy to bring Anita home and back into the fold. She told them the Commander had plans to blow up the casino and the diner. It's not right. Ben and Murray were so much in love. They were perfect together. Now my little girl will suffer for the rest of her life like I did when my Brodie died. But Ben . . . oh, my poor Benjamin. He was so strong and brave. And young and handsome."

Leona took one of Isabel's hands in hers and said, "Maybe there's still hope. Didn't you say the doctors aren't sure?"

Isabel's lower lip quivered. "I saw the look in the doctor's eyes."

Isabel's phone rang. She wasn't going to take the call until she saw it was Ben's mother. "Oh no." She collapsed her arms and head on the table. "I can't take this call. I can't take anything anymore."

Chase answered the phone. Julia's plane had just landed at the Fort Wayne airport. "I'll send a car for you," Chase said. "Look for my man with your name on a sign. No, no. It's no trouble at all. Yes, Isabel is here at the diner. Yes, he's alive. We don't know how he is at this point. He's just out of surgery. Okay, we'll talk in person when you get here. Bye now. See you soon. Glad you're here."

Leona and Isabel stared at him when he ended the call. He held up both hands like he was being frisked. "What? We really don't know what's going to happen with Ben. And even if it is completely hopeless, I wasn't about to tell her on the phone that it looks like her son is dying."

Isabel softened her glare. "So, what are we going to tell her? He's gonna be fine?"

Chase looked to Leona for advice, as he often did on delicate matters. Leona looked him in the eyes as she thought about what to do. Then, she shook her head. "We're not going to tell her anything. We'll let the doctors do that. In fact, Chase, wait a minute. Tell your driver to take Julia straight to the hospital. We can all meet her there."

"I can't go back into that hospital right now," Isabel said. "I just can't. I know I should, but I'll just give it away that he's dying. I saw him bleeding to death. And Murray told me how awful it was in the ambulance."

Chase nodded in understanding. "I think it's a good idea for you to go home and get some rest. You might need medical care yourself. I'll get you a driver and a security detail. Rest up and see how you feel. Leona and I will head out to the hospital. Call us if you need anything."

Isabel nodded numbly and said, "There's something I need to show you both." She rose slowly from her seat as if grief had aged her thirty years. "Come on," she said as she walked them out the front door and around to the back of the diner.

"There," she said, pointing to a wooden section of the wall that had been cut out just above the foundation and was now leaning against the building. "That's how they got in." Isabel shook her head sadly. "They cut it out, then nailed it back up once they planted the bomb. If the bomb squad hadn't found that cutout and gone in after the device, I wouldn't be standing here talking to you. The bomb-squad dogs were barking at the floor, which caused the team to search around the foundation."

Isabel scanned the area. A delivery truck could have driven up close to the diner and blocked the view while men with tools and a bomb slipped around the back. A stand of pine trees kept the rear of the diner hidden from the interstate and even from the service road.

Chase spoke softly to Isabel. "I can tell you're nearing a complete breakdown. I'm a wreck too. The bad news about Ben is hitting me hard."

Isabel seethed in anger. "We all know who did this. When are we gonna blow him up like he blew us up?"

Chase tried to sooth Isabel. "Let's not worry about all that. Right now, I'm worried about you. Are you ready to go home and rest?"

Isabel did not respond as Leona and Chase led her to the front of the diner where a car was already waiting. She went inside the restaurant to grab her keys, then got into the car and waved a sullen goodbye as it left.

Julia walked briskly and bravely into the hospital, leaning forward slightly as if she were walking against a strong wind. Chase and Leona greeted her in the lobby near the front door. One look in their eyes and Julia fell apart. All pretense of composure evaporated into overpowering sadness as she held her head and fell to her knees. "No, no, don't tell me he's already gone."

Chase helped her up as Leona said, "He's not gone, Julia. The doctors don't know how he will respond to the surgery. He's still alive."

A spark of hope flickered in her tearful eyes. "Oh, thank God. I thought you were telling me he was gone and that's why I had to come directly to the hospital. All right, let me try to pull myself together. I know it's not good. I'll try to be strong. Can I see him?"

"Yes," Chase said. "The doctor is waiting for you—but only you. We'll wait here until you call for us."

Chase and Leona had never met Julia, but no one had the emotional time for introductory pleasantries.

Chase summoned a nurse he had talked to upon arrival. She approached in disheveled scrubs and uncombed hair. Hospital staff were still reeling from the overload of casino victims. "You're here to see Benjamin Fitzgerald?" the nurse asked. Julia nodded. The nurse tried to smile, but she was sniffling and fighting back tears of her own. "Come with me. I'll take you to him."

Julia did not turn around to say goodbye. She followed the nurse, who was telling her to not be shocked by her son's situation. "He's on a ventilator now, and he's in a coma. He won't be able to communicate or even know you're here."

Julia did her best to prepare for the worst. It didn't do any good. One look at her helpless son and his entire life flashed before her eyes: holding him as a baby, teaching him how to walk, making him breakfast before his little league baseball games, every time she kissed him goodnight, and every time he kissed her back. Memories flooded her mind as she drowned in sorrow. She clung to the nurse and staggered to Ben's bedside. She let out a wail in agony.

The nurse stepped away from her in startled response to the loud screams of maternal horror and grief. Julia grasped her son's hand and tried to control her outburst, but she couldn't. The wail was her primitive and desperate attempt to wake him. It ended abruptly when she sensed his total lack of response. His cold, lifeless hand caused her to recoil emotionally into a dark silence.

The doctor came in and explained Ben's diagnosis, course of treatment, and prognosis to Julia in detailed terms she could not comprehend and would not remember. She nodded like she was listening, but she wasn't. All she could hear was Ben's voice from his youth, calling for her to come watch his latest bicycle trick.

She stayed in the hospital room with her son for nearly an hour. At one point, she thought his hand twitched, but she realized her mind was playing tricks on her. Ben's body was motionless and still. It was time to leave. She couldn't take it anymore. Any thought of sleeping in the room with him had vanished the moment she saw and heard the dreadful mechanics of the ventilator and life-support equipment. She left the room in search of anything, or anyone, who could confirm she was not dying herself.

Chase and Leona were surprised to see Julia back so soon.

She looked exhausted and completely wrung out. All they could do was hold her and walk her to the car. Julia was in a shocked state of emotional shutdown.

Leona spoke once they were on the road. "I know you're staying with Isabel, but I'm not sure that's such a good idea."

"No, I know what you're trying to say," Julia said with the clarity of someone having a sudden realization. "Isabel is exactly the person I need to be with. She needs to see me too."

Chase and Leona looked at each other warily, but neither tried to talk Julia out of going to see Isabel. The car arrived and the three of them got out slowly. Leona felt like she was wading in waist-deep water.

They walked Julia up the steps to Isabel's house. Chase's two security guards were not in plain view until they approached to identify the visitors. Isabel opened the door and stepped onto the porch to bring Julia into her arms. The two women cried together until they shook their heads at each other in tears and disbelief.

"This is an awful way to finally get together in person," Julia managed to say.

Isabel almost smiled. "I know we both look wretched, but I'm so grateful you're here. Come on in. I'll make us some sausage, biscuits, and gravy. We can talk. I can't sleep. Seeing you reminds me that I haven't eaten in days. Did you go see Benjamin?"

"Yes, I did." Julia hung her head and then raised it up again. "Let me help. I need something to do with my hands besides wringing them out like a wet dishcloth."

The four of them sat down to an 8:00 p.m. breakfast. Leona made a fruit salad and Chase helped with the coffee. They felt relieved to be doing something nearly normal. After the first few bites, though, no one ate much. Chase and Leona told Julia all about Ben's progress in their management agency and in supervising construction of the Trucker Nation Casino. "He is such a fine young man," Chase said, his voice cracking with emotion. "You should be proud. We love him like a son."

"We can always count on Ben," Leona said. "He is the most honest, hardworking, and kind young man we've ever been around."

"Thank you for being there for Benjamin," Julia said. "He loved all three of you so much. He told me all the time how much he . . ." She lowered her head and sobbed softly. Wiping her eyes with a napkin, she raised her head and continued. "I'm sorry. I just can't believe all this is happening. I want to wake up and realize it was all a bad dream. But I am so very grateful we're together. I know I can't get through this on my own."

Isabel grabbed Julia's hand to her left and Leona's hand to her right. Chase completed the circle as Isabel prayed, "Dear Lord, we come to you with terrible sadness in our hearts. We pray that you help Ben recover. We pray that you help him heal. We pray for all those who lost their lives in the bombings and for all those who were injured. We know that you are with us in our suffering. We humbly ask that, as the four of us find strength in each other, we may also find solace and faith in our union with you, our loving and all-knowing God."

"Amen," they said.

There was a knock on the front door. It sounded like God approving of the prayer. Murray walked in. She ran into Julia's arms, and the two of them cried so hard it was impossible for everyone in the room to hold back their tears.

"Julia, I am so, so sorry. He was being brave. I was right behind him. We couldn't—"

"Murray, Murray, Murray. He loves you so much. We all do," Julia said as Murray scooped Isabel and Chase and Leona into their hug.

Murray tried to lighten the mood. "Mom, do I smell your famous sausage, biscuits, and gravy? Why didn't you call me? I'm famished."

It was a tough crowd at a rough time, but Murray managed to get a weak laugh out of them as she sat down to eat. The others watched her wolf down a plateful before she finally looked up and said, "I don't know about you guys, but I'm not giving up on Ben. He's too young and strong to die."

"Oh, Murray, I hope you're right," Julia said. "With all my body and soul, I do hope you're right."

"I love your fighting spirit, Murray," Leona said. "Nobody here is giving up on Ben."

"We'll keep our prayers going strong," Isabel said.

CHAPTER TWENTY-SEVEN

The bombings instantly became a national tragedy. So many truckers rallied to The Highway Diner that they nearly shut down the truck plaza. Isabel and Murray held a press conference to thank truckers for their support. "But please," Isabel said to a tangle and gaggle of microphones, "don't come to The Highway Diner. And if you're already here, please get back on the road. We can't get our trucks and heavy equipment in to clean up the casino bomb site."

Outrage spread from coast to coast. The bombing was roundly condemned and described as an act of domestic terrorism. Late-night talk-show hosts eulogized the victims and paid homage to Trucker Nation and The Highway Diner. People in restaurants, bars, and at family dinner tables across the country watched the television coverage in shocked silence and horror. Children asked their parents why bad things had to happen. Mothers and fathers had no answers.

The President of the United States did not miss his political opportunity. He flew into a press conference at The Highway Diner on a Sikorsky helicopter. Noise from the choppers sounded like an invasion. Heavily armed personnel poured out of the aircraft and spread out around the area. In moments, federal snipers were on every nearby rooftop.

Chase and Leona ushered President Robert Denison and his secret service detail to the stage. He walked up the steps and hugged Murray, Julia, Isabel, and Naomi. He took time to speak with each woman individually as the cameras of the world rolled.

"We are all deeply saddened by what happened here two days ago," President Denison began. "Thirty-seven people were killed and many more are left fighting for their lives. This is clearly an act of war—an act of mass murder that will be met with military resolve. We will find those responsible and bring them to justice. Our response will be swift and decisive."

———

The Commander was watching the speech on television at his bunker headquarters in Michigan. Cal Mavis and Josh Nelson sat with him, drinking beer and whiskey, and smoking high-grade marijuana laced with opium.

"Look at that asshole, Denison," the Commander shouted at the television. "Always on the campaign trail, no matter how bloody it gets. What he's trying to say about a swift response is they don't want another siege that killed all those Branch Davidians and a few ATF agents at the Koresh compound in Waco, Texas."

"What year was that?" Mavis asked.

"Nineteen ninety-three," the Commander answered.

"And how long after that did Timothy McVeigh kill all those women and children in the Oklahoma City bombing?" Nelson asked.

"April 19, 1995," the Commander said. "Exactly two years after Waco. McVeigh was a goddamned hero. He sent a message. You give us Waco, we'll give you Oklahoma City. Gave the feds a dose of their own medicine. Took ''em till 2001 to execute him."

"Amazing," Mavis said. "I can't believe you know all the dates and numbers."

"Don't forget Ruby Ridge," Nelson said. "When was that?"

"That was in August of 1992," the Commander said. "That was the Randy Weaver standoff. The feds lost a US Marshall in a shootout. Then they killed Weaver's wife, his fourteen-year-old son, and even the family dog, Striker. Typical federal overkill."

"So, why do you know so much about this stuff?" Mavis asked.

"It's why we're here today," the Commander said. "We're talking about the rise of the American Militia Movement. It's bigger than all of us. Michigan Militia 714 is one of a thousand units across the country just itching to take this country back."

Nelson and Mavis nodded and waited for the Commander to continue. "Look at that son of a bitch, Denison. He's grandstanding today, stuttering away like always, pretending he gives a shit about the people who died."

The three men listened to a little more of the president's speech before the Commander turned off the television. "That's it. They're coming here. They'll do the same thing to me that they did to Koresh. They'll get a search warrant for suspected stockpiling of illegal weapons and probably one for me for that undercover agent getting killed."

Mavis and Nelson looked at each other in shocked silence.

"Time to buckle up, boys. It's gonna be a rocky ride. First armored vehicle on my property is gonna get blown sky high by my M1 Abrams tank." The Commander had acquired an amazing array of weapons by paying big cash to unscrupulous arms dealers.

The two men did not know how to respond to the Commander's insane belligerence until Mavis finally blurted out, "You're gonna get us all killed if you bring out that tank against the feds."

"What makes you so sure they're coming here?" Nelson asked.

The Commander laughed as he got up to get another bottle of whiskey. "Well, for starters, Josh, you killed their undercover agent. Then Cal here let that little diner girl get away with probably more information than they need to get their warrants."

"So, maybe we should all get the hell out of here," Nelson said.

"Or maybe," Mavis said, "we should let them serve the warrants and fight it out in court."

The Commander poured out three shots. "There's no place to run, Josh, and the courts are all rigged."

"Can anybody prove we planted the bombs?" Mavis asked. "I mean, I don't really have any idea who did the bombing."

"Let me just tell you, then," the Commander said. "It was Jenkins and Alexander, my demolition buddies from Afghanistan. You've been hearing their test explosions for weeks now, so don't try to play dumb. It was supposed to look like gas leaks. But they got to the bomb at The Highway Diner before it exploded. I don't know why it didn't go off with the casino bomb. Somebody must have set the timers wrong. We can't ask Jenkins and Alexander. They moved out of the compound in the dark of night. Didn't even say goodbye. They knew the shit was about to hit the fan. Do you know what it means that The Highway Diner bomb didn't explode?"

Mavis and Nelson shook their heads.

"It means they have all kinds of evidence against us. They can take that bomb apart and track down where every element came from, straight back to the compound. Not to mention fingerprints and DNA. So here, let's have a toast."

Nelson and Mavis looked at each other warily as they raised their glasses. The Commander continued, "Let's drink to going down in a blaze of glory. With any luck at all, militia attacks will break out all over the USA."

Nelson and Mavis downed their shots much more slowly than usual. The Commander's phone rang at the same time his Cobra radio went off. He answered the phone, talked briefly, then issued his order on the internal radio system, "Battle stations. This is not a drill. The feds are moving in. Battle stations."

"They're already here," he said to Mavis and Nelson. "It's go time. We're as ready as we'll ever be."

Mavis and Nelson scrambled to the back room for their gear and weapons. "Shit, shit, shit," Mavis muttered as he fumbled with his body armor. "I didn't sign up to die at the Alamo."

Nelson kept a cooler head. "The Commander is right. There is nowhere to run. Especially now. Stay low. We'll see what happens."

———

Strike teams from the Federal Bureau of Alcohol Tobacco and Firearms had been stealthily closing in for the last hour. Two Navy SEAL teams were also in the hunt on special assignment from the president himself. Support units from the Michigan Army National Guard, more than thirty FBI agents, and Michigan State Police were also in the process of tightening the noose.

There were 123 men and fifteen women in the compound when they all realized it was too late to leave. Federal forces were spotted on multiple perimeter cameras. Once the alarm was sounded, everyone scrambled to his or her defensive assignment. The Commander had convinced his people that he would personally execute anyone who tried to surrender.

The Commander's schoolhouse and adjoining central bunker were on slightly higher ground than the surrounding acres of gently rolling farm fields. The school had been built in the remote location to serve a large rural area. The compound did not look like a military installation. It blended in as part of the landscape.

Militiamen were heavily armed with FGM-148 Javelin anti-tank missiles and surface-to-air missiles. Firing positions were reinforced concrete trenches, covered by plate steel roofs with natural overgrowth. The bunkers could withstand mortar attack. The narrow shooting gap between the concrete foundations and steel tops made them hard to take out with missiles. Each bunker had a tunnel connecting it to the main bunker. The Commander had spent more than ten years and millions of dollars creating his circle of defense. Twelve combat bunkers surrounded the schoolhouse like numbers on a clock. The compound had a diameter of half a mile.

Government undercover intelligence had reported all this and described the compound as "a tough nut to crack." Sending a SWAT team in an armored vehicle to serve arrest warrants would only be a suicide mission. A siege was out of the question. The casino bombings warranted immediate attack to prevent additional loss of life.

All news outlets shifted coverage from the president's speech at The Highway Diner to what television reporters were already calling the Battle of Newaygo. News media vehicles gathered quickly, just outside the front gate of the compound on the south side. The entrance had ten-foot pillars of stacked stone columns connected by an ornamental steel gate. A chain-link fence with slanted barbed wire on top stretched out from each pillar to surround the compound. The place looked like a luxury retirement community from the front gate if one didn't notice the barbed wire.

The federal public relations officer outside the compound

told all members of the media that Militia Unit 714 had been informed by electronic communications of its options. "Basically," the officer said as he shook his head sadly, "they've been given good notice that failure to surrender will result in an immediate military attack on their facility. They have elected to not surrender."

As the officer spoke into the cameras, a Javelin missile from the militia screamed into the area and exploded the CNN news truck, killing one reporter and seriously injuring three others. No one had suspected an attack on the media. Panic took over as reporters abandoned their cars and trucks in a mad scramble to get as far from the gate as possible.

The public relations officer instinctively hit the ground as the news truck exploded. He got to his feet quickly, doing his best to remain calm under fire, knowing this was perhaps his best and last chance for fifteen minutes of fame. "There you have it," he said. "The compound has openly declared its disdain for the rule of law." With that he discontinued the interview.

Federal mortar fire unleashed a deadly barrage and homed in on the bunker nearest the front entrance to the compound. The militia responded with heavy machine gun fire from M2 Brownings on tripods. As three militia bunkers opened fire, full-powered magnum rounds cut down trees on either side of the fencing and riddled news vehicles with bullet holes.

As the battle raged near the front gate on the south side of the compound, a Navy SEAL team surprised militia defenders at a bunker on the northeast side. One SEAL silently slit the throat of the only guard outside the bunker. The team entered the militia firing position through the back door. Four militiamen were killed before they had time to turn around.

The SEAL team found easy access to the tunnel system by

way of a steel door at the back of the bunker. They entered warily. It was pitch black, but they were well prepared. They turned on their headlamps and moved cautiously underground toward the center of the compound.

———

The Commander saw the north bunker, number twelve, being blasted by mortar fire as he watched his monitor system in the command bunker. At the same time, he saw a bunker on the east side, number three, on the brink of losing its battle with federal armored vehicles. A Dingo 1 mine-resistant vehicle was on the bunker roof, firing into the compound with its remotely controlled 7.62 mm machine gun.

"Looks like everybody wants in on this party," he shouted to Cal Mavis, who was shocked into silence by the fury of the federal assault. "Time for me to get to work. Watch the monitors, Cal. You're in charge of the command bunker now."

Mavis turned to Josh Nelson once the Commander had left and said, "I don't want to be in charge. Why don't you take over?"

"Take over what?" Nelson asked. "We're getting hammered on every monitor screen."

The Commander ran through a tunnel from the command bunker to the half-buried steel Quonset hut housing the M1 Abrams tank. His gunner, loader, and driver were waiting and ready, each man a well-trained and angry veteran of the war. "About time you got here," the gunner said. "Are we ready to kick some ass or what?"

"Let's go get 'em, boys," the Commander ordered as he jumped in and took command. The massive killing machine roared out with its main gun blasting 120 mm artillery shells. The Dingo 1 on top of bunker three, the east bunker, was demolished by a direct hit from the Abrams. Two more armored vehicles were destroyed between bunkers one and two before the tank swiveled on its tracks to charge south at nearly forty miles an hour.

The site of a rogue M1 Abrams on a mission of annihilation struck terror into the hearts of all attackers who saw it coming. The tank was equipped with the latest Active Protection System, which used radar and computer processing to knock down and intercept rocket-propelled grenades and anti-tank guided missiles. The Abrams destroyed three incoming RPGs in rapid succession as the Commander continued to dominate his combat arena.

As a US Army Apache helicopter swooped in to attack, the hunter tank looked like it was about to become easy prey. But the Apache came in too fast and low. Its missiles overshot the tank and exploded an entire hillside outside the compound. The helicopter made a steeply angled turn to come back for another attack run.

That gave the militia all the time it needed. Two SAM missiles were launched by gunners outside the command bunker before the chopper could line up another shot. The Apache took a direct hit from the first SAM and exploded into a ball of fire. A hail of metal shrapnel from the obliterated helicopter caused casualties on advancing federal forces. Both pilots in the Apache's tandem cockpit were dead before the flaming wreckage hit the ground.

Militiamen cheered as the singed-kerosene smell of exploded helicopter fuel permeated the area. The Commander shouted into his helmet microphone, "Looks like we got us a no-fly zone, boys. Keep pounding the bastards."

The tank avoided mortar and other fire by moving at a high rate of speed on a road grid designed by the Commander for evasive maneuvers, all the while delivering brutal blows against federal forces on the perimeter of the compound. The Abrams ammunition loader was well trained and fast, which meant the sixty-eight-ton tank could fire one round every three to five seconds. The murderous barrage inflicted heavy casualties on the attackers.

Even so, all militia-firing bunkers were under relentless attack from the Army National Guard, which arrived with Javelin missiles of its own. The vicious, nonstop explosions could be heard miles from the raging battle. It sounded like a war zone, which is exactly what it was.

Losses from missile, tank, and small arms fire were mounting steadily on both sides.

An Army Javelin missile struck a direct hit on the southwest militia bunker number eight. It penetrated through the shooting space and blew off half the roof. Machine gun fire stopped abruptly. National Guard forces advanced on what they had assumed was an empty bunker.

Three militiamen in the bunker had been killed, but two men survived because they were in the tunnel when the missile struck. One of the machine guns, amazingly, was still operational. Bunker reinforcements used it to kill four Guardsman and injure many more. "Is that all you got," a militiaman screamed as he paused his killing spree. "Come on! Keep coming! I got more where that came from!"

Militia bravado notwithstanding, the number eight bunker was silenced and buried within minutes by a vengeful concentration of mortar fire.

Still, the tank continued to dominate all 360 degrees of the compound. It was fast and deadly and occasionally disappeared into long trenches designed to protect it from rocket attacks. Bunker number four was being overrun on the southeast quadrant of the compound's circular defense. The Abrams tank leaped out of the trench like a lion on the hunt. Its big gun blasted the position to keep federal forces from advancing.

As the tank kept attackers at bay, the Commander's luck finally ran out. The Abrams tank took a federal Javelin missile hit that disabled its right tread. It came to a steel-crunching halt even as it fired another round. Seconds later, the top hatch of the tank popped open. It was hard to see through all the dust and fog of war, but it looked like the crew might begin evacuating.

Then, lightning struck. The tank was blasted to bits by a drone strike before the tank crew got out. No one saw it coming. The drone was high enough in the sky to be invisible to the human eye. To anyone on the ground, it looked like the tank exploded from within. The drone missile turned the most powerful tank in the world into bits of metal too small to be identified.

The terrifying blast of what amounted to a death ray from the sky left a sudden and sullen silence on the battlefield. All witnesses were spellbound by the shock and awe. The Commander had mistakenly assumed the federal government would not have clearance to use a military drone on American citizens, no matter how anti-American they had become.

Once the tank vaporized into a plume of smoke, militia fighters began surrendering. Losing the Commander burst their bubble of revolutionary zeal. They could see they were heavily outgunned by a military force much more determined than they thought possible. Many who feared they would be fighting to the death found themselves vastly relieved to still be breathing after such a horrendous firefight. Militiamen emerged from their bunkers with hands raised. A few turned T-shirts and soiled rags into white flags. Federal troops were so stunned by the surreal vaporization of the tank that they held their fire long enough to see the compound had given up the fight.

Mavis and Nelson watched the surrender from video monitors in the command bunker. Mavis looked on in stunned curiosity as Nelson grabbed two hand grenades without saying a word and headed for the door. "What the hell you doin'?" Mavis called after him.

Nelson only shook his head sorrowfully as he walked slowly out of the command bunker, shouting that he wanted to surrender. His hands were behind his back, not over his head. As a squad of ATF agents approached, he rolled out a grenade that exploded, killing two agents, and severely wounding a third.

Then Nelson clutched the second live grenade to his stomach as it blew him to bloody bits.

Mavis watched Nelson's suicide in trembling dismay on the video monitor. Nelson had told him many times that he would not be taken alive to spend the rest of his life in prison. Still, it was a shocking and sickening moment to witness. Mavis felt what little courage he had drain out of him as he realized he was pissing himself. His arms and legs were shaking. He did not want to die. His hands were frozen in fear as he remained in the command bunker, trying to think about what he could do to survive.

Federal agents surrounded the bunker and called out for anyone inside to come out peacefully. Mavis realized he was being thrown a lifeline. He opened the rear door of the bunker slowly and called out that he wanted to surrender. He threw out his rifle first, then his handgun, and then walked out slowly with his hands up, screaming, "Don't shoot. I got no weapons. No explosives. Don't shoot. I surrender."

Federal troops handcuffed Mavis and everybody else who surrendered, except the seriously wounded. The prisoners who could walk were herded into waiting transport vans and hauled across the state to the federal prison in Milan, Michigan.

CHAPTER TWENTY-EIGHT

The Highway Diner crew gathered around the television and watched in horror as the war unfolded before their eyes. The Commander's tank had exploded. Murray was shaking. *The bastard is dead,* she thought.

None of them were prepared for what they saw. News media had launched camera drones so the brutality of battle was captured on film, close up and in living color. Drones were feeding images back to news trucks until the moment they were blasted out of the sky by either the militia or the ATF.

"Oh my God," Chase groaned as the M1 Abrams tank rolled into view. "The Commander has gone completely mad."

"Somebody kill that bastard," Isabel hissed through clenched teeth. The hatred coming out of her mouth startled her. She was nauseated by the violence, but the fear building up for months had turned to anger.

"Serves him right," Murray said. "He's been waiting his whole life for this moment of glory. He knew it was a suicide mission. He planned for it. She hung her head in disbelief. The whole military mess was nothing but madness. She had wanted to see the Commander pay for what he did to Ben, but it was hard to watch it happen. Even the warrior inside of her wanted to cry.

Julia sobbed. "I wish my Benjamin were here to watch that crazy fool die."

It was hard for anyone to believe the tank had been

obliterated so quickly after looking so invincible only moments before. "Only a few seconds between the tank tread getting hit and the drone strike," Chase observed. "Nobody got out of that tank. The Commander didn't go down in a blaze of glory. He went up in a puff of smoke."

"So, that's it?" Isabel said. "The evil force is gone in the twinkling of an eye? Are we sure the Commander was even in the tank? Wouldn't it be more like him to have somebody else drive the tank while he escaped through one of his tunnels?"

"No," Chase said. "Neil, the undercover agent who got killed, told me the Commander was the only one who ever commanded the Abrams. It was his special toy, and he never let anyone else control it. He and his three-man crew trained in it all the time. They got very good as a team, but he was always in charge. He didn't call himself the Commander for nothing."

"The whole thing makes me so sad," Leona said as tears streamed down her cheeks. "Looks like a lot of people died for no good reason. I saw a woman go down. Did you see her running out of the bunker? She got hit by so many bullets it looked like she was dancing. You couldn't even tell which side killed her. Had to be dead before she hit the ground. I'm amazed they showed all that on live television."

"We all saw it, and none of us will ever unsee it," Naomi said. "I'm sure the television people were so glued to the screen they forgot to hit the edit button or whatever they do to cut out the really bad stuff. It won't be on the reruns, that's for sure."

Murray was consumed with combat adrenalin as she watched the battle and thrilled when the Commander's tank had been destroyed. "I still don't believe the Commander is dead. It hasn't sunk in yet. It doesn't feel real. It's like a movie that ended so fast you weren't ready for it to be over."

The Highway Diner team continued watching the militia

surrendering. Everyone was emotionally exhausted and disgusted by what they had seen on live television. Suddenly, Cal Mavis came out of the command bunker with his hands over his head.

"Shoot that little weasel," Isabel shouted. "He's the one who kidnapped Anita."

"Anita warned us about the bombs," Murray said. "She told us the Commander had plans to bomb the diner."

"Too bad she didn't get to us in time to save the casino," Julia said. "Benjamin wouldn't be in the hospital fighting for his life."

Nobody said a word as the truth of that remark settled in.

Chase finally broke the ice. "I've never seen anything like that on television. I don't think anybody has. But we all realize what this means, don't we?"

Isabel responded, "Don't try to tell me 'Ding dong, the witch is dead.' I'm sorry, but I don't feel that way. Not yet anyway."

"I know what you mean," Naomi said. "How many more commanders are out there?"

"At least the one who tried to kill us all is dead," Murray said.

"That's what it means." Chase pointed his finger at Murray. "Our enemy has been eliminated. We can all rest a lot easier now. In fact, it could be time for a little celebration."

All present groaned their disapproval at the thought of celebrating the carnage they had just witnessed. Chase nodded to show his withdrawal of the proposal.

Losses from the battle were horrific. Federal forces had 44 killed and 121 wounded. Michigan Militia 714 had lost 23 men and 5 women, 58 wounded.

Three weeks after the bombings, the casino wreckage was getting cleared away to the point that Naomi and Isabel were preparing to reopen the diner. Isabel was navigating a hectic Tuesday morning when Blake called.

"Hello, Isabel," he said, then waited for her to respond. She was too surprised to speak, so he continued cautiously. "Listen, I'm calling again to say I'm sorry. I'm not looking for forgiveness. I know all that's gonna take some time."

"It's good to hear your voice, Blake." Isabel collected her thoughts and interrupted his prepared speech. "And believe it or not, I'd love to see you again. But not for a while. We're all still going through quite a lot here. I know it's been hard for you, too, and I'm proud of you for trying to stay sober."

"The worst part of all this is not being able to be there for you, Blake said."

"Thank you, Blake. That means a lot. It really does. But let's not talk about it on the phone. Tell you what. I'll call you when I'm ready."

"All right, Isabel, I understand. Don't forget I still love you."

"Good luck with your program, Blake. We'll get together when you've got a couple months of clean time."

Naomi watched in awe as Isabel hung up the phone and sat down hard on a wooden chair. "I'll say one thing for that boy," Naomi said. "He's got a lot of nerve calling you after all he's put you through."

"The worst part is the sound of his voice still makes me remember all the good times we had. And I am *so* glad he called."

"What you got? A bad-boy thing?"

"No," Isabel said. "Blake's not really a bad guy. He just does stupid stuff when he's drunk and high, like everybody.

I hope he stays clean. I really do. In fact, I'm pretty sure he'll stay sober. He stuck it out to the end in rehab, anyway. That's a good sign. He sounded good on the phone—too good. That's the thing about Blake. I love his songs and his voice and all the sweet things he does, like send flowers and write songs he says are about me."

"Listen to you," Naomi chided. "If I didn't know better, I'd think you've still got it bad for him."

"I guess I do," Isabel sighed. "But we'll have to see how he does. I'm too worried about Murray right now to pay much attention to the Blake drama. And I hate to admit it, but I'm a little jealous of all the time she's spending with Julia at the hospital.

"We both know they're just bonding over Ben dying . . . I mean, I hope he's not dying. But you know what I'm saying. Besides, you and I spend most of our time together at this diner and all that's going on."

"I know. Maybe I just feel guilty for not being with her more. But every time I go visit, I feel like a third wheel on a bicycle. Murray and Julia were so much closer to Ben than I ever was. But—oh my sweet Jesus—Murray's going to suffer more than she knows. There's no end to it, losing the one man you thought you'd love forever. I'll never get over watching Brodie die so young."

———

Murray and Julia left Ben's hospital room to take a break in the basement cafeteria. "I'm afraid it's time," Julia said. They had been at the hospital every day since the bombings three weeks ago.

Murray grabbed her hand and said nothing as they stepped into the elevator. The two women had become inseparable as their vigil progressed. At first, they encouraged each other to be hopeful. But Ben's brain scans continued to show no active brain function. They got a sandwich and some tea and sat down at a small table in the back corner of the cafeteria.

"What about your daughter?" Murray asked. "Isn't she supposed to come visit before we do anything?"

Julia sighed so heavily she had to take a sip of tea to recover. "Stephanie's not coming."

"What? She doesn't want to see her brother?"

"Not like this," Julia said. "Says she doesn't want to remember him as a vegetable."

"Oh no! She didn't say it like that, did she?"

Julia lowered her head. Murray resisted the urge to call Stephanie a coward for not coming to help her mother through Ben's ordeal. Instead, she asked Julia a question that had been on her mind for some time. "She's not blaming me and Mom and The Highway Diner for getting her brother killed, is she?"

Julia's head jerked up so fast that Murray realized her question had resonated with the ring of truth. Julia looked like she'd been caught shoplifting. The guilt on her face revealed she'd had those feelings herself.

She recovered as best she could. "You know, I think there was a little of that at first. The Highway Diner rise to fame was so fast it made everybody wonder if it was real or if it would last. Stephanie thought—and I did too until I met you—that Benjamin had been blinded by all the hoopla. But she knows better now. We've had long talks about it. She knows Benjamin was only following his heart. Both my kids know that's the only way to live. So, no. That's not totally it. What might be truer is that you're here with me and she isn't."

"She could change that," Murray said. "We could change that. She could come out and I could stay away."

"Actually, no. Stephanie really does want to meet you. We were supposed to get together in Sausalito, you know, but you and Benjamin had to leave when that Anita interview made national news. So now we've been talking about how to get you two together. And I've been thinking about how to get the Intrepid back to California." She pursed her lips and raised her eyebrows.

"Yes, we will drive the Intrepid together, back to Sausalito, so I can get together with Stephanie," said Murray. "Maybe we could try painting again on the way."

Julia flashed a big smile. "That would mean so much to me. And, yes, we can try. It might be too soon to get creative, but we should try. I made a big mistake when I stopped painting after my husband left. I let the sadness take me down. I thought I would never do it again. I don't want to let that happen again. Life's too short. Plus, once I started making my comeback, I realized that painting is the best therapy for grief. After a while, it starts replacing bad feelings with good ones."

"We could help each other by doing it together," Murray said. "We might be able to actually start living again."

"Yes," Julia said. "We can even take Benjamin along for the ride in our hearts."

Murray broke down in tears again. Julia joined her. They both knew it was time. The doctors had told them it was time a week ago. What hadn't made sense a week ago now felt like the only thing to do. Neither woman had been able to make the final decision on Ben's condition until she had imagined a plan for her immediate future.

"There is no doubt in my mind what Benjamin would want us to do," Julia said.

"I know."

"Does your mother want to be here?"

"No, she knows it's up to the two of us."

They left their half-eaten sandwiches on the tray, took the elevator up to Ben's floor, and told the doctors they were ready.

Murray and Julia clung to each other like survivors in a lifeboat watching the *Titanic* sink. The medical team came in with somber faces. They said nothing as they disconnected the machines keeping Ben alive. Blinking lights disappeared with beeping blips of finality.

Nothing happened to Ben when the lights went out. No last gasp for air, no death rattle. Nothing. Ben had died in the ambulance three weeks earlier. His skin color had turned from gray to light blue.

Murray closed her eyes and turned away during the ventilator extubation process. The sucking sounds of the tube being removed made her wish she had covered their ears. Tears flowed as she opened her eyes and turned around to watch the body being removed from the room. She didn't follow down the hall. Benjamin Fitzgerald was gone but far from forgotten.

CHAPTER TWENTY-NINE

Anita came back to work at the diner to help Isabel and Naomi get ready to reopen it. It had been five days since Ben's official death, and Murray was a mess. Everyone was still in emotional shock from the murderous thunder of the casino bombing and the televised killing at the militia compound.

Half the workers decided not to come back after the bombings. It didn't matter how good the pay and benefits were or how glamorous the high-profile employer was. Many still saw The Highway Diner as a target for the far-right militia.

Chase was against reopening so soon after the attack. "It's only three weeks since the Commander went up in smoke," he said to Isabel. "You need to take some time off to heal. I know you think getting back to work is the best medicine, but it isn't. It takes time to get over something like this. Besides, you're in high demand now for television appearances and publishing deals. I could book you three hundred and sixty-five days a year. You should focus on telling your story."

"Let 'em do a story on how we're getting this place up and running," Isabel said loud enough for anyone working in the restaurant to hear. "I'll talk all day about how no Q-Anon thug with a tank is gonna run me out of business."

Leona clapped her hands in agreement. "Think about it, Chase. It's a better story this way. Isabel fighting back to reopen is bigger than the militia and the bombs. It's about women not being intimidated or defeated by men. It's about the economy not being broken by the politics of hate. Isabel's determination is a much more compelling narrative than a woman hitting the late-night talk-show circuit to talk about how sad and wounded she is."

Chase had no quick response. He looked at Leona, then at Isabel, who was nodding in agreement. Naomi joined in. "As far as The Highway Diner goes, Isabel needs to show the world that we're on the comeback trail."

Isabel and Leona and Naomi cheered each other in agreement and started dancing and high-fiving in what looked more like a war dance than a celebration. Isabella was chanting, "Open up, open up, open up."

Chase held up his hands. "All right, all right. I can see I'm outnumbered. And, yes, I do see your point. You can't keep a good woman down. So, how about this? All the interviews I book will be conducted outside the diner so as not to interfere with the reopening process."

"That's my boy," Leona said as she hugged him. Isabel and Naomi burst into laughter. Chase knew better than to try and tell his work-wife what to do. For all practical purposes, they were a married couple. Neither had ever married. Whether or not they were having sex was an oft-discussed topic among all who knew them. Mercifully, they had abandoned the blonde twin look. Chase looked much more distinguished as a silver fox.

As for Anita, she was working twelve-hour shifts at the diner with a two-hour break in the middle of the day to attend twelve-step Narcotics Anonymous meetings. The FBI sent her to psychiatric counseling sessions. The counselor released her with a glowing report that concluded, "Anita has made a remarkable recovery, considering the intense traumatic experience she endured during her captivity."

"Damn straight," Anita said out loud as she finished reading the report.

Murray and Julia came to work at the diner after Ben's cremation. They held off on their plans for California since they were obviously needed for the reopening. The frantic pace of business at the diner and truck plaza was therapeutic for all involved. Everybody focused on the reopening and tried not to talk about the grief and anxiety they were still trying to process. Most were seeing therapists. The Highway Diner paid all bills for mental health counseling.

Murray was pretty sure she would never get over the loss of Ben, although she did not seek psychiatric help. She was in emotional shock. Her life felt surreal without Ben. She wasn't wallowing in grief. She kept expecting him to walk in the door any minute. Murray was confused by her feelings. Part of her felt angry, like Ben had stood her up for the prom. Mostly, though, she felt empty, especially when she realized he was never coming back. That was the hard part, the finality of it all.

She started running with a vengeance at her old high school track. Quarter-mile sprints were her favorite since they hurt so bad at the end. The burn in her chest from lack of oxygen temporarily supplanted her emotional pain. Then, the sadness returned as she walked a cool-down lap. It was so overwhelming it nearly drove her to her knees. Tears blinded her. She was glad to be alone so she could talk to Ben. Most of the time she called out, "Where did you go? Why did you leave me?"

But she kept walking, and by the end of a quarter mile lap, she usually felt a little better.

She was inexplicably wary that the Commander might be alive. She bought herself two AR-15 rifles and spent considerable time at the firing range. "Shooting therapy is all I need," she was fond of saying. Even as she said it, she knew it wasn't true. But she kept saying it because it made her feel better.

Beneath the bravado, Murray was most afraid that vengeful thoughts had changed her into an angry, violent person who could never get back to being a creative soul. Life had taken a terrible turn for her since Ben's death. She had been on the comeback trail from trauma and drama at the diner when the bombing turned everything upside down and inside out all over again.

Isabel confronted her daughter. "You're stuffing your real feelings into an unhealthy bag of grief avoidance. All this running at the track and shooting at the range won't help you get over Ben. How many times do I have to tell you. You'll never get over this. I'm not over your father leaving me alone with you and a truck stop. I don't want to be over him. Won't you at least talk to me about it?" she pleaded.

"What's left to say?" Murray said. "I lost the love of my life, and you lost Daddy, and neither one of us is ever going to be the same. It serves me right for thinking I was gonna be the lucky one."

"Oh, my sweet, sweet Muriel," Isabel tried to comfort her. "I wish we didn't have to go through any of this. And, I hate to say it, but I've learned at least one thing in my forty-two years."

"What?" Murray asked as her toughness tumbled into tears.

"Nobody gets off easy in this life. Nobody." Isabel pulled Murray into her arms.

"That really doesn't help at all, Mom. What are you saying? I've just gotta suck it up like everybody else?"

"No, no. I'm sorry, honey. What I should be saying is that

things will get better in time. In their own sweet time, not on our schedule. The worst thing I did after your father died was try to get over it. This grief you're feeling isn't something you can get over. It's something you've got to go through."

"Why?" Murray cried. "What happens if I ever get through this?"

Isabel stroked her hair and whispered, "You'll get him back. Not physically. It's a spiritual thing. You won't see him or touch him. But you'll be able to feel him and take his heart with you wherever you go."

"Is that the way it is with you and Daddy?"

"Absolutely, my sweet, sweet Muriel. Absolutely."

———

Murray caught up with Anita in the kitchen late one afternoon. "I haven't properly thanked you for being so brave," Murray said. "You saved the diner by escaping. If you hadn't run from the Commander, we wouldn't have gotten the warning and found the bomb before it blew."

Anita looked at Murray with deep sadness in her eyes. "I'm so sorry about Ben. I haven't had a chance to say that to you up close and personal. It's got to be so hard. You two were perfect together."

Murray's eyes filled with tears. "Thank you, Nita. I never knew it could be this hard. I mean, we lost my little sister and then my father. But this is worse. It feels like my heart and soul got crushed by a giant steamroller. I never hurt this bad emotionally—and physically too. It feels like someone beat me all over with a hammer. I can't sleep. I don't want to eat. Don't get me wrong. I'm gonna carry on . . . I know that. But right now, I don't know how."

"Wish I'd made my break a few days earlier," Anita said. "But I ran as soon as I could after hearing the Commander talk about blowing up the diner."

"You should not feel guilty about anything," Murray said.

"No, I'm not blaming myself," Anita said. "I know the bastards who did what they did. I was lucky to get out of there alive, especially after they got me all doped up."

"I knew it wasn't you talking on television," Murray said.

Anita nodded and lowered her voice. "I'm glad to be clean, but I've been having terrible thoughts lately."

"About what?"

"I don't think he's dead," Anita whispered. "I can't explain it. He was such an evil force. I'm not feeling any relief that he's gone. If he was really gone, I'd feel it, don't you think?"

Murray nodded as Anita continued. "He's coming to me in my dreams. I'm telling you, it's so real I can smell the whiskey on his breath and that funky odor he always got from his damned tunnels. In the dreams, he's always saying shit like, 'The two of us should hook up now that Mavis is in prison.'"

Murray covered her mouth with her hands. Then she spoke in a hushed, awed whisper. "I can't believe you just said that. I've been having dreams too . . . bad ones about Ben. He comes into the bedroom and wakes me up with a gentle kiss. Then, he gets serious and tells me to watch out for my mother. He says the Commander isn't dead and he's coming after us."

"You know," Anita said, "if he is alive, he'd be the one to seek revenge on The Highway Diner for destroying his world. He'd need to blame somebody. Otherwise, he'd have to take responsibility himself. But here's the worst part: every time I think of him, I get to feeling violent. Like I want to hurt him. This is new to me. I never wanted to hurt anybody in my life."

"Even if he is dead," Murray said, "I feel the same way you

do. It's like he's ruined us for life. I find myself daydreaming about ways to hurt him if he is still alive. And I mean hurt him physically. But the worst part is, I'm so angry inside I can't paint anymore. Every time I try, I see people dying. I hear the screams and feel the explosions in my chest."

"Yes, yes, I know what you mean. It's like the old me has been replaced by some bad-ass bitch who wants to—"

"Who wants to hurt anybody who ever caused her pain," Murray responded.

Anita nodded. "Exactly. And that makes it hard to even be kind. I have to force myself to smile and say nice things. So, I can see why it would be a real problem with trying to be creative."

"It's more than a problem," Murray said. "It's life and death for an artist. I'm hoping it's something I'll get over, but it doesn't feel that way right now. Julia and I are already beginning our painting therapy. It's not working yet, but she says it will in time."

Anita shook her head in sorrow. Murray asked, "Here's something I've been wanting to ask you. It's about the Commander. You spent time with him, and you got to know him. What was he like? Why was he so hateful?"

Anita sat down on a stool and motioned for Murray to join her. "This might surprise you, but he had a lot of good qualities. For one thing, he was a good-looking man. He would have looked like a movie star if he'd shaved his beard and cut his hair."

"Maybe that's why you dream about him?" Murray teased.

"Easy, there, girl. I'm just saying. He's a hard worker and smart as hell."

"You do realize you're talking about him like he's still alive," Murray said.

Anita's eyes widened as she nodded her head.

"So, why was he so mean?" Murray asked. "I mean, it seems like the man killed people for sport."

"He killed too many people when he was serving in Afghanistan to ever come back to any kind of peace. He's got zero peace of mind. That's why he drinks and takes drugs. He thinks it helps, but it only makes it worse. That kind of violence gets stuck in your head so deep you can never get it out. We know, now it's in our heads too. It's deep, deep grooves. I saw it at the compound. Most of the men who lived there were ticking time bombs. Anger and violence eat them alive. Even the female vets. Cal Mavis was the only one with any semblance of mental health. That's because he never went to war. I'm not saying all veterans are mentally ill. But most of them who join these fanatical groups are truly sick. Some of them are so mad at the world they're suicidal, or close to it. There were two suicides in the compound just in the time I was there."

"So, it's true," Murray said.

"What's true?"

"The militia is caused by all the wars we fight that never end."

"They'll say it's gun rights and too much government," Anita said, nodding. "But it's all about the wars. Violence causes violence. We've got armies of emotionally crippled veterans coming home every day to prove it. We've got what? Seven thousand suicides a year? These are more than individual tragedies. These are cries for help from a sick and psychologically wounded nation."

"Whoa," Murray said. "I never figured you for being such a radical thinker."

"Watch it, girl," Anita said with a smile. "You're dangerously close to saying you're smarter than me. You always thought that. I didn't mind. I knew it wasn't true."

The two were laughing together when Isabel walked into the kitchen. "What's so funny, ladies?"

Murray straightened up enough to answer. "We're just joking around about which one of us is smarter."

"I say you're both pretty damn smart," Isabel said. "And I, for one, am happy to hear some good cheer around here. We can't make a comeback until we can do it with a smile."

"We were also talking." Murray hesitated before opening a topic that might worry her mother. She wasn't going to mention it until Anita said she was having the same kind of dreams and intuitions. Her mother waited until Murray continued. "We were talking about the feelings we're having that the Commander is not dead."

Isabel paused to consider her response before saying, "It doesn't surprise me. He was one frightening man. None of us are gonna get over him any time soon. It might help you both to know that I'm not having dreams about the man. In fact, I don't care if he's dead or alive. We kicked his ass either way."

"Don't you believe in dream messages?" Anita asked.

"The only dreams I'm having are nightmares about the bombs and the killings. I wake up three or four times a night with explosions in my head. That, and ones about trying to get this place back open." She turned to leave the kitchen and said over her shoulder, "Speaking of the reopen, I've got a potato delivery to handle."

"She sounds so confident," Anita said after Isabel left.

"She's not," Murray said. "She's a pro at covering up. I can tell she's scared by the way she throws herself into all this work. She and Naomi never stop. I don't know if you've noticed."

Anita chuckled and pointed at Murray. "Neither do we."

The Highway Diner reopened on Friday, September 22, 2023. Isabel and Naomi picked the day because the calendar said it was American Businesswomen's Day. "It's not exactly a national holiday, but it's as good a day as any."

Chase and Leona talked about having a big media event for the reopening with a press conference and maybe even bringing in Diamond Lil for a guest appearance.

"No, no." Isabel waved both hands. "This thing is already out of control. The media will be here anyway."

"Isabel is absolutely correct," Naomi added. "We've got a severe parking shortage with all the casino construction going on. Nobody will be able to get within a mile of this place as it is. Trucker Nation is gearing up to make a big-rig statement. Our phones are ringing nonstop. We can't answer the calls. The website is blowing up all day, every day. We're viral on social media. Let's hold off on Diamond Lil until we at least get the casino built."

Leona had to agree. "One thing about you, Naomi: you know how to lay out the basic facts to support your position."

Isabel was giving five interviews a day, no more, no less. Chase and Leona scheduled them quite ethically. They did not allow the media to pay for access. Murray participated in as many sessions as she could handle without falling apart over Ben.

Television interviews were conducted beneath the new neon sign over the front door that said, "The Highway Diner." The sign was twenty feet long and ten feet tall. It could be seen at night from half a mile away. The neon changed color from blue to green every ten seconds. Chase wanted it to flash, but Isabel and Naomi vetoed that in a hurry.

"You're gonna make us look like a casino," Isabel scolded. "Let the casino look like a casino. We need to look like the little old diner we've always been. You know, the little engine that could."

The masses flocked to the diner on opening day without any apparent concern for their personal safety. They did have plenty of difficulty navigating the parking madness and making slow progress through crowd-controlled access corridors.

Fox News and CNN covered the opening in a rare display of television unity. Reporters from each news outlet interviewed people as they arrived and as they left. One middle-aged woman from Bend, Oregon, told CNN, "My husband and I wouldn't miss this for anything. We drove more than two thousand miles in an eighteen-wheeler to get here. I drove half that myself. We're here to meet Isabel and Murray and tell them how much we love them."

The interviews demonstrated that Isabel and Murray had become influential new faces for women's rights. As one woman told Fox News, "Don't you think it's great that two gals from Indiana can run a truck-stop flag right up to the top of the pole for equal rights?"

All the women of The Highway Diner had learned not to take sides on political issues, particularly not the right-to-life, right-to-an-abortion drama. Chase had been carefully coaching them about not commenting on the US Supreme Court overturning *Roe v. Wade* in 2022. "The Highway Diner stands for bringing the country back together," he said. "You'll never do that by taking sides in an argument neither side will ever win."

Naomi said her favorite television interviews about the diner were people leaving after eating and shopping. "They all loved the food and the prices and the service," she said. "Unbelievable, everything went smoothly. We served more than twenty-five hundred people today, and they all went away happy."

"That must make us the world's largest truck stop," Murray said.

"No, that's on Interstate 80 in Iowa," Naomi said. "They park nine hundred trucks a night, up to five thousand visitors a day."

"They don't get the news coverage we do," Murray said.

"They will once some militia group blows them up," Leona said.

CHAPTER THIRTY

By the middle of October, Julia needed to get home to California, and Murray was determined to help her get there. They each hoped a road trip would begin to fill the hole in their souls from the loss of Ben.

"Sure you're going to be okay, Mom?" Murray asked as they were saying goodbye.

Isabel nodded. "I'll be fine. I'm already taking two days off a week, no matter what. We've all been working too hard."

Julia hugged Isabel. "You are one amazing woman, Isabel. I'm so happy I got to play a small role in your comeback. I'm proud to be your friend."

Isabel's eyes were brimming with tears of appreciation.

"We all love you, Julia," Naomi said. "Take care of Murray. Don't let her enroll in art school just yet. We still need her."

Murray hugged her mother and whispered, "I'll be back soon. I love you. Don't ever forget you're all I've got."

Once the goodbyes were finally said, Murray and Julia climbed into the Intrepid and rolled out of Fort Wayne under cover of darkness, headed for Chicago and the Art Institute. From there, they would take Interstate 80 across the country. Murray had her Glock 9 mm in the glove box by the front passenger seat.

"This road trip is exactly what we both need," Julia said. "I've never suffered like this before. Not even close. I always heard how hard it is to lose a child, but I really had no idea. Some days it feels like I'm the one who died."

"A big part of me died, for sure," Murray said. "Losing my father was horrible. But losing Ben has been so much worse. All our dreams of building a life together ended violently. Nobody killed my father. That's what makes it so hard about Ben. Knowing the evil that took his life makes it impossible to accept. How many times a day do you have to remind yourself that Ben is really gone?"

"More times than I can count," Julia said. "It hits me at the strangest times. Like putting on lipstick and looking at my sad face in the mirror."

Murray thought about that image for a long while as they each slipped into their own grief. They rolled on through the night as occasional headlights pierced the darkness. Long stretches of empty highway became meditative. Murray was driving. She looked over at Julia and noticed tears streaming down her cheeks as they passed beneath a lighted road sign.

"You've got to help me start painting again," Murray said. "How long did it take you to come back from your divorce?"

"Too long," Julia said, drying her eyes with a crumpled tissue. "I was on the pity pot way too long. I was afraid to try because I didn't think I could. But once I got started, I realized that painting itself is the best therapy. We're both going to have trouble for a long time. All we can do is keep painting, one brushstroke at a time."

Murray considered Julia's point for at least ten miles until she said, "It's so good to hear you say that. I've been afraid to take the first step on the journey."

"We'll take it together," Julia said. "We'll do it for Ben, and for each other, and for ourselves. I've been on the comeback trail before. The trick is to believe the rocky path up the mountain will lead to a much better view."

"Oh, I love that. We better write that down."

"It's already been written thousands of ways. All we've got to do is believe it."

———

Julia had booked a room with a view of Lake Michigan at the historic Drake Hotel in Chicago. Somehow, she arranged for the hotel to provide valet parking for the Intrepid. She also made an appointment for lunch with her long-time friend from college, Casandra Ashton, who was a tenured professor at The Art Institute.

"I'm excited to meet Casandra," Murray said as they floated toward Chicago at sixty-five miles an hour. "I looked her up online. Love, love, love her paintings. It's so great you went to school together."

"Ah, yes, Stanford was wildly creative in the nineties. Casandra and I showed our work at a little art gallery in downtown Palo Alto. We sold a few paintings. Benjamin's father was my best customer. He was a dashing young doctor. We fell in love and got married to live happily ever after, fools that we were."

"So, why didn't you tell me about Casandra when I was in Sausalito, and we were talking about The Art Institute of Chicago?"

Julia cleared her throat and spoke in a low, confessional tone. "Well, I haven't talked to her in years. But that wasn't really it. I'm sorry to say I was more interested in having you move to San Francisco at that time. I was being selfish. I wanted Benjamin nearby."

She raised her voice to a cheerier level. "But I'm beyond all that mother-in-law manipulation at this point. Now that I know you and your mother, I can see that Chicago is your obvious choice. And now, sad to say, Benjamin won't be coming home."

"I felt it strongly when I was there with Ben . . . I mean, that Chicago was the place. We both did." Murray's voice trailed off in sad reflection.

"Let's not go there," Julia scolded gently as she shook her head and shoulders. "Let me just tell you that Casandra is looking forward to meeting you. We had a good talk, getting caught up on the phone. Evidently, you made quite an impression when you audited that drawing class. Not to mention you're a media celebrity."

"Oh no, that's the last thing I want to be. I'm sick of 'media celebrity,' as you call it. And please don't tell me they want me just because I'm kind of famous."

"Actually, no," Julia said. "Casandra sees that as a distraction that you and the university will have to overcome. You don't want to be another celebrity painter. You want to get in the trenches and learn how to make a painted canvas come alive."

Murray leaned forward in the driver's seat and gave the horn a good, long blast. "You know I love it when you talk like that."

They laughed together. Then Murray got serious and turned to Julia. "What do you think about me going to art school?"

Murray had never asked so directly. Julia thought about how to best respond. "I'm going to answer that question with a question of my own," she said, then paused. "Why did you want to be an artist in the first place?"

"Ah," Murray said. "I see what you're doing."

Julia waited for an answer until Murray responded. "I

remember drawing with crayons as a toddler. It's my first memory. I loved my crayons right away, and I was good with colors. Mom encouraged me from the start. One morning, she took away the coloring books and gave me a big roll of brown paper. Said I was too talented to stay in someone else's lines. That was the moment I knew I wanted to be an artist. I started drawing animals and people and stars in the sky. And then one day, Daddy put one of my drawings on the refrigerator. Maybe that was the moment I knew I wanted to be an artist."

"You know you want to be an artist when you keep having moments like that," Julia said. "So, back to your question about art school. You're obviously an artist at heart, and you've got special talent. That's the main reason you have to go to art school, Murray. The people you'll meet and the things you'll learn…it's so much fun. You will absolutely love it. And let me just come right out and say it: you owe it to your talent. Talent needs training to blossom."

"That is so true. I never thought about it like that. But what about the diner?"

Julia paused, knowing she needed to be diplomatic. "The diner is your mother's artistic expression. It's her way of bringing love and light into the world. And, yes, she needs you. But Naomi is there to help. You can go back any time you want. That's why Chicago is so perfect."

"I know my mother is an artist. Her cooking alone qualifies her. But she's also got this crusade going. She's saying what women need to be saying: stop the hate and keep the trucks rolling."

"Isabel is more than amazing," Julia said. "The two of you make a powerful team. But let me say this about art and life. The more art you create, and the more life you live, the more you realize that lifestyle is the ultimate artistic medium."

"That is so good . . . I think. I mean, what are you saying?"

"I'm saying that every action we take is a brushstroke on the canvas of our lives. What we wear, who we spend time with, how we help others. Lifestyle is an art form. It can be good art or bad art."

"Wow," Murray said. "I'm gonna steal that for the rest of my life. Lifestyle is the ultimate artistic medium. I can't believe I've never heard it before. Did you make that up?"

Julia laughed so hard she leaned as far forward as her seatbelt would allow. "Maybe I just did. But the concept is nothing new. I'm sure the sculptors who built the Parthenon in ancient Greece were talking about the same thing. Isn't it fun to think about? We're making some beautiful art right now with this road trip."

"So, if everybody's an artist," Murray said, "why go to art school?"

"Oh, Murray," Julia laughed. "Just when I thought I had it all wrapped up, you turn it into something else. Most people don't see themselves as artists. Art school puts you in contact with people who know what it means to be creative. They know you don't start out as a great painter. You've got to learn drawing and anatomy and printmaking and sculpture. Picasso spent years studying with his father and in university. He didn't jump right into cubism."

"So, you're saying lifestyle is the ultimate artistic medium if you get the right training?"

"No, I'm saying it's the ultimate artistic medium if you live your life creatively."

———

Murray and Julia slept until 10:30 a.m. Even then, it wasn't easy getting up since they hadn't gotten to bed in their hotel room until 3:00 a.m. Once awake and showered, they had to take an Uber to the Art Institute. They had planned on walking the Lake Michigan shore, but they didn't have time.

Casandra was waiting for them at the entrance when they arrived only two minutes late. She greeted Julia with a squeal of delight and an extended hug. "You look younger than last time I saw you," Casandra said. "How long has it been? Five, ten years?"

Julia responded with tears of joy, grief, and relief as she let herself go in the arms of her old friend. "You lie so well, Casandra. The sad truth is I feel thirty years older since we lost our Benjamin. But wait, this is my dear friend, Murray."

Casandra pulled Murray into a hug. "Oh, Murray, it's so good to meet you. I've heard so much about you." Then she released the embrace. I am so, so sorry about Benjamin. I can't imagine how hard this must be for both of you."

The three women bowed their heads together in an impromptu moment of silence.

Julia was the first to recover. "So, let's not be sad. It's time to have fun. Where are we going for lunch?"

Casandra dried her eyes and smiled. "I have an exciting afternoon planned. We'll have lunch at the Museum Café, and then we'll paint together in my 2:00 p.m. oil painting class. I've got you both set up with easels and paints. And Murray, your friend, Tyra Cooper, will be there. She's one of your biggest fans."

"And I'm one of hers," Murray said. "She was so kind and is such a wonderful artist. I'll never be able to thank her enough for getting me into my first college drawing class."

The Museum Café was filled with happy chatter and the clatter of silverware on colorful ceramic plates. It smelled like baking bread and coffee. All the excitement of her first visit to the Art Institute flooded back. She kept expecting Ben to walk around the corner at any minute.

The three women talked excitedly about the Art Institute, Chicago, the diner, and Julia's painting career in San Francisco. "You should see Julia's painting porch in Sausalito," Murray said. "It is paradise."

"I've painted on that porch," Casandra said. "It is so perfect. And, oh, how I miss the Bay Area, especially when it's below zero in the Windy City."

"You need to come visit," Julia said. "I've got lots of room and I'd love the company."

After lunch, Casandra introduced Julia and Murray to her painting class of nine students. Tyra gave Murray a welcoming high five. She felt like an old friend to Murray. The two of them had only spent one afternoon together, but they stayed in touch by texting and the occasional phone call.

Casandra got right down to business. "So, we're here to paint, not listen to me talk" she said to the class. "You each have a black-and-white photo on your easel. Today's exercise will be to paint that scene in color. I'll be walking around to critique and encourage each one of you. Remember, it's not a race. Finishing first might not be a good thing."

A half hour into the class, Casandra came over to check on Murray's landscape. The painting was stiff and clunky. "Sometimes, it's hard to let go," Casandra said. "After all you've been through, it's going to take a while. Just remember where to shine the light."

"What do you mean?"

"Where to put the spotlight. If the light is on the artist, we've got trouble. Try to shine the light on the painting."

Murray stood up and threw her arms around Casandra.

"You are so right. Now, if I could only do it and stop feeling sorry for myself."

"Start with the sky," Casandra suggested. "Give me a brighter blue wash over all that gray. And remember, it's a process, not an event."

Murray returned to her work with a lighter heart.

Julia's painting stopped Casandra in her tracks. "Look at you, girl. Just when I thought you couldn't possibly get any better." She raised her voice to address the class. "I want each of you to check out Julia's work. It's nice to have an experienced professional in the class. We're all professional painters by this point, but Julia's got more time on the easel. That's really what it's all about: time on the easel. Practice makes perfect. No, I shouldn't say that. None of us wants to be perfect. Perfect is somebody else's idea of what's good. We make our own creative decisions around here."

Murray was thrilled by these thoughts. Casandra was saying things Murray had often contemplated but had never been able to put into words.

The class lasted two hours. When the time came to hold up artwork for class comment, Murray had a much brighter painting to share. "I know it's still a little stiff," she said, "but I'm taking baby steps on my path of art therapy."

"You've made some serious progress today, Murray," Casandra said. "Think about how good your next paintings will be."

"I love your sky," Tyra said.

After class, Julia, Casandra, Murray, and Tyra decided to carry on at The Drawing Room, an ornate hangout at the Chicago Athletic Association Hotel. After a few cocktails, Tyra asked Murray, "So, when are you enrolling?"

Murray didn't hesitate to answer. "Actually, "I'm planning on applying for the upcoming semester." She turned to Casandra. "Can I do that?"

"Not only can you do that, but we can fill out the paperwork in my office tomorrow," Casandra said.

CHAPTER THIRTY-ONE

It happened back in August when the M1 Abrams tank took the crippling hit from a Javelin missile fired by government forces. A few witnesses saw through *the dust that the tank turret* had popped open. No one saw anyone escape before the tank was wiped out, seconds later, by a drone missile.

But one person did escape. The Commander flipped himself out of the tank in a move so smooth it defied detection and was somersaulting into a trench when the drone missile struck. A blip on the tank's radar system had alerted him that something big and bad was incoming. Bailing out in a catlike contortion, he shouted down to the crew to get out. It was too late. His warning had barely registered when they were obliterated.

As the Commander was falling into the trench upside down, only his legs were exposed to the exploding tank. The blast stunned him unconscious for a short time. He came to with a painful throbbing in his head, and an unidentifiable shard of metal from the tank stabbed almost entirely through his right thigh, just above the knee. His mind was shell-shocked into confusion by the concussive power of the blast. It took a few minutes of head shaking and deep breathing to remember who he was and where he was. Instinctively, he looked at the sky and realized what had happened. *A drone. They're treating me like a terrorist. Execution without a trial. Totalitarian justice.*

He didn't look over the earthen mound of the trench to survey the damage. Why risk being spotted when there'd be nothing left to see? No one in the tank could have survived. It didn't matter to him. Personal survival was now his only concern.

Buying the abandoned school years earlier had saved what little was left of him to save. He threw everything he had into developing his shooting range. It became like a child to him, an unwanted stepchild he felt obliged to raise.

Now, as his mind came back into focus from the tank explosion, he knew the ambitious project was surely doomed. He didn't have to watch the battle. Without the tank, the compound would fall quickly. The paid soldiers of his private army would soon be dead or on their way to prison. Their fate did not concern him. He wouldn't have said goodbye to a single one of them, even if he could. Except maybe Cal Mavis, his only lifeline back to a time when he still had hope.

The Commander dragged himself down the tank trench until he reached an access point to the tunnel system. The searing pain in his right leg made it difficult to move. He pulled the circular steel hatch open and crawled inside. Once the hatch closed behind him, he marveled at his situation in the total darkness. Using a light could give away his position. *They couldn't even kill me with a drone*, he gloated.

Severe pain in his head and leg brought him back to the harsh reality that his militia compound was being overrun by federal forces. He sat down in the tunnel to slowly wiggle out the jagged piece of metal from his thigh. He tried not to rip too much flesh. The pain almost blacked him out. The eight-inch metal fragment made a nasty sucking sound as it finally came out. Blood spurted and gushed out of the wound. He tore off his right shirt sleeve and tied it tightly around his leg.

Getting up on his feet made him clench his teeth to keep from screaming. Putting weight on the injured leg sent lightning bolts of pain directly to his brain. Not a good situation. *Must be a broken bone or nerve damage.* He couldn't walk, and his only weapon was a cell phone. He felt for it in his Kevlar vest and was relieved to find it in the inside chest pocket. It operated half the compound, including his secret escape tunnel.

The tunnel was nearly a mile long and led to a remote and completely overgrown bunker outside the compound. He had built it for just such an occasion as this. The Commander couldn't help but admire the brilliance of his foresight. He didn't stop to think about the insanity of building the tunnel system in the first place. Narcissism had closed in on him to the point where every window was nothing but a mirror.

The door to the escape tunnel was not far, a hundred yards down the main tunnel at the most. He tried to hobble, but he couldn't do it. He got down on his good knee and began dragging himself through the main tunnel. The pain in his right leg was fast becoming unbearable, and he was losing too much blood. He stopped to tighten the shirt sleeve. Time was not on his side. He had to keep moving.

He crawled forward until he reached the well-disguised access panel to the escape route. To anyone with a light, it looked like tree roots, rock, and earth. The Commander knew how to find it in the dark by feeling for the slightly raised roots on the side of the tunnel. He was just about to open it with his cell phone when he saw headlamps coming around a corner, thirty yards away. Whoever it was hadn't seen him yet. He could tell from the downward angle of their lamps. They were moving slowly and carefully.

The panel made no sound as it opened inwards on a programmed command from his phone. He had his back to the approaching headlamps and held the phone close to his chest to hide its operational light.

The Commander rolled through the opening and silently closed the panel. He waited, motionless, until he heard a squad of men passing by as a piece of their gear banged against the raised roots on the side of the tunnel. Now all he had to do was make it to the remote bunker.

The escape tunnel was his pride and joy, sealed and lined by a circular plastic tube five feet in diameter. The other tunnels were supported by wooden frames like mine shafts.

He used the cell phone light to visually inspect his wound for the first time. The makeshift wrap was oozing blood at an alarming rate. He became lightheaded to the point of nearly passing out. Only adrenaline from the battle and his narrow escape kept him going. Martial arts training took over. He made the most of his movements and kept their economy of motion repetitive. His pace was steady and determined. Upper body strength showed its worth as his arms became his legs. Even so, he was completely spent by the time he reached the remote bunker.

Once inside, he flipped on the lights and located the medical bag. He cut the shirtsleeve bandage off his leg and grabbed a large bottle of water from the cooler. He gulped most of it before using the rest to clean his wound. He gave himself two shots of morphine in his right thigh. A wave of wellness washed over him as the narcotics took effect. It would have knocked him out had he not developed a tolerance for the drug through recreational abuse.

He poured a small amount of gunpowder from a .45 cartridge into the hole in his leg and ignited it with a match to cauterize the wound. Forcing himself to maintain consciousness despite the pain even the morphine couldn't control, he stuffed the hole in his leg with antibiotic cream and gauze and wrapped a clean bandage around his thigh. Only then did he allow himself to pass out.

———

The Commander dreamed of his former captive, Anita. Sexually at first, and then nursing him back to health. She was cooling his brow with a moist cloth when the dream took a violent twist. He was lining her up with all the women from The Highway Diner in front of a firing squad that he commanded. He awakened to the sound of his own voice barking the orders, "Ready. Aim. Fire!"

There were enough provisions in the bunker to keep two men alive for two weeks. He drank beer and water once he regained consciousness, wondering how in the world he had forgotten to stock the bunker with whiskey. He ate very little, only a few ready-to-eat military meals. The escape bunker was not connected to the compound's monitoring and communications circuit. It had its own generator but no independent communication system. The Commander was cut off from news of the outside world.

He thought he would hide in the bunker for at least a week before venturing outside by way of an exit hatch disguised as a rock that opened to a deserted section of white pine trees. But after three days he had used up the entire supply of morphine. The pain forced him to seek medical treatment. He had $150,000 cash in a bug-out bag, and he knew who to call.

Dr. Harold Aikens, a militia sympathizer from north of Grand Rapids, Michigan, answered the Commander's call. It was after midnight.

"Jesus Christ, Andrew," the doctor gasped. "How the hell are you still alive?"

"Did anyone see me get out of the tank?"

"No, we were all pretty damn sure we saw you explode in a tank on television. Everyone thinks you died in the drone strike. I can't believe I'm talking to you. My God, man, you're back from the dead. We all saw you die. You were commanding the tank, weren't you?"

"Yes, and I bailed out as fast as I could once the tank was immobilized. I wasn't out three seconds before the drone hit. Did they say it was a drone?"

"Oh my, yes," Dr. Aikens said. "It's been described in detail and analyzed by every military expert they could get on camera. Even did a big story on the drone operator. You'd think he bagged Osama bin Laden."

"Well, he didn't bag me. So, here's what I need you to do. Come pick me up in your car. Right now. Alone. Tell nobody. Are you ready for this?"

"Yes, yes, of course," the doctor stammered. "I'm still having a hard time believing I'm talking to you. Give me a minute. I'm still in shock that you're alive."

"Okay. I'll make it worth your while. You know I'm good for it. I've still got tons of cash. So, take the county road that runs north and south on the east side of the compound."

"The one that goes past the deserted Standard Oil gas station?"

"That's the one. Head north until you turn right on the old logging trail by that rundown log cabin near the top of the hill. You know where I'm talking about?"

"I know the cabin and I know the trail. When do you want me there?"

"Can you make it in half an hour?"

"I'm leaving right now. Are you injured?"

"My leg's bad, doc. Bring some morphine. Where can we get an MRI? It must be broken. I can't put any weight on it."

"I've got everything we need at my private clinic."

"Make sure you turn off your headlights before you make the turn onto the trail."

"Way ahead of you. But I still can't believe I'm talking to you. I'm gonna slap myself around to make sure I'm not dreaming."

The doctor hung up the phone, and the Commander began packing his gear. In forty-five minutes, he was waiting outside the bunker when he saw Dr. Aikens's car creeping down the logging trail. There was plenty of moonlight. The doctor stopped the car and got out to help his surprise patient into the vehicle. He gave him a shot of morphine before they even buckled the seat belt.

"Got any whiskey?"

"Right there in the glove box. Help yourself. I figured you could use a drink. Those government bastards killed half your people. Funny, I haven't heard any report saying they never found your body."

"The bodies inside that tank were emulsified and scattered so far it'll take them forever to identify anybody."

"Oh my God, that's terrible to think about," Dr. Aikens said. "What's gonna happen with these federal drones? They can blow anybody to kingdom come."

The Commander groaned in pain as the car bounced back up the trail. "That's exactly what we've been trying to tell everybody for years. They won't listen until the drone lords start blowing up private homes because they don't like their voting record."

The doctor drove in silence until he reached the county road and turned on his headlights. "You smell like a bad infection. Glad you didn't wait any longer to call. We'll get you on some good antibiotics and I'll patch you up proper. What's your plan?"

The Commander answered like he'd been pondering that very question since his escape. "Revenge, plain and simple. Revenge, first on those bitches from The Highway Diner. It was them and that Nashville agent of theirs who brought the feds down on me."

"Did you blow up the casino?"

"Hell yes, I blew it up. And those Highway Diner bitches are lucky they didn't get blown up too. It was that goddamned Anita who tipped them off. Mavis let her get away. She knew too much."

"Now, Andrew," Dr. Aikens said. "As your doctor, I advise you to settle down. We need to keep at least a little of that hot blood inside your body. And, as your friend, I'd advise you to slow down on all that talk about revenge."

"I'll slow down when I'm dead."

CHAPTER THIRTY-TWO

Murray and Julia made their way across the Great Plains and into the Rocky Mountains on their journey to Julia's house in California. It was a struggle for Murray. As wonderful as Julie's painting lessons were, Murray couldn't get over or around the helpless feeling of watching Ben bleed to death. She found herself sobbing at the easel every time she tried to start painting.

Julia had tears of her own, but she was able to loosen up much quicker than Murray. "Don't worry, Murray," she said one afternoon as they were painting in Colorado. "I've been down the comeback trail before. Trust the process and it will set you free. Believe me."

"How can I be free when all I see is Ben lying in that hospital bed waiting for us to pull the plug? I was getting better after everything I went through at the diner until that bastard killed Ben."

Julia put her arms around Murray. They cried together until Julia backed out of the embrace and looked Murray in the eye. "If you don't keep moving forward, the grief will catch up and consume you."

Murray sat up ramrod straight as Julia's message resonated. She dried her eyes with a paint rag, leaped to her feet, and screamed at the sky, "That's right. I'm gonna keep running. It's never going to catch me. And if it does, I'll blow it up sky high."

Julia wasn't ready for the violent outburst, although she seemed relieved to see fire returning to Murray's eyes. "We won't have to get violent," she said. "That's what we're trying to overcome through the creative process."

Murray held her hands over her ears like she didn't want to hear herself scream again. "It's not the sorrow that's killing me. It's the anger. I'm mad at the world for what happened to us, and I want revenge for Ben."

"Believe it or not, "I understand completely," Julia sighed. "I wanted to kill my husband for a long time after he left me and the kids. I used to dream up ways of doing him in. I wanted to waterboard him and shock him with electrodes on his balls. Believe me, I spent way too much time dreaming up ways to torture him. My bitterness ate me alive for almost a year. And then one day, a recovering alcoholic friend of mine warned me that holding on to resentments is like drinking poison and expecting the other person to die."

"So that cured you?"

"No, but it turned me around and got me on the path to a creative recovery from grief. And let me say this about grief: it's not something you want to try and get over. Grief has a job to do. You've got to go through it to understand the benefit." Julia smiled. "Bear in mind I'm talking to myself as much as to you. I'm nowhere near through my grief over Ben. But the whole point of the grieving process is to be able to take the good parts of the person you lost with you wherever you go."

"That's exactly what my mother said. It must be true if two of the women I admire most are saying the same thing. And I guess I've been able to do that with my father," Murray said. "It took a few years, but I talk to him all the time now."

"It's gonna take us both some time to be able to think about Ben without tears on the canvas."

Early on the journey, they visited the world's largest truck stop on Interstate 80 at Walcott, Iowa. It was the Disneyland of truck stops. It had a museum, trucker rodeos, live country music, and every imaginable service for travelers. Julia looked at a brochure and said,

"They've got barbershops and chiropractors and dog groomers and even dentists at this place. It's impressive. But it feels like a tourist trap."

Murray nodded. "I'm afraid The Highway Diner is headed that way, especially once the casino opens."

"I can't believe they don't have a casino here," Julia said.

"Maybe the owners are too wholesome," Murray said. "Or maybe a casino doesn't really fit into the mission of a truck stop."

"You know, I've been thinking the same thing ever since I heard about the casino going up next to The Highway Diner," Julia said. "Kind of overshadowing, don't you think?"

"Absolutely," Murray said. "That's a good word for it—*overshadowing*. I've been wondering why the casino didn't feel right. Once you put it that way, I understand how I feel. It's overshadowing."

"That's definitely something for you and your mother to discuss," Julia said. "And you better do it soon. That casino's going up fast."

Murray and Julia became an efficient traveling team in the Intrepid. The trip to California took two weeks and they only stayed one night in a hotel. Julia got the double bed in the rear of the Intrepid; Murray slept in one of the pull-out bunks. They shopped together at the folksiest grocery stores they could find in the smallest towns along the way. They cooked marvelous dinners and made fires in National Park campsites for late-night entertainment, except when it got too cold in the mountains.

Murray taught Julia how to drive the RV. Julia was overly cautious at first but quickly got the hang of being behind the wheel of an oversized vehicle. "The only thing we need is a big air horn to blow any time somebody gets in our way," Julia said.

Julia read the owner's manual out loud while Murray drove. "This vehicle is truly amazing," she said. "I'm glad I've got the time to read about everything it can do."

Emptying waste from the toilet was the second hardest thing Julia and Murray had to do. They laughed themselves silly when Julia said, "I can't believe two sweet girls like us can make smells this terrible."

The most difficult task was changing a flat tire. A well-meaning man at their campsite in Utah offered to help when he saw them studying a deflated right rear tire. "No thanks," Murray said. "We got this."

"Are you sure we got this?" Julia asked after the man walked away.

"Believe me," Murray said. "My daddy taught me how to change truck tires when I was a little girl."

Murray had a tough time getting the spare out from under the vehicle. It was on a long bolt, and she had to get the nut off with a hand wrench. They both got dirty trying to keep the tire from falling on them once the nut came off the bolt. The jack system was a little easier, but they both had to get on the lug nut wrench for a couple of stubborn turns. They got the job done, not as fast as a racing crew, but in pretty good time. Murray was strong enough to handle a tire by herself, but Julia insisted on lifting her half of the load.

"You're not going to believe this, but that's the first tire I've ever changed," Julia beamed.

"With any luck, it'll be the last," Murray said, wiping her

brow and leaving a smudge mark of tire dirt. "That was a lot more work than I remember."

———

Murray stayed in Sausalito long enough to meet Ben's older sister, Stephanie. She looked so much like Ben that Murray burst into tears when they met. Julia and Stephanie began crying too.

The tears didn't last long. Stephanie and Murray were happy to finally meet. They were soon chatting and drinking wine while they went through every family scrapbook Julia could find. Benjamin lived on in their communion. They were helping each other make peace with his passing. After a couple bottles of wine, Stephanie opened up and said, "You know, Mom and I have talked a lot about The Highway Diner. At first, it seemed a little like a flash in the pan, but we know better now."

She had Murray's absolute attention as she continued. "It's gotten to be this symbol of women trying to make peace in the world. Women resisting men and their stupid war games."

"Thank you so much for saying that," Murray said. "But here's the problem. Ben getting killed by that monster who calls himself the Commander has made me feel a violent streak inside myself that just won't quit. I still want to shoot him right between the eyes."

"Me too," Julia said. "Wish I'd killed the bastard."

"That makes three of us," Stephanie said.

The women laughed and poured another round of wine. Murray was getting loose enough to share her fears that the Commander wasn't dead, but she decided against it. She'd already told Julia about her Ben dreams. No need to worry Stephanie.

"I'm sorry I didn't come to see Ben in the hospital," Stephanie said without warning. "I know I should have been there for Mom, but I just couldn't do it. I wanted to remember him tall and handsome."

"It was awful," Murray said. "But I understand how you feel. Julia and I talked about it. And now, I'm glad to be with you."

Julia raised her wine glass and said, "I'd like to propose a toast to Benjamin." Murray and Stephanie lifted their glasses. "Here's to a wonderful, kind-hearted man. My son, your brother, your best friend. May he live forever in our hearts and always be remembered in our friendship."

The immediate sisterhood she felt with Stephanie gave Murray strength as she attended a celebration of life for Benjamin at a seaside restaurant in Sausalito. Julia had organized it by phone as they drove to California. She kept it small to ensure it wouldn't become a media event. After the celebration, Murray, Julia, and Stephanie snuck off to pour Ben's ashes into the choppy salt water beneath the Golden Gate Bridge.

"I'm guessing this is what Benjamin would have wanted," Julia said. "He was too young to think about what should be done with his ashes."

The three women bowed their heads in silence until Stephanie said, "I'm pretty sure he wouldn't want to be in a vase on somebody's mantel."

Julia and Murray smiled wistfully and nodded their heads in agreement.

Murray knew she had to head home soon after the event, especially after Ben appeared to her in dreams on her fourth night at Julia's house. He awakened her with a kiss like he always did. But this time he didn't say anything. Murray could tell by the look in his eyes that he was warning her of danger. His gaze was too steady.

"What is it, Ben?" she asked. "What's wrong? What are you telling me?"

She woke up to the sound of her own questions, crying in frustration.

Murray made arrangements that morning to fly home. There was no doubt in her mind that Ben was telling her to get back to her mother as soon as possible. There was also no doubt he was warning her about the Commander. She knew he wasn't dead. She could feel the fear and anger tingling up and down her spine every time she thought about him.

Julia drove her to the airport the next day. "What's the matter, Murray? I can tell something's wrong. You're too quiet. Did Benjamin come to you in a dream again?"

Murray nodded. "I should know better than to try to hide anything from you, Julia. And yes, he did. He didn't say anything. But he gave me a look that I can't get out of my head."

"About the Commander?" Julia asked.

Murray nodded. "It's always about the Commander. I hope he is still alive so I can get my chance to—"

"Murray, please don't talk like that. We all feel that way, but we've got to stop saying it out loud."

Murray always surprised herself as her creative juices turned to battery acid when she thought about the man who'd killed Ben. But she needed to change her attitude to have a proper goodbye with Julia. They had been through so much together. She was sad to see their monumental road trip coming to an end.

"Don't worry, Julia," she said, getting out of the car. "I'm going to be all right. I'll stay in close touch. I don't know how to thank you for everything, especially the painting and helping me get into art school. Please tell Stephanie I said goodbye."

Julia got out of the car to hug Murray goodbye. "You know I love you, honey. Sure you don't want me to walk you to the gate?"

"I'll be fine. My phone says the plane's on schedule." She grabbed her bag and started rolling it toward the terminal entrance. Then she turned and waved to Julia as she yelled, "Love you, Julia. Long live Benjamin Fitzgerald."

Isabel was waiting for Murray during the first week of November when she arrived at the Fort Wayne Airport and headed for baggage claim. "Muriel! My baby girl. So good to see you. Feels like you've been gone forever. You look more beautiful than ever."

Murray threw her arms around Isabel. She could smell the diner in her hair. "Ah, my gorgeous mommy. Looks like you've lost some weight. You look great. Thanks for picking me up. I know you're slammed at the diner. How are Naomi and Anita doing?"

"They're slaving away as usual, trying to keep up with the nonstop rush. We've all been laughing about getting a chiropractor and a dentist since you told me about that giant truck stop in Iowa. We can't believe they have all those services at a truck plaza."

"What's the latest on Blake?" Murray asked. "You haven't mentioned him the last few times we talked on the phone. I figured you got some bad news, so I didn't want to bring it up."

Isabel looked toward the empty luggage carousel for a long moment. It wasn't moving yet. She turned back to Murray and said, "Well, if you must know, he's gone back to his ex-wife and kids. Said he realized that once he got sober, they should have been his top priority all along. He's not touring with the band. He's going to meetings, and he's got a sponsor. I'm happy for him."

"Mom," Murray scolded gently.

Isabel shook her ponytail defiantly. "Okay, you know it hit me hard. And you know I'm going to get over it. It all takes too long, as you know. These men in my life keep coming and going. But I will say this: the longer he's gone, the more foolish the whole thing looks."

"It wasn't foolish, Mom. You two had a ton of fun."

"Yes, we did," Isabel said. "I was crazy about that good old country boy."

Her mother looked so sad that Murray decided to change the topic. "Speaking of meetings and sponsors, how's Anita doing?"

Isabel breathed a sigh of relief to be talking about something else. "Anita is working her ass off. She and Naomi get along great. Maybe too great. They spend a lot of time together after work. I'm starting to wonder if they're planning a new business."

"Mom," Murray gasped. "Those are two of the most loyal people we'll ever know."

Isabel laughed. "I know, I know. I'm just jealous because I miss having time with you, my favorite woman in the whole world. It is so good to have you back. We're all thrilled about you going to art school. We'll miss you, but everybody knows it's what you should do."

Murray sighed. "I'm not anywhere near getting over Ben. I feel like he's still with me everywhere I go. I don't know how long I can keep this up. I don't ever want to forget how perfect we were. I keep playing the same memories over and over. And the bad ones are taking over."

"That's not something you'll ever get past," Isabel said. "Not something you'll even want to get over. Good memories will win out in the end. I still talk to your daddy every day. You'll get to the place where Ben will be a friend by your side. It'll take time, but you'll get there. I didn't think I ever would, but I did."

"I know, Mom, but I'm so angry and frustrated. Half the time I want to scream. I can't believe some crazy person could take him away forever. And these dreams about the Commander still being alive are driving me crazy. I'm worried about you too."

"That you can stop worrying about," Isabel said. "Chase is in touch with the feds. They're all completely convinced the Commander is dead and gone. Chase is here for a few days, by the way. So is Leona. They both want to talk to you."

"About the Commander?"

"No, they've got some news of their own."

"Oh my God," Murray said. "They're getting married."

Isabel beamed. "Not only that. Oh, I shouldn't tell you. They made me promise."

"She's pregnant," Murray shrieked so loudly the passengers turned around from staring at the luggage carousel, which had just started moving with an annoying buzzer and a flashing red light.

Murray hushed her voice and said, "Isn't she a little old for that? How old is she? Forty-five?"

"She just turned forty."

"That's still pretty old to be raising kids," Murray said.

"She'll have her hands full. Chase claims he'll be the head diaper changer. We'll see how long it takes him to hire a nanny."

CHAPTER THIRTY-THREE

Trucker Nation Casino was halfway rebuilt when a stop work order was issued by the Allen County Superior Court. A lawsuit filed three weeks before Christmas by the Concerned Citizens of Fort Wayne, Indiana, claimed the project was in violation of state construction and gaming laws.

Concerned Citizens was a conservative consortium of churches, charities, and colleges that didn't want a casino coming to town. It had taken them months to gather the funds to hire an attorney and get a suit filed. Opposition had been strong at the Planning Commission and Zoning Board hearings, but plans for the casino moved ahead because the area had long been zoned for commercial use. The court granted the Concerned Citizens' request for temporary injunction until a hearing could be held. Casino construction came to a court-ordered halt.

Chase and Leona called an emergency meeting with Isabel and Murray. Naomi and Anita were also present. As usual, they all sat at the round table in the corner of the diner.

Isabel surprised everybody but Murray when she said, "You know what? I don't think this stop work order is all bad. The more I think about building a casino, the more I don't like it. Casinos bring in too much trouble. Do we really want to be a tourist trap? Or wouldn't it be better to build a high-end hotel with a big performance venue?"

Chase and Leona looked at each other in shock. The notion of building a casino had become so ingrained in their plans that to question it now sounded like blasphemy. Chase recovered first and said, "That's basically what a casino is, a hotel that features entertainment. We've been planning this casino for nearly a year, Isabel. We've got a fortune in architects and infrastructure for a casino. Are you really jumping ship on us at this late date?"

Murray moved to her mother's side and took her hand. "Nobody's jumping ship, Chase. We're just beginning to wonder if the casino is less about truckers and the supply chain and more about mobsters and drugs and too many old smokers gambling away their monthly social security money."

Chase sounded dismayed. "Come on, Murray."

"No," Murray said. "I'll tell you what the real problem is with the casino. It will overshadow The Highway Diner. The casino will overpower the diner. We'll be more about gambling than trucking."

Leona attempted to mediate. "I'm sure the Concerned Citizens, or whatever they call themselves, are afraid of mobsters and drugs. But that's not what casinos today are all about. It's all about service, and it doesn't have to be overshadowing or overpowering. It can serve the same people the diner does. It can be family oriented. That's what we're going to be. We've talked about this, Isabel. Our casino will offer truckers a nice place to stay and play. The truckers of tomorrow aren't going to be sleeping in their cabs every night."

Naomi and Anita kept their heads low as the debate continued. They were working for Isabel and Murray at The Highway Diner, but Chase and Leona were increasingly involving them in plans for the casino. Naomi had the professional background to help design kitchens and dining rooms. Anita was proving herself to be trustworthy and capable of any task, much like Ben had been.

"How about this?" Murray asked. "Why don't we have our lawyers meet with their lawyers and lay out our plans for a family- and trucker-friendly casino? Instead of spending a fortune for legal fees, we could agree on providing a service to the community. We could even ask the Concerned Citizens for suggestions on what they would like to see from the new hotel."

Chase saw his opening. "Great idea, Murray. That we can certainly do. Let's meet with the lawyers and see what can happen."

"Maybe we could offer up services, like a chiropractor and a dentist," Isabel said. "Murray says that's what that giant truck stop in Iowa is doing."

Naomi raised herself slowly and purposefully from her chair. "How about we don't call it a casino at all? The word itself has tons of negative emotional baggage. And casinos are everywhere. They're *passé.*"

The group looked at her in stunned silence, waiting for her to continue. She smiled politely and said, "A casino is not what The Highway Diner started out to be. We're about truckers, not gamblers. So, why not make the Trucker Nation building a place with everything a trucker, or any traveler, could ever need? I love what Murray said about chiropractors and dentists. We could still have some gambling, but we wouldn't call it a casino."

Chase was intrigued. "What would we call it?"

Naomi yielded the floor to Isabel, who said, "How about Trucker Nation Headquarters?"

Everybody thought about that for a moment until Leona said, "Sounds a little too military. How about something snazzy like Trucker Nation Plaza? You know, like the Plaza Hotel in New York City."

Anita jumped in to brainstorm. "How about just Trucker Nation? We don't have to add anything to that name. Everybody already knows what it is."

"And if they don't know by now, they'll find out soon enough," Naomi said. "I love it. Trucker Nation." She held her hands over her head like she was showing off a big, neon sign.

"That would make a great sign out front," Isabel said.

Chase spoke in a conciliatory tone. "You know, the performance center is already in the design. And we could cut the gambling arena in two and turn one half of the space into an event center."

"You could get married there," Murray said.

Leona frowned and held her four-month baby bump. "We can't wait that long. But while we're on the topic, Chase and I would love to get married at The Highway Diner."

With that, what could have been a disastrous clash of wills ended up being a wedding planning session that happened to change the course of Trucker Nation.

Within two weeks, the new concept for a "community center," as Chase's lawyers presented it, had been accepted and approved by the Concerned Citizens of Fort Wayne, Indiana. Construction was back on track. A different track, to be sure, but back on track.

———

Once Chase announced the new plans for Trucker Nation, every service provider in the area scrambled to lease space. Barber shops, computer and cell phone repairs, dentists, nail and pedicure parlors, massage therapists, truck cab designers, tax preparers and accountants, medical clinics, pet groomers, and every service imaginable clamored to jump on the bandwagon.

Trucker Nation Corporation bought acres of adjoining land for additional parking and space for special events like truck rodeos and jamborees.

Isabel had conflicting emotions regarding the rapid expansion. As a major shareholder of the corporation, she could see the financial benefit, but she worried The Highway Diner and her truck plaza were getting lost in the shuffle. Chase assuaged her doubts by suggesting they could triple the size of the truck wash and fuel pumps and double the size of the overnight truck parking.

"We'll have an upscale restaurant in the new hotel, but it won't be in competition with the diner," Chase said. "If anything, it'll handle your overflow. And all the events will be in the name of The Highway Diner. That's our focus now, and we can all make sure it stays that way."

"Oh, Chase," Isabel said. "You are one sweet-talking guy." Once again, she marveled at Chase's ability to get his point across without becoming confrontational.

As construction got back on track, Murray had little time to wait tables or work in the kitchen at the diner. The architects hired her to do drawings for the newly imagined Trucker Nation project. The drawings were technical, but she was good at it right away. It turned out to be excellent therapy, a bridge for her return to painting. Before long, she began to have a design influence on the project. Seeing her drawings come to life during the building process reminded her of the importance of art in all aspects of life.

She had been accepted into the School of the Art Institute of Chicago and was scheduled to start her first semester on

January 27, 2024. Murray was already in the process of renting a modest apartment near the Art Institute. The rent was high. Murray could afford it, especially with the help of her soon-to-be roommate, Tyra Cooper.

Julia encouraged her on the phone from California. "Drawing is great discipline for painting," she said. "Looking back on it, that's how I started getting over my ex-husband leaving."

"You're the best. I wish I were painting with you again," Murray said.

"We'll arrange something exciting for next summer," Julia promised.

Murray's favorite art project of the season was hanging Christmas decorations on The Highway Diner. She worked with Naomi and Anita, completely overdoing everything. They draped colored lights along the entire roofline and around all the windows. Anita wrangled a big sled with an electric waving Santa and all the reindeer. Of course, it had to be well lit for the holidays. Spotlights that rotated from red to green were installed.

The three of them had been inseparable once Murray returned from California. Anita remained strong in her program of addiction recovery. Naomi was encouraging her to go back to school to study hotel and restaurant management. Despite being young and single, the three friends almost never talked about men. Murray was having a rough holiday season without Ben. Anita was still recovering from her kidnapping. Naomi had been treated cruelly and harassed racially and sexually by her white male bosses in Nashville.

The one man they did discuss was the Commander. Murray and Anita were convinced he was still alive. They couldn't believe anyone so cruel could die without them feeling it in their bones. Naomi wasn't so sure. "The only reason I would ever wonder about him still being alive is from what you two have told me about your dreams. But those dreams are probably caused by what he did to us. We're all going to have nightmares about the man who murdered our friends and tried to kill us all."

Anita drained her glass of water with lemon and said, "I got a letter from Cal Mavis yesterday. He's in federal prison. He knows he's not getting out any time soon."

"No way," Murray said. "What did he say?"

"Said he's sorry for the way he treated me. Which is funny because he didn't really treat me that bad."

"Except for that crazy little crime called kidnapping," Naomi reminded her. "And holding you hostage, and drugging you up, and making you say terrible things about The Highway Diner on national television."

Anita laughed nervously. "Well, there was all that." Then, she said quickly, "I shouldn't laugh. It was horrible. They had me on so many drugs I didn't know what I was doing. I did develop some feelings for Cal Mavis, but I wouldn't be standing here now if I hadn't run away from that whole sick scene."

"Did he say anything about the Commander?" Murray asked.

Anita lowered her voice. "That's the thing. He said he was watching the video monitors in the command bunker when the tank first got hit. Said he thought he saw something, or somebody, fly out of the open hatch before the tank got blown away."

Murray gasped. "How could you not tell us about this right away?"

Anita shook her head. "I don't know. Guess I'm still trying to process it myself. I just got the letter yesterday. But I'm telling you now."

Naomi, ever the analytical thinker, said, "If he was still alive, he would have tried something by now. There's no place for him to hide or run. His mug's on the news more than the president. He'd have made his move much sooner. He'd want to do something before he gets caught."

"Damn," Murray said. "Just when I thought my dreams about Ben were all grief-related."

"We've all had bad dreams since the bombing," Naomi said. "I'm afraid I have to go with Chase and his federal sources on this. The Commander is dead. And just like Elvis, some people are always gonna say they saw him at the diner or wherever. One thing for sure: I wouldn't be paying much heed to a federal prisoner who used to be in his cult of military insanity."

CHAPTER THIRTY-FOUR

It took the Commander three months and two operations to recover from his injuries enough to begin walking with a bad limp and a cane. He still thought of himself as the Commander even though there was nobody left to command. His paid soldiers were all dead or in jail. Options for the future were not good. Even hiding out with another militia group was not a real possibility. Sooner or later, somebody would talk, and he'd be off to prison.

Dr. Aikens kept him well hidden in a small house near the medical clinic. Only the doctor knew he was there. Even nurses who assisted in the surgeries did not know the identity of the patient. His face was always covered. They were paid well to not ask questions.

Three months of solitude should have been enough time for the Commander to reflect on the absurd criminality of his militia compound. But the doctor kept him so high on whiskey and morphine that he lived like an addict, fading away in the wooden crib of an opium den. The only thought pattern that developed during this time was his hatred of women. His shame became all-consuming. His rage turned into rants. "Losing everything was bad enough," he often screamed near the end of a tirade. "Losing it all to the women of The Highway Diner is not something I'm gonna live with."

The Commander had convinced himself that women had

treated him horribly his entire life. His mother became an opioid addict after losing her premature baby during childbirth. It was a male child he always thought should have been his younger brother. His mother became distant and emotionally vague after the loss. She still did the laundry, shopping, cooking, dishes, house cleaning, and gardening, but she became incapable of showing any kind of affection. She never came to her only child's school functions or football games.

As his parents' marriage unraveled, the young man blamed his mother for making his father unhappy. She overdosed on Percocet and died shortly after the divorce had been finalized, leaving a hole in his soul he pretended not to notice. It never occurred to him that he and his father had treated her like a slave.

He blamed his own wife for not understanding how the war had strangled his ability to feel kindness or compassion. Humanity had been shocked out of him like a convicted killer in an electric chair.

His wife had no idea what she was dealing with. Every time he came home on leave from the combat zone, his moods were darker, and he was angrier and more withdrawn. He berated her concern for his mental health. As far as he was concerned, she only made things worse by demanding he get help. How dare she think anyone could help him after what he'd been through?

The Commander eventually asked Dr. Aikens to help him sober up. He told the doctor nothing about his plans as he developed an attack strategy against The Highway Diner.

Life was over for him anyway. He'd thought about trying to escape to a foreign country, but he'd be captured eventually. It might take the government years to execute him, years he would spend in federal prison, probably in solitary confinement. He didn't want to go out like Timothy McVeigh, the Oklahoma City bomber. Why die alone by lethal injection when he could take out enemies and leave his cruel world behind in one last blast of defiance?

The Commander and the doctor rented a box truck to retrieve weapons and explosives from a farmhouse titled in the name of a fictitious corporation. The feds hadn't searched the property since it had no apparent connection to either the Commander or his compound.

"What exactly are you planning to do with all this?" Dr. Aikens asked once they'd loaded enough explosives and weapons into the truck to wipe out half a city.

"Nothing," the Commander lied. "I just don't want people getting hurt in case there's a fire at that house."

The Commander glared at the doctor, daring him to ask more questions. The doctor looked away and said nothing further.

The Commander picked December 27 for his attack, knowing that Chase and Leona were getting married at 6:00 p.m. on that date at The Highway Diner. He also knew that many celebrities, including Leona's friend, Diamond Lil, would be in attendance. News of the private wedding had been in all the entertainment mags, not to mention being a buzz on all levels of social media.

No one suspected the danger lurking in the twisted and battered heart of the Commander.

The Commander had inadvertently divulged the details of his suicidal mission to the doctor during a blacked-out, drunken rage. But the doctor couldn't call the authorities without going to prison himself as an accomplice. He was harboring the man who would have been America's most wanted fugitive had anyone known he was still alive.

Finally, in a panic of desperation, the doctor called The Highway Diner at noon on December 27, five hours before the Commander's attack on the wedding party was to begin. Murray answered the phone. The doctor slowly and nervously told her what was about to happen. He did not identify himself.

"What kind of truck will he be in?" she asked.

"He'll be in disguise, driving a Mason's Flower truck like it was delivering last minute for the wedding. He'll be alone. Arrival time 5:00 p.m."

Then he hung up.

———

Murray stood up and walked quickly to find Chase. He was already at the diner, making last-minute wedding preparations. His face fell down several flights of emotional stairs as he learned his wedding was about to be the scene of an attempted mass murder.

He looked her in the eyes as he wiped away tears of frustration and sadness. "Murray, this has got to be a crank caller. We all saw the Commander get killed in his tank on live television."

"I know it's the real deal, Chase. The man was terrified. He sounded professional. He knew too much about the Commander. He said the Commander got out of the tank just before the drone took it out. And I didn't tell you this before, but Anita got a letter from a guy in prison—Cal Mavis, the man who kidnapped her. Mavis was at the compound when it went down. He was watching the video monitors in the command bunker. He said he thought he saw someone get out of the tank before it exploded. That's exactly what the man on the phone said. It must be true."

Chase lowered his head. We did see the tank turret pop open. There was a lot of smoke and dust. Do you think he got out?"

Murray grabbed Chase by his shoulders and got in his face. "I know he got out. I feel it deep down. Ben's been telling me in my dreams." Murray's eyes were so intense and the tone of her voice so convincing that he believed her despite his doubts.

"Goddamn it," Chase hissed. "There goes my wedding." He looked at Murray. "You know I trust you. Plus, we can't afford to ignore this warning, even if it turns out to be false. Let's get Naomi and Anita on this right away. I want all the guests warned not to come. Thank God we don't have that big of a guest list. Tell them we have to change the date because . . ." He thought about it for a long moment, then raised his right hand as an idea came to him. "Let's say Leona is so sick she had to be hospitalized. The doctors are worried about a possible miscarriage. Yeah, that ought to do it. And tell them not to tell anybody what's going on and to please respect Leona's privacy. I'll get security to park a bunch of cars and limousines out front so it doesn't look like we suspect foul play. Tell your mother what's up. I'll get ahold of Leona. Goddamn, she's gonna kill me. There goes our wedding. Okay, okay. Go. Cancel the guests. I'm calling the FBI. Hell, I've got my own security guards. Don't worry, we'll stop him."

Isabel tried to remain calm as Murray told her what was happening. "Mom, breathe. You're not breathing. Stay with me. We've got to get all the staff out of here without anybody noticing we're vacating the building."

"Right," Isabel said as she snapped back into emergency-action mode. "We can put everybody in the back of the wedding planner's truck. It's empty. All the tables and chairs are out. It can fit twenty-five people. That's about what we've got. Should we do it now?"

"Let's get everybody together in the bar," Murray suggested. "They're going to need to know what's going on. The last thing we want is a bunch of panicked staff running around. We'll take them somewhere in the truck and keep them at a secure location until all this is over. We can't have them spoiling the trap."

"What trap?" Isabel asked.

Naomi and Anita came running up and overheard the word *trap*. "What's going on?" Naomi asked.

"All right, people," Murray said. "We need to put our heads together here. I just got a call from a man who said the Commander is alive and he's coming to the wedding on a suicide bombing mission."

"I knew it," Anita shouted. "What did I tell you, Naomi?"

"How can you sound so happy to be right?" Naomi asked Anita. "This is terrifying." Then she turned to Murray. "What are we gonna do?"

"We're going to stop him before he gets into the parking lot," Murray said. "The caller said he'd be driving a Mason's Flower truck. The feds plan to trap him at the gate."

"So, we're all leaving?" Naomi asked.

"I'm not going anywhere," Isabel said. "I'll be staying right here, locked and loaded. Nobody's blowing up my diner. I've had more than enough of the so-called Commander's bullshit."

"Me too," Anita said. "I'm with Isabel. Get me one of your AR-15s, Murray. I learned how to shoot like a pro at the militia compound. The Commander taught me himself."

"Whoa, Anita. You never told me all this," Murray said.

"You just earned yourself an AR. You know I don't just pass them out to anybody."

Naomi nodded. "Looks like we'll all be here. What kind of weapon do you have for me? I know how to shoot."

"You can have my Glock," Murray said. "We'll put Anita on the roof with an AR and a scope. I know just the spot from hanging all the Christmas lights. She'll have a three-hundred-and-sixty-degree view."

Chase came jogging up, out of breath, to join the circle of women. He had a Colt .45 strapped to his hip. "I've got the FBI and my security team setting up a perimeter and a trap, complete with SWAT units and armored cars in the truck wash bays. What about you guys?"

"We're staying," Isabel said.

"I figured that much out by looking at you," Chase said with a smile. "I need to know what positions you'll be taking. I'll be at the front door. If some lunatic is gonna ruin my wedding, I'm gonna take him out myself."

Chase got so excited about organizing the women at the diner and trapping the Commander at the entrance gate that he failed to assign any of his security personnel to guard the diner. Likewise, no federal agents were positioned at the diner. The feds thought Chase had the diner covered with his private force. Everybody was so focused on defending the perimeter that they forgot about protecting the diner.

The women of the Highway Diner were now their own last line of defense.

CHAPTER THIRTY-FIVE

The Mason's Flower truck arrived at the front gate of The Highway Diner parking lot precisely at 5:00 p.m. It was *immediately surrounded* by SWAT vehicles with two armored cars blocking its forward path. An officer from one of the cars shouted through the speaker, "Step out of the truck with your hands in the air. This is the Federal Bureau of Investigation. Step out of the vehicle. Now. You are surrounded. Step out of the vehicle."

No one stepped out of the vehicle. Teams of armed men deployed from SWAT vehicles and surrounded the flower truck. The command to exit was repeated several times. Still no movement from inside the truck.

Anita had her scope on the truck from her rooftop perch. Naomi and Isabel were at the big window in the diner, Chase was at the front door and Murray was at a window in the convenience store. The SWAT team yanked open the driver and passenger doors and hauled out the driver—a gray-haired Mexican man in a green uniform with a Mason's Flowers logo on his shirt. Anita could see through the scope that he had pissed his pants. He screamed as he fell flat on the ground, "No, no, no. I do nothing bad. Only flowers. Check and see. I do nothing."

Agents searched the truck and found nothing but flowers.

Anita swung her scope back to the parking lot in front of The Highway Diner. A chilling calm took control of her senses.

Her muscles relaxed; her breathing steadied. Fear faded into a hunter's hyper focus. She slowly scanned the lot back and forth. Nothing unusual. She did a slow 360-degree swivel to check the entire perimeter. Still nothing.

She returned to scan the parking lot with her scope. Something terrible was about to happen. She could feel it. Her hair felt like it was on fire. Then she saw the glint of a reflection from a moving SUV windshield heading straight for the diner. *It must be him*, she thought as she made herself wait.

She surmised instantly what had happened. The Commander paid extra to Mason's Flowers for a truckload of flowers to be delivered to the diner at 5:00 p.m. It was a diversion. It must have been the Commander, or one of his lackeys, who'd called on the phone with the warning.

It worked like a diabolical charm. The entire security force was preoccupied with the flower truck while the Commander began his attack from inside their circle of defense. He took full advantage of what had been a major tactical blunder on the part of law enforcement.

The vehicle moved too fast toward the diner to be anyone but the Commander. Anita couldn't see through the windshield, but she didn't need to. It was a black Denali SUV that looked like the FBI. She wondered if he entered the parking lot by falling in line with the other FBI vehicles.

"That's him," Anita screamed as she fired two rounds into the windshield before realizing it was bulletproof. She fired four more rounds into the engine area. Her bullets had no effect. The vehicle was armored. All law enforcement eyes turned in surprise and horror to watch the SUV skidding to a sideways stop in front of the concrete pole barricades thirty yards in front of the diner. Chase had them installed after the casino bombings.

As the attacking SUV was coming to a stop, smoke grenades bounced out the front passenger window and exploded into clouds that made the vehicle disappear. The smoke was so thick and widespread it temporarily blinded Anita with her own tears. The federal armored cars wheeled around to head toward the diner.

Isabel and Naomi looked out from their positions at the diner's front window in confusion as the smoke enveloped the restaurant and clouded their view. They held their fire. No one had any idea what kind of smoke or poison gas was creeping over the diner. It felt like a B-movie monster from another planet. The air inside the diner smelled like exploding fireworks and burning paper.

They didn't have to wait long to find out what was coming next.

A high-explosive anti-tank warhead from a Javelin missile blasted out of the cloud and through the front door of the diner. It made a high-pitched shrieking noise that sounded like the terrified screams of school children.

Chase was behind a concrete wall on the side of the front door. Mercifully, the missile went right through the glass, past Chase, and exploded into the rear of the building forty feet away, leaving a hole large enough to drive a truck through. Chase was hit by shrapnel and debris in the back of his left arm and leg, but he was still standing. He fired his .45 handgun into the smoke.

As Chase paused to reload, the Commander lurched toward the diner, still hidden by the smoke, firing nonstop with an AK-47. One shot went through the diner's front window and hit Naomi on the upper right shoulder. She fell to her knees in pain, then rose and emptied a clip from her Glock into the smoke.

Miraculously, only one agent in the parking lot had been hit in the leg by friendly fire from Chase and Naomi or ricochets from Anita's rounds.

Isabel looked through the broken window and saw the muzzle flash from the Commander's rifle pointed right at her. She ducked behind the block wall as bullets spit by her and into the restaurant. The Commander went through multiple thirty-round clips as he got within twenty yards of the entrance to the diner.

Chase was pinned down and having trouble reloading. Only he could see the Commander, who was walking with a bad limp through the smoke. There was nobody to stop him.

Murray was at a window in the store, twenty yards from the entrance to the diner. She instinctively knew the Commander would try to follow the missile through the front door. She sprinted across the store with her AR and took cover behind the wall next to the blown-out glass doors. She saw Chase on the other side of the entrance, struggling with his weapon. She knew what she had to do. Peeking around the wall, she saw fire coming from the Commander's AK. Bullets whizzed past her head.

She ducked back behind the wall. Months of fear, anger, and shame turned into a steely resolve. She peeked around the wall again. He was close enough for her to see his face as she looked down the sight of her AR-15. She was in position to kill the man of her nightmares, a man she had only seen in photographs. The man who killed Ben. The man who wanted to destroy everyone and everything she loved. The man who was charging at her with a blazing automatic weapon.

His face was contorted in pain and anger. He was pathetic and terrifying at the same time. In an instant, Murray realized he was just a man, not a monster. His misery was complete. He clearly wanted to die. She had no time to feel sorry for him. The rifle felt like an extension of her body. The world wound down into slow motion. She had never killed a human being. Now it felt inevitable.

The moment of truth felt nothing like Murray thought it would. The warrior in her took over and she became a savage beast, focused on nothing but killing its prey. No thoughts of triumph or revenge or justice. Just killing, completing the task at hand.

Chase had his gun reloaded by then and yelled that he was ready to fire. "Stay down," Murray screamed. "I got this."

She aimed right between the Commander's eyes. She clenched her teeth in an emotion somewhere between rage and reluctance, and pulled the trigger. Her first shot missed, as did the second. He kept coming. His head was too small a target, especially when he was spinning and limping and firing his weapon.

He was fifteen yards away and closing in fast.

Murray decided she had better hit something to stop him, so she aimed her third shot for his chest. She wouldn't have missed if he'd been fifty yards away. The bullet struck home for the shocking surprise of her life. The Commander's explosive suicide vest blew him up in an explosion that left a crater ten feet deep and thirty feet wide. Bits of his body parts splattered the outside of the diner like the devil's own graffiti.

Anita was blown off the roof and crash landed in the pine trees behind the diner. The blast destroyed most of the diner's front facade. Naomi and Isabel were not in front of their window or the explosion would have shredded them. They were thrown to the floor by the immense power of the bomb. It felt like the casino bombing all over again.

Chase and Murray were blown into the back wall of the building, near the blast hole from the missile. A piece of shrapnel had gashed the right side of Murray's head down to the skull. The wound was grisly and bleeding profusely when Naomi found her, covered in broken blocks and mortar. Murray sucked in a shallow gasp of air and regained semi-consciousness. The concrete wall she and Chase had been standing behind saved their lives.

"I got that son of a bitch," Murray croaked weakly. "I don't know how I blew him up with one bullet, but I got him. I got him before he got us."

"He must have been strapped up with explosives," Chase groaned from underneath the pile of rubble. "I'm amazed he didn't take us with him."

Naomi dug frantically to unbury the two of them, ignoring the stabbing pain in her shoulder. Murray tried to get up but couldn't budge. "I'm hit," she cried as she tasted her own blood.

Chase was able to struggle into a sitting position. He rubbed his eyes like he was amazed to still have eyes. "You did it, girl," he said to Murray. "You saved the day. I couldn't stop him. My gun was jammed until just before you shot him. You stepped up to the plate and hit a home run. Talk about keeping a cool head under fire. Where'd you learn to shoot like that?"

Murray did not respond. She was passed out. Naomi took off her gray flannel shirt and used it to apply pressure to the head wound. Her own wound was bleeding profusely. "Stay with me, Murray," Naomi shouted. "Stay with me." The scene felt sickeningly like the one that cost Ben his life.

Isabel rushed in to hand Naomi a tablecloth she grabbed on the way. "Oh no, Murray." She fell to her knees, sobbing, as she turned to Naomi and asked, "Is she going to make it?"

"I hope so," Naomi cried. "It looks like a bad head cut. I don't know what else might be wrong with her."

Naomi and Isabel dug their friends out of the debris. Isabel ripped up the cloth to tie a bandage around Naomi's shoulder. Federal agents rushed in and set up a defensive perimeter in case the Commander wasn't the only attacker. Besides a few orders being barked, nobody said a word as medics took Chase and Murray to the hospital. Psychological echoes of the explosion had shrouded the diner in a terrible silence.

Isabel looked at Naomi with a new fear in her eyes. "Where's Anita?"

"I don't know," Naomi answered, draping what was left of the tablecloth around her exposed shoulders. "Let's go find her. She was on the roof."

They ran to the back of the diner. Naomi climbed the ladder Anita had used. "She's not up here," she called down.

Isabel turned around and walked through the small stand of pine trees behind the diner. She took three steps and saw Anita in a crumpled heap at the bottom of the tree farthest from the diner. "Here she is, Naomi. Here she is. Oh my God, she's hurt bad."

Anita's right arm and left leg looked broken, and her face and chest were badly cut from sliding down a pine tree. She was covered in her own blood. It looked like she had already bled to death. Isabel knelt beside the body. Sorrow choked her neck so tightly she couldn't speak. Then she noticed Anita was still breathing. "Anita," she pleaded. "Can you hear me?"

Anita fluttered her eyes partly open, smiled faintly, and asked, "What happened?"

CHAPTER THIRTY-SIX

Three days after she killed the Commander, Murray watched news of his Kamikaze attack from her hospital bed. Surgeons had reset her broken bones with titanium plates and stainless-steel screws. Her punctured lung had been repaired, but she could barely breathe, even on oxygen. The pain from her broken ribs and collarbone was mostly masked by a morphine drip. She was floating.

The story, "Last Stand at The Highway Diner," was still breaking news. The world couldn't get enough of the heroic women who defended their iconic truck stop and killed the most dangerous man in the world. But even as Isabel and Murray were glorified, the FBI was being condemned and investigated for leaving the women to their own defense.

Murray watched her mother on television, giving a statement to reporters on the day of the attack. The interview had been shown many times over the past three days. Now Isabel was holding her hand and watching the news clips with her. Murray became disoriented seeing Isabel on television and holding her hand at the same time.

"It's okay, honey. I'm right here. You're in the hospital getting better. We're watching a press conference I gave a few days ago. And, oh my, do I look ragged. You've seen this many times, but you're still having trouble remembering."

In the news clip, Isabel was telling reporters how grateful she was for Murray and Anita. "My daughter was the first one to open fire on the Commander when he came to kill us all. By the way, we've got to stop calling him that. He was a cruel, hateful man. He deserved to die. He needed to die. We should just call him the Hateful One from now on."

"Right on, Mom," Murray said, squeezing her hand.

Isabel continued in the interview. "And my daughter, Muriel Paterson. That young woman deserves the medal of honor. She stepped into harm's way and fired the shot that blew up the hateful one. She was our last hope. If she hadn't gotten the job done, we'd have all been killed. She's in the hospital now, but it looks like she'll make a full recovery."

Isabel turned off the television.

"Where is Anita?" Murray asked.

"She's right here in this hospital, about four rooms down."

"How's she doing?"

"Just like you, she's going to be fine."

"I'll bet she's jealous I'm the one who got to shoot that bastard."

"Now, Murray, don't talk like that. We all killed him. More like we put him out of his miserable existence. The important point is he's dead and gone, and he won't bother us anymore."

"Then why am I still dreaming about him?" Murray moaned.

Isabel said nothing. All she could do was hold Murray's hand. Murray was still confused, frustrated, and caught in a state of high anxiety from the concussion. She did manage to ask, "How are Chase and Naomi?"

"They're going to be all right," Isabel answered. "Naomi got shot in the shoulder, but she's going to make a full recovery. You know, I've told you this. Chase might be in the hospital the longest. He had some tough internal injuries. But he's going to make it."

"Unlike Ben," Murray slurred as she fell asleep.

———

Chase and Leona were finally married on April 22, 2024, in a private ceremony in Nashville, Tennessee. Leona was nearly eight months pregnant. She didn't want media attention. Her friend, Diamond Lil, attended under cover of secrecy and disguise, as did a few close friends and family members. Leona insisted on keeping the guest list short.

Murray and Isabel attended with Naomi and Anita. When they arrived, Diamond Lil rushed up to Isabel like a long-lost friend and gushed, "People call me a gutsy broad, but you four ladies take the cake. I want you all onstage with me when I do my show up there to open Trucker Nation. The phenomenon, not the casino."

Isabel laughed. "I know you understand why we're not calling Trucker Nation, a casino."

"Oh yeah," Lil said. "There are casinos all around Diamond World. I don't go in them. Too depressing. And the smoking all night long. I can't tolerate it. It takes forever to get the stink out of your hair and off your clothes. No, I'm with you, Isabel. Trucker Nation was never about gambling. Keeping the supply chain moving is no game of chance."

Isabel put her hands over her heart. "That's a great way to put it. I'm gonna steal that every chance I get. Oh, and Lil—here, I'd like you to meet the three women who saved The Highway Diner. This here's my daughter, Muriel. And Anita and Naomi are like family to me. Come on, ladies. I'd like you to meet my friend, the one and only Diamond Lil."

Anita, Naomi, and Murray were completely starstruck as Isabel introduced them. They could barely speak. "Oh my," Lil said as she noticed the awe in their eyes. "I'm the one getting all nervous meeting you three, so don't you be shy about meeting me. I'm not out there facing down suicidal terrorists. Me and the whole country are so proud of y'all we could pop."

Murray managed to say, "Diamond Lil, it is such an honor to meet you. You've been our inspiration forever. Since we were little girls, right Anita?"

"Absolutely," Anita said. "My friends are going to be so jealous when they find out I met you in person."

Lil laughed and said, "The whole world's gonna be jealous of me when they find out I know the women of The Highway Diner."

———

Murray finally went to the Art Institute in Chicago after the wedding. Her injuries had delayed the scheduled January start. All the hustling and shuffling of college life was a welcome distraction from the nightmares of Ben's death and the Commander's attack on The Highway Diner. Her roommate, Tyra Cooper, was a huge help as Murray waded through the fog of violence and traumatic concussion. She couldn't believe it had already been a year since she and Ben had met Tyra at the art museum.

"My memory's coming back slowly," Murray said to Tyra one morning as they were walking to art history class. "I mean, I know what day it is, and I know I did the reading for art history. But I don't know what's going to happen once we get to class. It's been so frustrating. I was making so much progress after Ben got killed. I battled uphill until I finally got to where I could paint again. Then all that progress went right out the window when I had to shoot that suicidal maniac. My anxiety is worse than ever now. I actually feel bad about killing him. I keep seeing the fear and anger in his eyes. I always thought it would feel good making him pay for all the people he killed. But it doesn't. It's more like I added to the body count."

Tyra stopped walking and drew Murray in for a hug. "You did what you had to do. And that's all you did. Right now, your brain is playing tricks on you. You've been through too much. But wait and see. You'll come around."

"I hope you're right," Murray said. "Sometimes I have panic attacks because I don't know what I'm supposed to be doing. And you know the worst part is what we've been working on for weeks. Every time I try to paint, all I do is sit and cry."

Tyra nodded as she took Murray's hand to encourage her to continue talking.

"And then this crazy warrior thing inside me takes over and slaps me around and tells me to buck up. Which is all well and good. But the warrior can't paint. She's too busy surviving her suffering. So, there I am, not crying, staring at an easel, too pent up to create."

Tyra took both Murray's hands in hers so they would stop walking. She was shorter than Murray, but they could always look each other in the eye. "You know I love the story about you and the giant statue of the Native American woman. You always said the quilt she was holding up was a symbol of her own bravery."

Murray nodded and smiled at remembering her South Dakota epiphany.

"What we've both got to remember is that quilt she's holding isn't just a shield against danger. It's a work of art. Something she created. Not for herself, but for all the world to see. I know you get this," Tyra said.

Murray's eyes lit up. "The Native American woman was an artist. I can't believe I never saw her that way. I only felt her as a warrior."

Tyra grabbed her by the shoulders. "She wasn't carrying a weapon. She was carrying a work of art. Think about it. I'm not saying art is a weapon. But I am saying that artists must be warriors."

Murray opened her mouth and leaned her head back in a flash of realization. "Yes, yes, that's it. Warriors in the sense of having the courage to create. Art is a confession. It takes guts to pour out your heart and soul for the world to see. I get it. It's just that I'm not sure I can do it anymore. It's impossible to feel artistic when you still hear explosions in your head. I thought I was dying when I got blown up. I was flying through the air and then I was out. Sometimes I wonder if I ever really came back."

Tyra knew that what Murray really needed was a good listener.

Murray looked up to the sky and held out her arms to all the bright lights and neon of the cityscape. "I keep thinking about Ben and how he never got a chance to come back from the dead. He still talks to me, but I know I'll never see him again. That makes me remember how lucky I am and how I've got this chance to kind of start over. And yesterday, in afternoon painting, I slipped into a peaceful, creative space. Just for a minute, the brush felt right again. The oil paint smelled like a Sausalito breeze. So cathartic, but only for a short time. But if it can happen a little, it can happen a lot. Right?"

Tyra hugged her and said, "That's the spirit. And remember, you're not alone. We've all got to find a way out of anger and fear. We're all little bundles of scared shitless."

Murray laughed. "There's a lot to be afraid of. And I'm pretty sure the anger comes from fear. It makes me mad that I'm afraid I might not recover. It's an evil, endless cycle of emotional dirty laundry. But when I paint, it's the only time my head doesn't spin."

"Do not despair, my friend. You'll get there. We're gonna get there together. Creativity is the cure, not the goal."

It took months, but Murray's painting gradually became more colorful and bolder as she realized a return to painting would not be an event but a process. The more she painted, the more she could paint. Her brain was clearing, and her mind was relaxing. She felt it most certainly one morning listening to the birds singing outside her open window. She asked herself, *How long has it been since I heard birds singing?*

Everything was getting better for Murray except for one thing. The gaping hole in her heart from losing Ben still made her feel empty and alone. "I wonder if I can ever learn to love again," she wondered out loud to Tyra after they said goodnight to their friends at the bar one evening.

"Wait," Tyra said. "You love me, don't you?"

"Yes, of course I do," Murray said. "But you know what I'm talking about. Falling in love with someone like I was with Ben. I'm so balled up in myself I'm not sure I'd see love coming if it knocked me down on the sidewalk."

The two women walked on in silence until Tyra said, "Art is pretty much the same thing as love."

Murray stopped walking so she could grab Tyra by the shoulders. "Tyra, did you hear what you just said? It's so true. I can't believe I haven't thought of it before. But you're absolutely right. Love is all about giving and so is art. The artist loves creating, and people love the art."

Tyra nodded and grinned as she completed her point. "So, if art is love, and you can learn to create art again, you can learn to love again, right?"

Murray was bouncing on her toes. "Yes, yes. You make perfect sense. I just hope you're right."

Tyra and Murray carried the spirit of that conversation into their work for the next several months. They each generated incredible paintings. A friendly competition to one-up each other developed. They rose to new heights, taking chances and breaking rules. Murray began to feel how grief and grieving could strengthen her process rather than taking it away.

"It's like the deeper I feel, the more emotion I can put into my painting," Murray said. "Nothing ever cut me like Ben getting killed. I thought I was bleeding to death. But now it feels like I can brushstroke some of that blood onto the canvas."

"Oh man, that's a tough way to put it, but it's so true," Tyra said. "No doubt about it. There's a lot of pain in this world. You got your regular pain of people treating you like you don't matter. And then the extra pain of not knowing what we're doing here in the first place. One thing for sure, though: art is the best pain relief in the world."

"Couldn't agree more," Murray said.

The two friends took long walks together as spring blossomed in Chicago. Tyra was a positive person. She reminded Murray of herself before all the death and destruction. With Tyra's support and good example, Murray was healing, slowly but surely. But deep down, she wondered if she would ever be able to give her heart to another man. She was still crying herself to sleep over Ben on too many nights.

<hr>

One hot, sunny day at the beginning of the summer semester, a young man in paint-stained jeans and a black T-shirt walked into her painting class. He was tall and square shouldered with a short-stubble beard and long, brown hair. His long, easy gait reminded her of Ben.

"That's Nathan Ranier," the woman next to Murray leaned

over and whispered. "He's a grad student and a fabulous painter."

Murray knew and admired his work, but they had never met. She couldn't help looking at him even though she didn't want him to catch her staring. Suddenly, Nathan turned his head before she had a chance to look away, as though some disturbance had attracted his attention. They made eye contact. His eyes were blue and kind and curious. Murray quickly averted her eyes as the brief encounter awakened slumbering notions of romance buried in her heart. She returned her gaze to the painting in progress on her easel and adjusted her thinking. *The last thing I need right now is a man*, she thought. *Maybe later, but right now, I need to paint.*

She dipped a fine-detail paintbrush into a mix of yellow and orange paint. She marveled at the lush shade of amber on her palette. The painting was of a dirt footpath winding into a dense evergreen forest. It had given her trouble since there seemed to be no place for the path to penetrate the trees.

Suddenly, her brush had a mind of its own. It came alive in her right hand and used the amber color to highlight tree branches as if sunlight was showing the way forward. Brown dirt turned yellow brick with a single amber brush stroke. The path ducked under a massive pine limb and beckoned all to follow.

Murray surrendered to the magic as the painting took shape by a creative force she no longer needed to control. Her heart soared as she felt herself floating into the forest. Freedom called.

The path before her was one she would walk alone.

ABOUT THE AUTHOR

Mark Paul Smith is the author of *The Hitchhike, Honey and Leonard, The Reporter,* and *Rock and Roll Voodoo.*

After an around-the-world hitchhike in 1972, Mark became a newspaper reporter and then played in a rock and roll band on Bourbon Street and on the road. He was a trial attorney from 1982 until his retirement in 2021.

Mark and his late wife, artist Jody Hemphill Smith, own Castle Gallery Fine Art in Fort Wayne, Indiana.

OTHER BOOKS BY MARK PAUL SMITH

Mark Paul Smith graduated college on an Air Force scholarship with dreams of becoming a pilot. He had some downtime after graduation and before reporting for duty, so he decided to hitchhike the world. A decision that would change his life forever.

As he traveled, his approach to life and his future decisions changed. He hitchhiked through the Iron Curtain and worked on a collective farm in Hungary only to find that communism wasn't our real enemy. He met people from North Vietnam who showed him the real enemy was the U.S. war machine. Being an American was not popular in those days, but the people of the world showed Smith kindness and kept him alive when he ran out of money. The long road to decision showed him that people everywhere want peace, not war.

Mark Paul Smith's hitchhike from Indiana to India in 1972 changed him from being an Air Force Officer into a conscientious objector. His faith in the United States of America was restored when he sued the government and won his case in federal court. His journey is one of faith, contemplation, and awakening, mixed with the freedom and abandonment of the seventies.

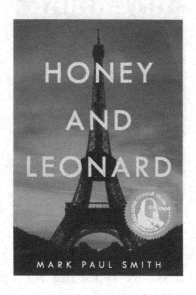

Honey and Leonard are in their seventies when they fall in love. Leonard is in the early stages of Alzheimer's and Honey thinks her love will cure him.

When their heirs try to keep them apart, they flee to France in violation of court orders. Pursued by police, press, and private investigators, they become an international media sensation. In a time just before cell phones and the Internet, they become the Bonnie and Clyde of love.

Their whirlwind romance encompasses arsenic poisoning, elder law, Alzheimer's, an Eiffel Tower arrest, and a Paris jail break. And through it all, Honey is in the middle of the difficult process of discovering that love does not conquer all. Or does it?

During the 1970s on a magic mushroom harvesting adventure in the Bayou, a young aspiring rock and roll musician discovers the voice of Voodoo, which not only alters his life, but the life of his band, the Divebomberz.

When the band is on the verge of making it big, tragedy strikes and Jesse is confronted with the hard truth that life is often a spiritual obstacle course designed to see if you can get over yourself.

A book for rock and rollers of all ages and for restless souls who have chased a dream only to discover that what they really needed was with them all along.